Dear Target Guest,

I hope you can help me. I need answers.

I'll be straight with you: I set out to write a funny book. A funny book telling funny stories about body parts. And, you know, it is pretty funny. There's a good bit with a biology teacher and an alphabetical list of all the rude body parts I could think of.

But as I was putting it all together, the body parts—and the characters they belonged to—began to misbehave. They reacted with one another, formed associations, made choices that caused my main character Ivo to become seriously ill. I built these characters body part by body part, and they presented big, complex questions that a writer can ask but can't really answer. Like: What happens when head meets heart? Or: We all make mistakes, but why doesn't everyone pay for them in the same way?

It's no spoiler if I tell you that Ivo has developed an illness that has put him at war with his own body. He finds himself obliged to live an entirely disciplined and healthy life at the notoriously ill-disciplined and unhealthy age of twenty. How does anyone manage that? I mean, I've tried to maintain a sensible diet through January, and it's no joke. Why does it feel so good to live in the present when it can take away your future?

Of course, we might recover from our mistakes through the care and attention of a few good friends or a lover, but what if you don't have those kinds of friends? And what if you can't live up to love?

As I said, big, complex questions.

This is my first novel, but I've been writing for twenty years. It's how I make sense of my world and the people I share it with. So imagine my delight when early readers of this book started to come up to me with answers. Not *the* answer, but *their* answer. Big, serious answers, gnarly and changeable. They brought the book to life.

I've been moved, humbled, and inspired by some of the responses I've had— often from people who have experience caring for someone, or loss. I'm proud that this lighthearted book became a much more poignant one. I'm proud that it became a love letter to the hospices and caregivers who are there for us when life runs out of answers.

I really hope you find this book means something to you—if not now, then maybe later. Thank you for picking it up.

THE A TO Z OF YOU AND ME

Praise for *The A to Z of You and Me*

"Spare, poignant, and with a quirky charm all of its own, it reminds us how kind people can be."

—Rachel Joyce, author of the *New York Times* bestseller *The Unlikely Pilgrimage of Harold Fry* and *The Love Song of Miss Queenie Hennessy*

"Beautifully constructed and hugely moving. Deserves to be a smash hit."

—Lissa Evans, author of *Crooked Heart*

"Genuinely one of the best books I've ever read."

—Lisa Jewell, author of *The House We Grew Up In*

"It's been ages since I read a book that affected me as much… It is so immensely beautiful: technically and stylistically innovative, there's much to admire."

—Susan Barker, author of *The Incarnations*

"Wonderful and heartbreaking."

—Claire Fuller, author of *Our Endless Numbered Days*

"So beautiful… A stunning, unique debut."

—Caroline Smailes, author of *The Drowning of Arthur Braxton*

THE A TO Z OF YOU AND ME

James Hannah

sourcebooks
landmark

For Sheila &
For You

Published by Sourcebooks Landmark, an imprint of Sourcebooks, Inc.
P.O. Box 4410, Naperville, Illinois 60567-4410
(630) 961-3900
Fax: (630) 961-2168
www.sourcebooks.com

Originally published in 2015 in Great Britain by Doubleday, an imprint of Transworld Publishers, a Random House Group Company.

Library of Congress Cataloging-in-Publication Data
Hannah, James (Fiction writer)
  The A to Z of you and me / James Hannah.
    pages ; cm
  (softcover : acid-free paper) 1. Man-woman relationships--Fiction. 2. Middle-aged men--Fiction. 3. Terminally ill--Fiction. 4. Memory--Fiction. I. Title.
  PR6108.A558A62 2016
  823'.92--dc23
                    2015029220

Printed and bound in the United States of America.
VP 10 9 8 7 6 5 4 3 2 1

I know exactly what you'd be saying to me now.

You'd be telling me that I have to try.

To try to try.

But I want to give up. I want to just lie here, in this bed, in this room, with nothing to look at but the wall and the window, the magnolia tree beyond.

A little robin's flitting in and out of the branches. That's enough for me. Away she goes. She'll be back.

So now—familiar thoughts start to build up. They never leave me alone. What have I got to keep them down? You? If I could sit here and think of you, I would.

No, no. I can't go there.

Sheila understands. She knows there's a problem. But what answers does she have for me? The same old ideas. Stupid mental exercises like the A to Z game.

Maybe the older patients are content to keep themselves occupied with parlor games. But I don't want any of it. I'm forty. My mind's too active. I need it deadening.

I want to ease the mental churn. The foam. I want it all to stop.

You have to try. You have to keep going forward.

You never let me get away with anything.

You're better than this.

Adam's Apple

Adam's apple means the Reverend Cecil Alexander.

Adam's apple means me coming out of church, down the stone steps trailing in the wake of my mum. We leave the chapel every Sunday and take our turn in line to bid thankses and good-byes and see-you-next-Sundays to the Reverend Alexander. I'm a kid. Short trousers, short legs. I'm actually scared by his enormous Adam's apple. It's the biggest I've ever seen. It leaps and bounces around, like an angular elbow fighting to free itself from his throat. It makes me feel sick even looking at it. I just think, how doesn't the man choke? What if he got punched right in it?

I know it might not be the right thing to do, to point it out. But you know me.

"What's that in your throat?"

The kind of questions a minister must have to deal with on the hoof.

If there's a God, why must he allow the suffering of children?

Got your shirt on back-to-front then, eh?

So, what about the dinosaurs, then, mate? Explain that. See, you can't, can you?

Frank says you said he could do the flowers next week, but you told me last week I could do them. Did you say that to Frank?

"What's that in your throat?"

He must have been asked this question a lot. Despite the embarrassed gasp and laughter of my mum, and a censorious hand swashed about my face, he is quick with his answer.

"Oh, that's a piece of apple." I frown at it very hard.

"Why don't you swallow it?"

He's a great one for thinking on his feet. Part of the job description.

"I can't. Do you remember the story of the Garden of Eden? Well, it's put there as a reminder of the moment that Adam was discovered eating the apple that Eve had given him. It stuck in his throat, see?"

"My dad's got one of them."

"Well, yes, of course. All men have them."

"I haven't."

"Ah, no. No, no. Not yet."

He smiles as he says this, with the air of a chess player good-naturedly checkmating an opponent.

I'm very fond of Adam's apples for that reason. I was totally satisfied with it as an explanation. And it didn't put me off apples. But it was years before I understood all the repercussions that were echoing around his head as he said those words.

"Ah, no. No, no. Not yet."

You'll fall, he was saying.

You'll fall.

"Morning, Ivo!"

It's Jef. Jef the chef.

"Any ideas what you fancy for breakfast this morning?"

Jefrey with a single *f*. Since school he must have had one career in mind. Except in the end they called him a catering manager.

"Can I get you some eggs? Scrambled eggs? A bit of toast?"

They make him wear the black-and-white-checkered trousers and everything. Is that health and safety? In case his trousers fall in the soup, so he can ladle them out more easily?

"You didn't have any of your porridge yesterday, so I'm guessing you don't want porridge today?"

He's hiding behind his clipboard a little bit, lingering respectfully in my doorway. Half in, half out. He should have a black leather notepad, like a proper waiter.

I have never been less hungry. Not full, just not—

"Hallo, Jef." It's Sheila.

"All right, Sheila, you still here?"

"Yeah, I've got another hour and a half yet. You just got in?"

"I've been in about twenty minutes. I thought I'd get these breakfasts sorted before the electricians arrive. Do you know what they're doing?"

"It's nothing major, is it?"

"I don't know."

"I thought it was only going to be looking at the security lights outside. They can only get to them from the inside or something. Are they still on?"

Jef ducks to look out of the window.

"No," he says, "they've gone off."

"God, isn't that always the way, that it fixes itself before the electricians arrive?"

"Murphy's law."

Sheila looks down at me. "How are you supposed to sleep with a big security light on the whole time?"

I shrug inside, but I don't know if it reaches my limbs.

"I reckon it's the hedgehogs on the lawn," says Jef. "These sensors are really oversensitive."

"Safety from attack by hedgehog. That's worth three thousand pounds of anyone's money, isn't it?"

"Three grand, eh?" Jef tuts and raps his clipboard with his pen.

"Well, I suppose you'd better get a move on anyway, hadn't you?"

"That's what I'm trying to do here, but we can't make our mind up." He turns to me. "Scrambled eggs? Toast? I'll do you some porridge, if you want it. Whatever you want. Try me."

I don't want anything. I shake my head.

"No?"

"I tell you what," says Sheila to me, "how about if we get you something simple, and you can see how you feel when it gets here? I'd like you to eat something this morning, even if it's only a couple of bites. How about something soft and easy, like scrambled eggs?"

I can't answer. I don't want anything.

"Yeah? Scrambled eggs?" Jef is looking at me brightly.

"How about that?" says Sheila. "Or poached? Or fried?"

"I don't do fried," says Jef.

"Oh no, course! Well, scrambled then? Or poached?"

I can't answer this.

"I'd like you to have something. It'll get your strength up, and maybe everything won't look so gloomy, will it?"

So.

They're waiting.

"Poached."

"Poached?"

I nod.

"Right you are, poached." Jef notes it down. He stabs an over-zealous period onto his clipboard and sighs. "You have to choose the one that's hardest to get right, don't you?" Not without humor. He disappears through my doorway, and his footsteps drop down the corridor, cut off by the suck of the big double doors.

He could so easily have said, "That wasn't hard, was it?" That would have made me angry.

Sheila stays behind, gazing thoughtfully at the space in the doorway Jef has just vacated. She half blinks as she comes to, straightens the bedsheets, looking at me and squeezing out an eye smile as she does so.

I like Sheila. Everyone does. She's got that way about her—bright and sparky. But I like her hardness. She's a bit brusque, not fluffy. Mischievous, I'd say, when she wants to be. And it's as if she's got twenty-six hours in the day. Always unhurried in her conversations with me or Jef or Jackie the relief nurse. And I've seen it: people light up when they see her.

She checks my drinking water's fresh, making contact with everything, fully and firmly—one palm now flat against the reeded side of the water jug, the other patting the white plastic lid, her chunky gold rings rapping out her reassurance that it's secure.

There's something more deliberate about her as she carries out her ritual hardware-bothering this morning. I can sense it. She seems to want to stick around. Is she sizing me up? She thinks there's something the matter.

I'm having none of it. I fix my eyes on the wall opposite. I could look out of the window. I could look at the magnolia tree; the robin has returned. But I'll look at the wall. The wall that has seen it all. I'm staring it out. It's staring me back.

It's winning.

It pretty much always wins.

Sheila's moved on to the towels, using the entire front of her body to assist in the folding of a new clean one, stroking it liberally with her hands, before dropping it in half and bringing it around into a quarter. She gives it a final stroke and pat for good measure as she slips it neatly into the space beneath my bedside cabinet.

I wonder when this hospice was opened. It looks like the 1990s, going by the precision brickwork with forty-five-degree corners, bricks looking less like stone, more like solidified porridge, every course the exact same color, laid as if by a computer, not a bricklayer. And green plasticky-looking metal girders with friendly curves.

So that's a quarter of a century this wall has watched people on their deathbeds. A quarter of a century of hysteria and tears and pain and misery.

I shouldn't be here.

I don't want to be here.

I've been here almost a week and—nothing. No better, no worse. Are they disappointed or something? Such an effort to get here in the first place.

What was it—Dr. Sood said they'd sort out my symptoms, and then maybe they'd let me go home for a bit if things got better. But he could say that whenever, couldn't he? Even if I found myself coffined up and rolling along the conveyor belt to the furnace, old Dr. Sood could say, "We'll let you out if you start to show signs of improvement."

I'm not *ill* enough for this. I don't feel like I should be waited on by these people, using up their time when they should be tending to properly dying patients. Mopping up all these charity donations by the old biddies and the shattered and bereaved.

"Are you comfortable there?" asks Sheila, finally bringing her fussing to a conclusion. I nod automatically. "Well, you let me know if there's anything you need, OK? Or let Jackie know when she comes in."

"Mmm."

"You all right?"

"Mmm."

She weighs me up with a look, her jet-black eyes just as intent and penetrating as my mum's used to be, but with many more smile lines sunnying them up at the edges. "Don't you want the TV on?"

"No. Thanks."

"You sure? You won't get bored?"

I do a smile. "I'll look at the wall."

"Oh yeah? Look you in the eye, does it?"

I nod. "It's seen a lot of us."

"Oh, I daresay it'd have a tale or two to tell."

"Mmm."

"But there's a lot of wrong things people would presume about these walls. They've seen a lot of love and pleasure, you know." She gives me a gentle smile. "How are you doing upstairs?" She taps her temple. "Staying sane? I'm still a bit worried about you, you know. I don't want you going bananas on me, all right?"

"I'm not going bananas."

"How's your game going?"

"What game?"

Of course I know what game she means. I just want to pretend I don't know what she's talking about. "You remember I told you about that game the other day? The A to Z? Keep the old brain cells ticking over a bit. So what you could do is try to think of a part of your body, all right? A part of your body for each letter of the alphabet—"

I nod—yes, yes—I want her to know I remember now.

"—and what you do—"

Yes, yes.

"—is tell a little story about each part."

"I've done one. I started doing it, actually. Today."

"Oh yeah? See, well, that's trying, isn't it? How far have you gotten?"

"*A*."

She laughs. "Well, it's good to take your time over it."

"Adam's apple."

"Oh, great. I've had a few people say Adam's apple when I get them to have a go at this."

"Do women have Adam's apples?"

"Yeah! Yeah, I think so."

"I thought they didn't."

"It's the larynx, isn't it? They don't have the sticking-out bit so much, because they're smaller than men's. It's why they have the high voices."

"Is it?"

"Yeah." She lifts her chin thoughtfully and circles her forefinger on her throat. "Larynx. Anyway, you're not a woman, are you, so don't be so picky."

"The vicar when I was little said it was the apple sticking in Adam's throat. Adam out of Adam and Eve."

"D'you know, I've never once thought of it like that, but it makes sense, doesn't it? How funny. Well, that means you've already got a story then, haven't you? Sometimes I think we should collect everyone's little stories about their Adam's apples. We could put them up on the wall in the day room."

"What do you do when you get to *X*? Or *Q*?"

"Well, that's where you've got to get your thinking cap on, isn't it? You've got to be a bit creative."

What would I do for *Q*?

Oh, there it is. It's my sister Laura, isn't it, mocking me, just to look good in front of her new best friend Becca.

Doesn't he know what a quim is? Aw, bless—

Becca's tongue pushing between her pristine white teeth, hissing with laughter, leaning in to Laura and bonding against me.

We aren't born with all the information we're supposed to magically know.

Becca's hissing laugh echoes down the years.

I'm Queen Quim!

Nope. Enough. Snuff it out.

I look up at Sheila.

"You could end up with an alphabet of all the rude bits," I say.

"Well, you have to have rules. You've got to use the right name for a body part, or near enough, like. No slang. No rude words."

"Yes, but 'larynx' never would have turned up the story about 'Adam's apple,' would it?"

"No, true," she says thoughtfully. "But rules are there to be bent, aren't they? It's only a game."

Anus

Anus, I write.

I straighten the photocopied handout on the school desk in front of me and adjust my grip on my fountain pen. A potent blob of black ink spreads across my knuckle, working into the tiny lines and creases of my skin and cuticle. I wipe it on my trousers.

Black trousers, black ink, no worries.

There are two outlines of human bodies on the class handout, with straight lines pointing to various parts.

"And I'll stop you after ten minutes," says Mr. Miller, perching his wiry frame on the stool at the front of the lab, making the crotch of his musty trousers wrinkle up in a cat's whisker shape. "And use the proper names, please."

I draw my own connecting line from the word *anus* to the relevant area of the male silhouette. I don't know what's made me do it. There's no undoing it. It's in pen. But a real, slightly frightening sense of freedom is swelling in my belly. Maybe now is the time to say it: Mr. Miller, you, me, and biology, we were never meant to be. Let's call it quits, eh?

Kelvin and the new kid look at what I've written, and Kelvin laughs a silent and heartening laugh. The new kid doesn't laugh. His face smiles without his mouth smiling—maybe it's in the brow—and he watches on with a cool detachment.

Balls (hairy), I add, and then underline the *A* and *B*, before quickly coming up with *C*, *D*, and *E*, all from the same source. *Cock, dong, erection*. We both tense up with silent laughter.

Fanny, counters Kelvin, arcing a line out to the female. *Gonads*.
Horn.

Incest.

I frown at him. "Incest isn't a part of the body," I mutter.

"No, but when it happens, it makes a dysfunctional human. It's genetic." He connects it to a line to the male's midriff, and then the female's for good measure. "They're brother and sister."

I look at the new kid, and the new kid arches an eyebrow at me. We're not convinced. Still: *Jugs*.

Knob.

"Doesn't that begin with *n*?"

"Mine doesn't."

Lips.

Mammaries, nipples.

Orifice.

We're silent-laughing in that way that makes me kind of queasy. The mash-it-all-up childishness you can only get in a hot afternoon of triple science.

Prick.

Queer. A connecting line to the wrist.

Rim.

Slit.

Tit.

Urethra.

Vadge, wang.

Kelvin chews his pen while he mulls over the crowded diagram for what to put for *X*.

In the meantime I add *yum-yums*, *Zeppelins*, and draw lines to the boobs with a grand flourish.

Suddenly and with detached confidence, the new kid picks up his own pen, plucks off the lid, and writes *X chromosome*. He draws a line to the midriff. I look up at him, and he looks at me, and I don't get it. But he smiles, and I smile back, and I look at Kelvin. Kelvin doesn't get it either.

"I'll take that, thank you." The paper is whipped from beneath my pen, and Mr. Miller leans on the new kid's desk. "Malachy, I see it was a mistake to put you with these two. I'll see all three of you afterward."

"I still don't know how Jef poaches those eggs so well," says Sheila. "I try to do them at home, and they go all mangled."

"Mangled eggs," I say with a weak smile. I don't mean it as a joke. Just reporting what my brain is feeding back to me. But it's quite funny, I suppose.

"Ha! Mangled eggs. That could be my signature dish, couldn't it?"

Ah, I don't know, I can't eat. I'm made of stone inside. Honestly, I don't want to be difficult.

Sheila perches on the edge of the visitors' chair and slots her hands between her knees.

"I think it would be a good idea if you could manage just a little bit of it. You don't want to make yourself feel worse by not eating. I know the last thing you want to do is eat, I really do. But believe you me, I've walked up and down this corridor for eight years, and I tell you, it always helps. It always helps when you eat it. Sets you right for the day."

I should. I know I should.

"Do you want me to get him to make you some fried eggs? Honestly, it'll be no bother. And if he says no, I'll do them myself."

Bless her, she does try to make me laugh.

What passes for a laugh these days. Wheeze and cough.

"Or I could come over there and do choo-choo trains with you, if you'd rather try that," she says, unclasping her hands and absently checking the positioning of the little upside-down watch clipped to her breast.

I can feel myself being persuaded along, like a boat at rising tide, my hull lifting with the wash, scraping along the wet sand and stopping, scraping along and stopping.

It's you I need now.

If I imagine it right, I can…I can sense you, enthusiastic you, telling me, *Yeah, you can do it.*

I can do it.

Of course you can.

Of course I can. If I just…if I just remember you right…I can sense your face…the way it used to move when you'd decided on something.

This is going to happen.

Here it is. I love it. I love this blueprint of you, here in me.

This is going to happen.

It feels to me like you're here. I can hear the comforting tones of your voice. I can actually hear the sounds. Or the memory of the sounds. They remain in my brain. I can be persuaded.

What is that, when you can hear someone's voice without really hearing it through your ears? I'm not hearing you, but I'm hereing you. I'm H-E-R-E-ing you. You ignite my gray brain. Light me up. Spark me into being.

If you eat now, you'll thank yourself later.

I lift my heavy hand and reach out for the fork.

I know, I know. I need to try to eat.

Chew chew. Chew chew and think of you.

Ankle

Does it count in the A to Z game if it's someone else's ankle and not mine?

I can't beat the best ankle story of all time, which absolutely belongs to Laura. She went down in the history of our family with her ankle. I cannot believe how perfect the whole thing was, and I cannot believe how out of order I was.

What would I have been, about twelve? So she'd have been seventeen. I think I said to her—did I?—yes, I told her that her boyfriend at the time—what was his name?—I told her her boyfriend at the time had told me that he thought she had a fat arse.

He never did. He never said anything like it. Why did I ever even think to say something so cruel? I didn't feel the cruelty at the time. It was only a joke.

Her boyfriend must have delivered a persuasive explanation of not knowing anything about it, because she came storming back to me later in the day, absolutely spitting venom, and calling me a little shit.

Mum took my side, again. She told Laura I would never do something like that on purpose, and that it must have been some sort of misunderstanding. And she said—poor Laura—Mum said, "I wouldn't be surprised if anyone did say you had a fat backside, the kind of skimpy shorts you waltz around in."

Of course Laura rushed upstairs in floods of tears. And the irony, the beautiful irony of it was that Laura must have dumped herself down on her bed with such a leaden sulk that she fractured her ankle between the bed frame and her arse.

There's not a year goes by that I don't think what utter humiliation she must have felt, shuffling on her backside down the narrow staircase to tell us, wailing, that she needed to go to the ER.

It's no wonder she ended up going the way she did.

"Let me get that." Sheila lifts my abandoned plate away. I've managed a few bites. "All right, you've done well there, haven't you? How are you doing now? Have you been able to lie back at all?"

I shake my head.

"Starts you coughing, does it? Did you sit up all night too?"

Minimal nod.

Shaking your head means no. Nodding it means yes. Why would that be? I'll save that for *H* in my A to Z.

"It's a problem, that, isn't it? You try to get a moment's respite because you're cold, and then your lungs start filling up because you're lying down. It hardly seems fair, does it?"

She stands with her weight on one hip, as if she's never encountered anyone with such a problem before.

"I'm all right," I say.

Sheila rearranges the knife and fork less precariously on the plate and considers me for a while. "Give me a shout, anyway, if you want any blankets or anything. Or a nice cup of something warm. Although we've run out of mugs again." She lowers her voice. "I don't know why people can't read the sign and bring their mugs back to the coffee machine. It says it right there. It's not too much to ask, is it?"

She takes the plate away and puts it on a cart in the corridor.

"I mean, I don't mind washing all the dregs out if they just leave the mugs there, but I haven't got time to go around doing a collection every twenty minutes. Have you filled in your lunch card yet?"

"No. Will he make me some chicken soup? My mum always used to make me chicken soup when I was sick."

She smiles. It's a sweet smile.

She understands and leaves to make inquiries.

Stay lifted. Self-sufficient. I can do this thing.

What thing?

Look out of the window. Look at the wall. Look at the bed-sheets. Look at my arms.

God, look at them against the bedsheets. Like great big use-less horses' forelegs. What are they? A connecting piece between chest and hand. Between neck and hand. Between heart and hand. Well, what? They're arms, aren't they?

Look at them. The superhighway of the body. They're history. A hopeless historical map, plotting clots and craters of short-lived attempts to spark me into being. They have evolved into someone else's arms. An old man's arms, not the arms of a forty-year-old. Purple and yellow, brown and bruised. Every vein is collapsed. Every entry point blocked off. Lumped-up fistula scars now useless, no way in anymore. My insides are sealed off from the outside forever.

They're numb cold, my arms. Cold arms are the price to pay. I can't keep them under the covers. They feel like they're dead already.

Arms

I flick the syringe lightly with shaking fingertips, and the bubble unsticks itself from the plunger and creeps sullenly through the liquid toward the needle.

"Come on, man, the little ones don't matter."

"That's not a little bubble, though, is it?"

It settles up around by the needle, and I flick again. Flick harder.

"Careful, man. You're losing the liquid out the top."

"I'm not injecting bubbles."

"It's only a little one."

"Listen, man—fuck off. It's up to me, yeah?"

Mal sits back, surprised. I never talk to him like this.

I don't like this.

Feels wrong. This is not me.

All I can think of is you. What if this goes wrong? What if…
what if it changes me forever? What if you find out? I'll lose you.

No, no. All this is bullshit. This is exactly like I was before I
took my first trip. I was scared there would be no way back. But
there is a way back. And anyway, this is the first and last time.

Try anything once. Once only.

Sheila's head eclipses the television screen a moment as she walks
past. She's doing her Closing Ceremony.

"I'm just on my way, Ivo," she says. "Got to go home and see
what that useless lump of a husband's been up to overnight."

"You should…you should get him in here. Ask him to
come here."

"What? Come in here and I can look after everyone at the
same time? That's not a bad idea, that. Save me coming and going

every day, wouldn't it? Now, how are you doing? You're looking perkier than when I came in earlier. I want to see more of the same later, please. Do you need anything sorting out before I head off?"

I don't want her to go. Don't go, Sheila.

"No."

"You're comfortable, are you?"

I nod.

"How are your arms and shoulders?" She rests her olive-skinned hand on my arm, uninvited. I don't mind. Everything everyone does to me now is uninvited, and it's rarely so tender. "Are they a bit cold? Do you want me to get a blanket?"

I nod. "They are cold. They ache."

"It's always a problem," she says, opening the bedside cabinet and beginning to rummage. "Because with most people it's all these drips and taps and pipes, they have to keep their arms exposed for them. It's always the same. Where are these spare blankets? Honestly, people must just come in and—" She stands up and looks about.

I know what's coming.

"Oh, here," she says, reaching down into my bag. She's got the crochet blanket.

No, no. Don't ask.

"Put this around your shoulders. That'll keep you nice and warm, won't it?"

No, don't.

She casts the blanket about my shoulders, and your scent wafts up, perfectly preserved, and floods my senses.

I don't want her to see, I don't want her to see, but she's looking up at my face, and she can see now there's something wrong. My throat's so tight. Hot, tight, tight, dry. That's normally what passes for crying with me. It's a dry throat. It's not being able to breathe.

But this time, for once, gratifying tears begin to prickle.

"Oh, lovey…" she says, quietly.

She doesn't make a fuss. She must be used to unexplained fluids leaking from patients.

How weird, tears. I trickle water for you.

Sheila sits on the side of the bed, takes up my hand, and strokes the back of it.

"Is there anything I can do, lovey?" she says in the softest, gentlest voice.

My throat aches, hot. "Sorry, sorry. Stupid."

"Not at all."

"This blanket," I say. "Lot of memories."

"Really?"

"My girlfriend made it for me."

"Oh. I wasn't sure if you had a girlfriend or anything."

"Ex."

"Oh, I see."

She doesn't see, of course.

"Mmm." I sniff. "She crocheted it specially for me."

"No—she did all this? It's lovely."

"I've been thinking about her a lot lately. Been talking to her. In my mind."

"Special one, was she? It's a shame, isn't it? Sometimes."

"Anyway, you'd better go," I say.

"No, no. There's no hurry."

"No, I'm fine. And husbands don't just look after themselves, do they?"

"No, you're right there. Well, if you're sure you're OK? I'm happy to stay."

"No, no. Thanks."

She rises from her perch on the side of the bed and places my hand down on the sheets.

"I'll be back tonight, all right? Press the button if you want Jackie. Don't be shy, now."

She gives me a regretful little smile and leaves me. I'm wrapped up to my neck in crochet, up to my neck in you.

I would give everything I have ever had and everything I will ever have just to put my arms around you, have you put your arms around me.

Our bodies simply fit, yours and mine.

That's what I'm going to think of now. That will see me off to sleep. Those arms of yours, wrapped tight, tight around me.

_13_

Back

I'm lying facedown, with my head sideways on your pillow. My senses are wide, wide open. I have never, ever experienced anything like this while sober. My hearing is absolutely clear, and the scents I am breathing in are blossoming and blooming in my brain. The clean, fresh smell of your hair from the pillow, the smell of the resin of the wood of your bedstead.

This is the first time I've had my shirt off with you, and the feel of the sheets on my skin is just so vital.

And now I am tracking your lips in my mind as they prickle down from the base of my neck, down past my shoulders, down, down my spine. And your fingertips too trace back and forth, outward and back in, in the line of my ribs, delicate, delicate, your hair now hanging down, brushing softly from side to side on my skin, a tingling trace in its wake.

You find your way down to the lowest of my ribs, and I suddenly flinch and tense, almost fling you from me.

"*No*," I say. "That bit's too ticklish."

You lie up against me and murmur in my ear—"That's what I was looking for"—before heading back down, and kissing there again, *right there*. And now my whole back is unable to take any more, and I cry out and turn over, and I can see you there, laughing wickedly.

"I love that bit," you say. "It's torture."

Awake now.

I'm awake.

What?

I can see the gray-green plane of the lawn beyond the magnolia tree through the window. Did that light just come on? Or was it always on, and it was only me who flicked on?

I'm confused.

What woke me then? I'm sure there was—

((((Uuuuuh)))

Oh, oh no.

It's her next door again. The groaning woman and her groans. It's at a frequency where I can sort of hear it in the wall. Thin wall, then; hollow partition.

((((Uuuuuh)))

I put my hand on my brow, and for a moment that's all there is of me. A hand on a brow, swashing and scrunching and scratching, and knuckling the eyeballs now. Itch, itch, *itch* to get this sound out of my head.

((Uuuuuh))

But it won't go, of course. There's no stopping it. I can't believe she always starts up right when I'm trying to get to sleep. Just… just as I've dropped off into peaceful slumber, it's—

(Uuuuuh)

It's ruined. And it'll get worse. It always gets worse. If it was the sort of groan that stayed the same volume, I could put it out of my mind, but it changes. It grows louder and louder. Keeps you listening. It's like purgatory.

The light outside flicks off again.

(Uuuuuh)

Blood

Think blood. What can I say about blood? A complete history from start to finish.

Uuuuuh.

In the beginning, I was a few cells of blood and—whatever it is babies are made of before they're properly human. The abortable mush. How is it that embryos or fetuses can develop intricate veins and capillaries and auricles and ventricles and all that stuff? Amazing, really.

Uuuuuh.

So, birth, lots of blood there, but not mine, so much. The divvying up between me and my mum. Everything that was on the outside of me was hers, everything on the inside mine. And what shall we do with this bit? Cut it off, sling it away, snip snip, medical waste. We'll not talk of it again.

They fry it and eat it sometimes, don't they? Cannibals.

Uuuuuh.

Uneventful childhood, my blood would see the light of day through knee scrapes and head bangs, testing the coagulation—no hemophilia—then pretty much just ripped cuticles, before the great event of—what, about 1982?—when my sister tied my wrist to the back of her bike with her old jump rope and towed me off down the street on my ride-on truck. I distinctly remember how I imagined the wind would riffle my hair as Laura pedaled and the streets and houses would sail by at sixty miles per hour. This was going to be great. Three thrilling meters in, I was yanked from my plastic seat, and I traveled the following five meters on my face, before Laura stopped and turned to see why pedaling had become so laborious.

Then she dropped her bike and ran away.

That's probably the earliest drama for my blood, flooding onto my screaming face as I stumbled up the steps to my mum, the wooden handles of the jump rope jumping and hopping on each step as I climbed. Mum had been sitting on the edge of her bed, putting on her makeup.

She told me I staggered into her room like a murder victim.

I had to have an injection.

Dr. Rhys had half-glasses and was kindly and had lollipops in a tin on his desk.

"You, young man, have a blood type of AB positive, it says here."

The blood type struck a chord with me, because I was learning my ABCs. And AB seemed good. ABC might have been better, but, well… Maybe I should have that on my gravestone: AB positive. Alongside height and shoe size. For future generations to know, you know?

After I totaled my ride-on truck, the story had to be circulated on the family grapevine. Come Sunday, I was around to my grandma and granddad's to sport my scars. We stopped off there every week after church, even after Dad died. They wanted to see us.

"Stop *picking*."

Mum relished telling the tale of the ride-on truck to my grandma, carefully crafting every last detail to make Laura seem much naughtier than she actually was. It made me guilty and embarrassed, so I stopped listening. I looked at the TV. It wasn't on, but I looked at it anyway. Laura sat next to me, quietly fuming.

"He was bleeding like a stuck pig. He looked like a murder victim. But he only had one or two cuts—I couldn't believe how much blood… Anyway, Dr. Rhys was telling him he was AB positive, wasn't he, kiddo? Quite rare, he reckoned."

Granddad leaned over to me and muttered with a mutinous air, "What blood type was Christ?"

I didn't know what he was talking about, so he lifted his wine bottle and sloshed it at me.

"Ten percent by vol?" He wheezed in lieu of a laugh. "A nice bit of Beaujolais?" Wheeze. "That'd get me back to church on a Sunday morning!" Wheeze.

I was fourteen when I started seasoning my blood. 1989. What, twenty-six years ago. Over a quarter of a century.

That's probably the next chapter point after Laura ran for the hills and I lost my no-claims bonus on the ride-on truck. That's such a short time, 1982 to 1989. It's no time at all, is it?

That's actually shocked me a bit.

Vodka and orange in our school flasks. Me and Kelvin. We raided Kelvin's dad's liquor cabinet and filled Kelvin's Transformers flask with vodka and fresh orange. More by luck than judgment, seeing as vodka doesn't smell of anything, and we pretty much got away with it. I was cagier about it than Kelvin, but I sat in a haze through geography, and then in math Kelvin was sent out of the class for being boisterous. I've no idea if the teacher realized. Probably. They say they always do.

Anyway, we did get caught: Kelvin's mum had a big go at him for taking all that fresh orange juice. It was a luxury purchase in the 1980s.

I mean, it's amazing, blood. The quality of your blood makes for the quality of your life.

I seasoned my blood with a few choice herbs and spices. Nothing wrong in that. Everyone's at it, in one way or another.

Glug down blessed blood, or sup on fermented liquids, or draw in vapors or smoke—or whatever.

And the blood carries it around your body, flavors your brain.

And your heart.

And your lungs.

And your liver.

And your kidneys.

"So, you have a blood type of AB positive, it says here."

I nod. Dr. Rhys is still sporting his pretentious half-glasses after all these years, like some Harley Street big shot. What's it been, eleven, twelve years? Almost thirteen, actually, since the ride-on truck. He still has a tin of lollipops on his desk. Will I get one today? I still suck them. We take them into clubs, big baby-dummy-shaped ones, sucking them like children. Sweets and E, back to innocence, back to childhood. Pure pleasure.

"I should update our records here. Do you—um, are you a smoker?"

I nod.

"Roughly how many a day? Ten?"

"Twen—ahem—twenty." It's hard to talk quietly sometimes. Have to clear my throat.

"Alcohol?"

I nod.

"Units a week?"

I'm not sure what units are. I know pints.

"Pff—" I look at the ceiling. "Maybe about twenty pints?" Twenty seems fair.

Dr. Rhys writes it in and then scrunches up his nose. "Recreational drugs…?" Slight involuntary shake of his head, before peering back at me for an answer.

Here we are. We're here, and we've got to tell the truth. I don't mind telling him the truth.

"Um, grass."

"Marijuana?"

I nod.

"And speed too."

"Ecstasy?"

I nod. I'm quite impressed he knows it.

He makes a few notes. His ancient chair creaks as he adjusts his brogued feet between the wooden legs. I'm grateful for his professional silence.

So anyway, I tell him I'm thirsty all the time, going to the toilet all the time, and then there's the weight loss. I look at him closely. He knows what I'm thinking. He's got the notes. He'll be thinking the same. He'll be thinking about what my dad died of. He'll be thinking about what my dad died of. He'll be thinking, *Mmm, family history of early cancer deaths on the male side… What are the odds of…hmm.*

"I'm worried it might be cancer," I say. "I think that's why— well, it's taken me a while to come and see you."

"But you don't think about giving up the ciggies?" he says, without looking up from his piece of paper.

He must feel the silence beside him, because he looks up at me over the top of his glasses and pauses significantly.

"Your symptoms could indicate any number of things," he says, looking back down at the papers. "Best not to speculate. What I'll get you to do is take a short stroll down to the blood-test unit, and we'll take it from there."

My head's pounding as the bloods nurse leeches out the liquid. I should tell her. But I need to be strong. I should tell her I'm not feeling so good. The ceiling is bearing down on me, and this place is so hot. It'll pass, no doubt. I haven't had any breakfast, and I'm feeling weak and sick, hot hospital, waiting ages for my name to be called.

And those vials, filling the vials full of black. It's so *black*. Less red in those little vials, more inky black. And quite smelly. Smells like— like what? It smells like a *jungle gym*. Unpainted iron *jungle gym*. Is…is the iron on a jungle gym the same as the iron in your blood? I could ask, but I don't want… Stupid.

The floor falls away from me.

"Jean, we've got another one."

"It's always the men, isn't it?"

The results are right there in front of him. Right there, on paper. But all he's doing is sitting there in his chair, trying to get his mouse pointer to open the right bit on his computer screen. He totally knows my mind is racing away—

Cancer cancer cancer cancer.

—and the bottom's dropping out of my stomach.

He's punishing me. He's making me pay for not looking after myself and for taking drugs, and for leeching the NHS of all its resources, because he likes his job to be nice and easy.

Cancer cancer cancer cancer.

"Well," he says, exhaling through whistley nostrils, "your tests indicate a very high level of blood glucose—"

And you've got cancer.

"—which indicates to us that it seems your pancreas, which is a rather important organ situated here"—and he circles the air around my belly—"just, uh, just below your stomach cavity, is not functioning properly—"

And you've got cancer.

"Now, when your pancreas produces insulin, that insulin gets pumped into your bloodstream to help you absorb the sugars, you see?"

How long have I got? He's wittering on, and all I want to know is the answer. I should have asked my mum to come with me. I actually want my mum. No joke.

"Now, this is a major change."

That's it. He stops, and he looks me in the eye, and he says slowly, "This is a major change."

I nod, comprehendingly. What's a major change?

"People find it takes a good deal of adjusting to. But it's largely a matter of self-discipline. Before you know it, it'll be something you don't even think about. A little jab—*pop*—and you carry on just like everyone else."

"So I need to inject myself?"

"Yes, yes, but modern kits make it all very straightforward and easy, and a lot of the time people say they can do it without anyone even noticing. Or if it's an awkward situation, you know, you can take yourself off to the loos or wherever and sort yourself out there."

So I'm injecting myself? I have an image of grimacing and straining to pull the tourniquet tight with my teeth and jabbing a hypodermic into my throbbing vein.

"And then there's no reason why you can't live as long and happy and fulfilled a life as anyone else. There are tens of thousands of people living with type 1 diabetes in the UK, and they all get by just fine. Hundreds of thousands."

And this is the first time he has said *diabetes*. I'm completely sure of that.

So it's not cancer.

I have not-cancer.

"I was totally shitting it!" I say, the relief flushing through me at the Queen's Head as I reveal the verdict to Mal and Kelvin. "All I could think was cancer, you know? Cancer or AIDS. I'm telling you, though, if they'd told me it was cancer, I'd be straight up to Hephzibah's Rock, and I'd take a running jump, straight into the river. I'm not going through all that pain and agony. I would wait for a perfect sunny day. I would leap into the blue, slow motion at the top of the arc of my leap, my face warmed by the summer sun, drop into the Severn, and get washed out to sea. I wouldn't be scared. It'd be hep-hep-hoo-raaay—*splash*."

"No, don't say that," says Kelvin. "Don't joke about stuff like that."

"You'd be shitting it too much to do that," says Mal. "Unless you were completely caning it on E or something."

Something about me doesn't quite like this idea. Knowing that Mal most likely has a pocketful of Es makes it all a bit real. A bit seedy. A bit possible.

"No," he says. "You want to slash your wrists, don't you?" He draws back his sleeve to bare his wrist and draws along it with the nail of his little finger. "What you want to do is cut a line, from here, down to here. Along the arm, see? Most people try to go across, but it just closes back up. Don't *cross the path*, go *down the highway*. Job done."

"Ah, Mal," says Kelvin, squirming. "That's sick."

"What?" Mal shrugs. "Better that than being hooked up to a big bank of machines."

"Oh yeah," I say. "If I'm hooked up to a big bank of machines, just switch me off. I don't want to know."

"Hey, man, I'd switch you off," Mal says with comic earnestness. "I'll make sure you get a decent send-off."

"But would you then fling me off the top of Hephzibah's Rock?"

"For you, anything."

"Hep-hep-hoo-raaay…"

"*Splash*."

Electric click from outside as the security light switches my window out of darkness. Stark electric shadows branch from the tree, flee across my sheets, frozen now midflight. Shift minimally in the wind.

Uuuuuh.

The groans of the woman next door start up again, sparked by the light, no doubt. This is the world I live in now.

It almost doesn't matter to me.

That's how it is.

Out in the corridor the fire doors unstick and thud, and footsteps quietly approach.

Sheila appears at my doorway and peers in to see if I'm awake. I'm awake.

"Are you comfortable?" she murmurs in her twilight voice. "Do you need anything?"

"I'm awake," I say. "I'd rather be asleep."

"Oh, well, I'm sure I could get you something—I'll just have to take a quick squint at your notes."

"No, no, it's all right," I say with a sigh. "You can probably ignore me. I'm being grumpy."

"Well, I'm not surprised," she says, charitably. "It's enough to make anyone grumpy, having that light come on all the time."

"I thought they'd fixed it."

Uuuuuh.

"Useless, aren't they?" She pads over to the window and looks outside.

"Unless it's someone setting them off for a laugh. Kids, like."

"That's what worries me a bit," she says. "There's rich pickings in the store cupboards. Medication, needles. Some people will do anything to get their hands on that stuff."

Uuuuuh.

"Oh, hark at her, eh? You could set your watch by her, couldn't you?"

"It's the same every night. She doesn't know she's doing it, does she?"

"Oh, no. It's only snoring, really."

"She's not in any pain?"

"No, no. But it's the medication too, you see. That has an effect. Sometimes we can change it, which might ease things."

Uuuuuh.

"Every time she starts up, it snaps me awake again."

"I always think she's like Old Faithful, you know, comes out with a big burst of noise every hour on the hour."

"Is she all right?"

Uuuuuh.

"She's a very poorly lady, I'm afraid. Very poorly. But she's a fighter, definitely, bless her. She's fought every step of the way."

"Yeah?"

"Yeah," she says. "There are some people you meet who totally restore your faith in the job, you know? She's one of them. A genuinely lovely lady. Gentle, uncomplaining."

"Not like me," I say. Half joke.

"Oh, you're all right, aren't you? Keep yourself to yourself."

"Yeah, I suppose."

She sits now uninvited in my visitors' seat. Do I mind? No,

I don't mind. I quite like the presumptuousness. It's nice when nice people presume I'm nice. It makes me nice.

"Listen, I'm sorry if I upset you yesterday—that business with the blanket and all."

I look down at the blanket, which is now installed permanently around my shoulders.

"No, don't be," I say. "I'm sorry. It was a bit unexpected, is all."

"What was her name?"

"Mia," I say without thinking—and the shape of the word in my mouth, the sound of it in my ears feels—it feels strange. A sound I used to make every day, many times a day, but which I haven't for…for *years* now.

"Special one, was she?"

"Yeah. Another person who'd restore your faith. She was a nurse too, actually."

"Oh, right. Whereabouts?"

"All over. She only just got past the training. She worked a short while."

"Yeah, so many of them drop out in the early days."

"Mmm."

"What did she want to do in nursing?"

"She was into getting to the root of things. Alternatives, you know?"

"Yeah, like, um…holistic medicine? Reiki, hypnotherapy, stuff like that?"

"Yeah. She wanted to work with patients individually, depending on what they needed."

"Ouu, she'd have her work cut out there. They're under so much pressure, hospital departments."

"Yeah. Bum wiping and processing them on, isn't it?"

"Bum wiping if you're lucky. That's what I love about working here at the hospice: you get to spend time with people. They come in here and they're scared, because they don't know what to expect, and you can really turn them around. You can make a difference when they'd maybe spent their whole lives dreading the name: *St. Leonard's.*"

"'Come out feetfirst in a box,'" I say.

"You see, it's so bad people say that," she says a little agitatedly. "It makes me so cross, because it's not true. We do so many positive things here."

"Yeah. Sorry."

"Oh, don't be daft. I'm not having a go at you. So, what happened then, with…Mia, was it?"

"Oh—didn't work out."

"Tell me she didn't end up with some consultant."

"No, no."

"That lot, they all need bringing down a peg or two."

"No, no. It was all my fault. I messed it up."

She winces sympathetically. "That doesn't seem like you."

"Just…I tried to live up to… I really badly wanted it to work, but I could just never seem to make it happen. I couldn't get my act together, and I don't know why."

"Oh, Ivo."

I smile ruefully. "I'm just an idiot, I think."

"Well, my darling, you won't find anyone judging you here, all right? You know and I know there's plenty of people between these walls who've paid a very heavy price for doing nothing wrong at all. And you can bet there are thousands of people out there on the streets who'll never pay any price for being total—yeah—jerks. It's not fair, but there it is. It's for no one to judge."

She stands herself up from my chair.

"Listen, I say this to everyone, but I mean it with you, because you're one of my specials: if you want to talk about anything, then I'm here for you. You know that, don't you?"

"Thanks, Sheila."

"And if you *don't* want to talk about anything, then at least do yourself a favor and keep your thoughts in order. There's your A to Z game. Or think happy things. Maybe about this ex; if you had happy times together, no one's stopping you from going away back to them in your mind. It might be helpful, is all I'm saying."

I draw the sheets up around my middle.

"I don't mean to say anything untoward," she says.

"No, no. Not at all."

"It might help, is all." She sighs and scratches her arm a moment. "Anyway, sounds like Old Faithful's gone off the boil again. So give me a buzz if you want anything."

"Will do. Thanks."

She pads away down the corridor, and as I hear the double doors slip shut behind her, the security light flicks off once more.

It's been lovely to talk about you with someone who understands.

It's been lovely to feel strong enough to think about you at all.

Chesticles

"Chesticles?" you say.

"Yeah," I say. "Becca used to say it."

It's the joy in your face that takes me by surprise, and then your infectious and unfettered laugh.

"Oh, that's lovely!" you say. "And I suppose Becca ought to know. You wait, I'm going to use that *all the time*."

I can't remember the last time I heard anyone laugh so delightedly. And so delightedly at me.

I'm surprised.

I don't know what to do. I sort of shrug modestly that I thought to say it.

It's *nice*.

It's the little details that get to me.

⊂∘⃝∘⊃

"If I had a million in the bank, I'd totally get a boob job," says Laura.

I exchange a glance with Kelvin, and we agree with a micro-shift of eyebrows that we'll remain silent. I stare back down into my nearly empty pint. Look at us, two seventeen-year-old zeros who've gravitated like children to the two squat little stools drawn up to the sticky dark-wood table. But here we are with Laura's friends, all of them around twenty-two, and all sitting in proper chairs with backs. Laura's finally deigned to let me come out with her. She's in a bad place at the moment, having ditched her boyfriend of six years. I could almost persuade myself that she's glad of my company.

"Because men—society—it's such a pain, isn't it? They're either leg men, boob men, or bum men, aren't they? It's not fair. I mean, if you're a woman, you can't say you're, like, a chest woman, or a schlong or a butt woman."

"Oh, I don't know," says Becca. "I like a nice arse." She twists theatrically at the outside of her Afro and looks lustily across the room.

Oh, Becca.

If there is any benefit in the world to listening to my sister whine on about her woes it's that we get to sit at the same table as the goddess Becca. Smoldering eyes and flawless ebony skin—an instant magnet to everyone around. How pathetically feeble

Kelvin and I must look in the company of Becca. And yet here we are. We're on the stools.

"But it's men who make all the rules. And we're all supposed to play by those rules. It's bollocks. I think, you know, if you've got a lovely big pair of chesticles"—and she holds her hands illustratively in front of her imagined boobs—"you're already a step ahead of the game."

"So what are you then?" Becca asks Kelvin. "Are you a boob man? Do you like a lovely big pair of chesticles?"

"Well," he says, "I don't really know. Maybe a leg man?"

I'm suddenly aware of the crappiness of Kelvin's hair. He's got good-boy hair. Side parting. I run my fingers through my tangles, just in case. At least mine's long. Kelvin looks like an office junior.

"Not a boob man?" says Laura.

He reddens but plunges on, shaking his head. "I never understood the fascination with breasts. I mean, what's so amazing? They're just fat sacks, aren't they? Fat sacks with a cherry on top."

There's the tiniest pause, before both women collapse in laughter. I glance at him, and he looks bemused. They think he's joking.

"Any more than a handful is a waste," he adds.

Jesus, I don't want to be linked with this. I'm here trying to appeal to girls—to *women*—and he's giving out all the signals of inexperience. I catch myself actually shuffling my stool away from him.

"What about you then?" says Becca. She turns to me and gives me one of those smiles that could knock a man down. "Give me a shopping list so we can get you matched up. Are you a boob man or a leg man or an arse man?"

"You're a boob man, I bet, aren't you?" says Kelvin.

Here's the thing: Becca has I think the most magnificent breasts I have ever seen. Kelvin and I have spent hours dreaming up wonderful new positions to take in relation to Becca's breasts. We both know it, and we both know the other knows it. I fix my eyes firmly on her eyes, and then gaze up at the ceiling, lean back from the table, right back on two legs of my stool. "Well, I don't know," I say. "Beggars can't be choosers, can they?"

"Aw!" says Laura. "Are you reduced to begging?"

"You must have a preference," says Becca. "What's the first thing you look at? Go on, say you're lusty and forget everything about personality and being a gentleman and all that. You just want, y'know, a good *wooargh*. What is it?"

I'm thinking *boobs*. I'm thinking *Becca's boobs*. I know I really should just say "boobs." The word actually leaks into the middle of my tongue, but I clamp my teeth shut.

"Boobs. Totally boobs," Kelvin says with finality.

But I can't admit it to Becca. I've angled my position on the stool specifically to include her breasts in my composition of the room.

"Honestly, I really… I couldn't choose. I'd be all over the shop. It'd be everything. I don't think there is a boob man or a bum man or whatever."

Mal mercifully chooses this moment to return from the bar,

carrying three pints in his hands, a glass of wine in his top pocket, and a packet of scampi fries swinging from between his teeth.

"What about you, Bigbad?" says Becca, turning away from my wriggling deceit. "Are you a boob man, a bum man, or a leg man?"

Mal grits his teeth around the packet of fries as he knocks each glass out onto the table.

"I'm a cunt man."

He drops himself in his seat and tears open the packet.

"Jesus, Mal," I say.

"What?" he says.

Becca gives a great big hearty laugh.

"I hate that word," says Kelvin.

"Cunt?" my sister says brightly. "Oh, I like it. I think it's funny. Cunt, cunt, cunt." She puts a very deliberate clean *t* on the end of each word. She draws out a cigarette for Mal and one for herself.

And this is it: I'm getting the first possible stirrings of a tiny inkling that Mal and Laura have a little bit of a thing going on between them. She's laughing now very brightly and I see Mal smile to himself, a big smoky smile, looking down at the table. Pleased with himself. It strikes me because Mal never normally gives this stuff away.

How is this? How is it that this bloke can come along and be as horrible as he wants, and still come away smelling of roses? That's the magic of Mal, isn't it? People are just drawn to him. They do what he says. And they don't stop him doing anything.

"So, you're the only one who's not laid your cards on the table yet," says Becca, looking over at me. "Boob, bum, or leg?"

"Well, I don't know," I say, as honestly as I can.

"Aw, sweet!" says Laura.

"No, I mean, I think I'm all of those things."

"A sensitive lover?" says Becca, with a teasing little smile.

"Well, I'm seventeen. I've had one proper girlfriend," I say. "What do you think?"

Becca roars with laughter. "Honesty! You'll go far!"

"What do you think, Mal? Do you think I should get a boob job?" says Laura.

"Yeah, go for it." And now, all of a sudden, Mal's an expert on the pros and cons of cosmetic surgery. "People get too hung up about it. Some big moral thing. Especially with women. This major pressure that somehow you're not allowed to do this with your own body. It's stupid."

"Yeah!" Laura says sparklingly.

"It's just like dyeing your hair or getting your ears pierced, isn't it? It's the new makeup, a nip and a tuck here and there."

"That's what I think," says Laura. "You've got all the eighteen-year-old girls getting boob jobs for their birthday—it's totally part of the culture. It's just like a tattoo."

"I bet Mum would love to see you get a boob job," I say. "Because she absolutely loved your tattoo, didn't she? What did she call it? A slag tag?"

"Cranky old bitch," says Laura. "Just repeating some phrase from her church group. I bet she dined out for a month on that story. The prodigal daughter."

"I think she might want to get you exorcised."

"Do you know what they did in the nineteenth century?" Mal dabs the ash off his cigarette and speaks out the smoke. "When they were wearing corsets, anyway, they had these two ribs removed, here"—he grabs Laura by the wrist, lifts her arm, and chops his hand at her lower two ribs—"down here, they had them taken out so they could make the corset tighter."

"Ahhh! Mal!"

"And they'd lace these corsets so tight that all their organs would get pushed up into their chests."

"Is that true?"

"So, you know, I don't see the problem if you want to upgrade a couple of wasp stings into a pair of lovely fun bags."

There's a momentary process in Laura's eyes, before she bursts into unconvincing peals of laughter.

I think she's thinking, *What a funny guy.*

I think she's thinking, *He's lucky I'm so fine with how I am, to say something so daring.*

But I know he knows.

He knows she's not so fine with how she is. He *totally* knows.

The rubber tires squeak as I am trundled along the shiny corridor by Kelvin. Nice of him to come and visit me. Ah, man, why did I let them persuade me into a wheelchair? Is this humiliating? I could walk this easily. But I've always enjoyed being a passenger.

It's nice being pushed. The changing perspectives wiping themselves across my eyes. Vague shift of air in low drafts, subtly swirling temperatures, mixing with billowing acoustics as the rooms pass on by.

Could pleasures get any simpler?

"I bet you're sick of being asked this," says Kelvin from behind me, "but if there's anything I can do, you will tell me, won't you? Practical stuff or anything else. Anything."

"Thanks. I'm good. I'm all right. Better now I'm in here."

"You only have to ask."

"Yeah, cheers."

"Out the main entrance, is it?"

"Suppose."

The automatic doors trundle open, and there's the first thrill of unconditioned air on my knees and thighs. It envelops me completely as we push on through, lingers around my nostrils and lips, cradling my head, my neck, riffling my hair. We emerge into the open, and the brightness makes me squint. Magical nature. Makes me feel so dead and dusty and plastic. I'm an indoor animal. I don't belong out in the wilds like this. Uncontrolled, unregulated nature, coming to get me and whisk me away.

We roll down a paved slope, the chair now gently percussive over the regular gaps between the slabs. Soothing pulse. I close my eyes to the brightness. Sun warm on my eyelids. Natural warmth.

The tires of the wheelchair crackling consistently through microscopic grit. I register every grain, fresh and high-definition. My hearing has been calibrated for too long by the beeps of machinery, acoustics of plaster and glass, jangling fridge, throb of corrupt blood in my ears. The wind opens up the distance, wakens the trees; the leaves wash briefly and recede. It's beautiful. It's overwhelming. I want to inhale it all, breathe it, take it all in. But I can't. I can't draw deep. I manage only a pant.

We turn a tight little bend on the slope and pass through an archway into the hospice garden. And it's beautiful too. Grand lawn with paths ribboning its low banks and gentle inclines. High wall all around. Old-looking wall, soft blushing pink bricks, crumbly pointing. Tailored, tamed nature.

The sun chooses this moment to radiate through to me, through me. It feels like…it feels like *life*. I can sense my corrupt blood bubbling and basking beneath the surface. All these things remind me of you: you and me in our favorite place up at the top of the valley, gazing down.

"Beautiful," I say out loud to myself. Out loud to you. "Beautiful."

"Yeah," says Kelv, the only ears to hear.

Rolling peacefully forward, we pass the flower beds, all these carefully chosen specimens. Amazing, amazing, that these delicate petals have unfurled from the earth, vivid sunlit colors, calling out to nature, calling the humans to come, come and cultivate.

"Look at that," I say. "Still got their verbena. They're lucky."

"Yeah?"

"They were all wiped out the last couple of years. Hard frost. Must be the wall keeping them sheltered."

"Right."

"And alliums," I tut fondly.

Of course it's you I imagine I'm talking to, not Kelvin. It's you I can sense pointing at the seed heads, looking over at me, your eyes delighted at the collection of bobbing heads. You speak a sentence to me, all blurred enthusiastic tones, and I can hear you say—

Huuuge!

—and you grin and turn away.

"There are roses, and there are nonroses," says Kelvin. "I only see nonroses."

"The big globey flower heads, there. They're alliums. And look, there's scabious. Bees land on it, get the nectar, and it sends them to sleep. All zoned out."

"Oh yeah, look. Stoned."

"Yeah."

I've bleeped ten thousand little packets of allium bulbs through the checkout at the garden center in the late summer sales. *Plant early autumn.* I wonder how many of the ones I've sold are reaching out to this warm sun, dappled across the region's back gardens? I wonder if I sold these ones here? That could be my life's achievement. Maybe I'd settle for that.

We resume our journey and round a corner of gentle, wispy grasses that bow and flutter in the soft breeze. Poppies. The sun urges warmth onto my knees as it burns through the thin cloud.

Given time, you and I would have had a garden. We would have had a little plot, and we would have taken such good care of it. We'd have had a clump of scabious to please the bees, and wispy grasses lining a pond.

Given time.

I remember all the times you tried to get me to apply for the garden design course. All those reminders to get my résumé into shape.

I can see you now, pulling on your coat, gathering up your keys, pointing at your desk, saying, "It's all there in that bundle of papers. Three courses you could apply for. The deadline's in July, so you've got time."

I don't know why I couldn't bring myself to do it. Too soon, too soon. July was an age away. And how is anyone supposed to get enthusiastic about scratching their résumé together? A few aimless, basic qualifications. Who would ever want me?

"Just have a look through them," you said. "You totally know your stuff. Come on, one small change is all it takes. If you fill in this one piece of paper now, you'll thank yourself as you cherry-pick the best jobs and sip champagne through the summer."

It was a good fantasy.

Kelvin and I crest the top of a low rise, follow a gentle curve and roll down the other side, and arrive alongside a bench. Kelvin heaves the chair into a stable position and settles on the seat beside me. We exchange a brief look, a brief smile, before gazing at the garden, letting the silence set in with the sun. Kelvin takes off his glasses and begins to clean them with his T-shirt.

"I'm sorry I haven't been in to see you before now," he says, lifting and huff-huffing the left lens. "I thought you might want to get your bearings for the first few days. How was the move from your apartment?"

"It's all wrapped up. There's people here who're going to get it all cleared out when the time comes."

"I could do that for you. You only had to ask."

"No, no, it's all fine. St. Leonard's gets the proceeds, and that's what I want. I think they've done enough for the family to get a few quid out of me."

"Was your dad here then?"

"Yeah, yeah. At the end."

He replaces his glasses, using his middle finger to push their bridge precisely up to the bridge of his nose.

"Cancer, you know—they all end up here. I'm lucky they'd have me, kidney patient. But the place was going, so—you know."

Kelvin sits silent a moment, and I'm sure I detect a choked air from him. I don't want to look, in case…in case I have to do anything.

"Well," he says with a great sniff and a sigh, "whatever you need me to do, just let me know. If there's anything not taken care of. Getting your effects in order, like."

I smile at him.

We sit and watch as a maroon work van crawls along the driveway at the required five miles an hour. *NRG Electrical* painted on the side in yellow. I can hear the pneumatics in its suspension as it creeps over the too-high speed bumps. They are here about the security light, no doubt. I could talk about that with Kelvin, steer clear of tricky subjects. I could tell him about that. But I feel too heavy on the inside.

"I…I saw Laura yesterday," says Kelvin, his voice a little husky.

"Oh yeah?" I say, naturally.

"Yeah. She's thinking of you. She asked me to send you her love. She's really concerned, obviously. Concerned that you're all right."

"All right."

"She told me she'd been wondering about coming over to make sure you're settled in. But, you know, she doesn't want to upset you."

The van disappears off behind the wall.

I can sense Kelvin fortifying himself.

"OK, I'm just going to say this. I know it's not something you want to talk about, but it needs talking about, right?"

"Go on." I know what's coming.

"Well, how long is it since she's been in touch? Five years?"

"Seven."

"Seven years. And it's pretty obvious why that is, I reckon."

"Is it?"

"Oh, come on, mate."

"I want to know. Why does she think she hasn't been in touch?"

"Well, I think she's scared to. I think she thinks that you won't want to hear from her."

"I see."

"But the thing is, she really does want to come and see you."

"Right."

"So—would you be up for that?"

I shrug.

Now he doesn't know what to do. Kelvin's never known what to do. I could keep him dangling all day.

You'd be telling me to choose to be nice. *Be nice.* You're right, I know. This is not a sport. I should probably give him something to go on. God knows what, though.

"Why does she want to see me?"

He exhales a quiet little laugh. "Because you're her brother, I imagine, and because you're in a hospice, and she's worried... she's worried she's going to lose you without—"

"Without what?"

"Well, without—"

"Having eased her conscience?"

"If you like."

I laugh. "Tell her not to worry about it. Tell her it's fine."

Kelvin falls quiet a moment as he thinks through this solution.

"I...I don't think that's going to be enough, mate."

"Listen, Kelv, isn't it enough that I have to forget about everything just to make her feel better? I mean, she hasn't even got the guts to come here herself, has she? She's sent you, hasn't she? Do you think that's good enough? Do you think I should see her?"

"I think you should see her, yes."

"Look, when it really mattered to me, when she should have chosen to stick by me, she didn't, did she?"

"No, she didn't."

"Her instinct was to stick with Mal. So that's that. And if she wants to know if that's fine, then fine, that's fine. I accept that she did that. You can tell her she doesn't have to worry about it anymore. She did it, and there it is. But don't pretend she didn't."

"There's more to it than that, mate."

"What more? The last time I saw her was seven years ago, and that was only because it was Mum's funeral. That's a lot of time to show there's more to it than that. Sometimes these things are simple. You don't need to make it more complicated."

Kelvin sighs a deep and defeated sigh.

"It's just… It's breaking people up. Even now. It's breaking Laura up; it's breaking Mal's mum and dad up. And yeah, you know, it's breaking Mal up as well. And you're the one who can sort all that out. If you can find your way to just talk to her. You know it's not a normal situation."

"It's not me that made it not normal, Kelv. Ask anyone you like. What he did—"

"No one's ignoring what he did. No one. But if you can just talk to her, it would help."

I do my best to draw in a deep breath.

"I don't know why you're running around after her, Kelv."

"I'm not," he says.

"She'll have you wrapped around her little finger if you're not careful."

"All I'm doing is saying what needs to be said, OK?"

"Listen," I say. "I don't have a problem with you. You know this isn't easy to talk about."

"Yeah, yeah. Totally. But you wouldn't want me to lie to you, would you? I can tell you this stuff. You know I'm straight with you."

"To be honest, mate, I think I'd prefer it if you lied."

Fuck, fuck. This is bad. This is getting bad.

I can't. I can't breathe. I—

I can't…make my chest go *out* enough. I can't breathe *in* enough.

Chest

Breathe in, chest out. Breathe out, chest in.

Come on, now. Keep it calm, keep it easy.

Chest goes out. Chest goes in.

And now it's me, conscious, as I breathe.

Out in out in outinoutin…

My pounding heart.

I just want to—just want to heave a sigh.

Is it too much to ask? To heave a great and heavy sigh?

Mini, now. Mini, mini, mini breaths.

Is it—is it bad enough to—?

To push the button? Call Sheila in?

No visitors. I should have *no* visitors. All just fucking complication.

You'd think, wouldn't you, that all this shit would stop at some point. You'd think that there would be a point when the fucking past would leave you alone.

I don't have to forgive anyone anything anymore.

This is me.

I can't believe they thought it would be OK. I can't believe Kelvin thought it would be fine to swan in here and ask me if I'd meet up with her. What does he know about it? He knows nothing. He's just trying to get in Laura's knickers like he always did, and he never will.

They don't know me at all, do they? They don't know me at all. I could tell, the way Kelvin was saying it. None of them understand what I've been through. *Every day* I've had to live with this. Every day. Ten years. Putting my life back together. Losing Mum too, dealing with all that on my own. Fucking dialysis three times a week. That's something, isn't it, calling a dialysis machine your best friend, old buddy.

No one can just waltz up and suddenly fix all that. And it's not me they want to fix, is it? It's not me they care about. It's themselves.

Creatinine

That's it—if I'm going to do a real A to Z, then I'll need to include all the things I've got but I don't even know about. The things I never paid attention to in biology at school.

That must mean pretty much everything in my entire body.

My body is not my own. I don't understand it.

I don't know how the fucking thing works.

When Dr. Sood turned around and started talking to me about creatinine levels and dialysis and—

I didn't know what a dialysis machine was. I mean, I'd collected for a dialysis machine they had an appeal for on some children's TV show. Probably 1984. I got it into my head that a dialysis machine had flashing lights and numbers, but I think I was mixing up the dialysis machine with the totalizer they had on the show. Every time they reached a new landmark, a whole load of bulbs would light up, and the number would get higher.

My dialysis machine was dreary off-white. Perhaps I was given exactly the one I collected for, thirty years before. It looked like it was made in 1984.

What's the shelf life of a dialysis machine? How many different people's blood had chugged through mine? Now mine was chugging through, and it was cleaning out the creatinine.

I think it was, anyway.

Cleaning out all the bad, the buildups.

I imagined it like the buildups of acid in my calves when I'd been running around.

Ahhh—ah, my God. There it is.

I nearly made myself cry.

I haven't cried for—

There are some things that you can't… They're unexpected. I haven't thought about this for years. One of the clearest memories I have of my dad.

Acid cramps in the calves.

That's it:

Calves

I'm lying, crying on the floor in the lounge of our house, on that horrible old white-and-brown swirly carpet. I'm on my back, and my dad has a hold of my leg, and he's kneading the calf between his thumbs and rubbing it gently with his palm.

Up, down, up.

Rub it better, little man. They're just growing pains.

The agony of it. The worst ache I'd felt to date. And I could not get away from it. It was inside me, and I didn't know what was causing it.

It'll pass, don't worry. It'll pass.

I never wanted him to let go.

I kept the crying up for as long as I could, but I think he could tell when the pain had subsided. But he didn't send me away. He patted the sofa beside him, and I hopped up.

Ha; ha; ha.

Fucking hell, this is…this is my heart. Is this my heart? A heart attack? No, chest pains.

What if it was?

Push the button?

She should have sided with me, Laura.

Fucking—*I* was the one she should have supported. Her own brother.

She made her choice.

Trying to have it both ways now.

No.

Fuck, fuck, this is it. Fuck.

Push the button. Where's the button?

There. Did that push?

Did that click?

There. I set that buzzer off down the hall. I think that's what I did, with the button. Too late to go back now. Can't unpush.

How many die of politeness?

C… C… Corpse.

Body. My body.

No.

"Hello, you all right?"

Sheila.

"I'm… I can't…"

"Trouble breathing? OK, wait a minute. I'll be back in a tick, OK?"

She knows. It was the right thing to do. Push the button. Not making a fuss.

"Here we go." She wheels an oxygen canister before her and carries a mask. Serious shit. Big deal, big deal. "OK, I'm just going to get you to sit up more here. And then we can get you some oxygen."

"I'm—"

"Don't talk, now. Let's get you sitting up. Right, now, if you hold this mask. I'm just going to—"

Small olive-skinned hands fumble with knobs on the canister.

"OK, I think that's… Can you just give me that?" She takes the mask back off me and looks at it. "No, it's… This is the one that's been playing up a bit." She fumbles more. "Sorry, sorry, wait a minute. I'll go fetch Jef to give us a hand."

She walks out briskly, comes back to deactivate my buzzer, then walks out briskly.

No panic, now, no. She's on the case. Sheila's on the case. Trained and able.

Come on, come on.

Your hand in mine, mine in yours. Tight, tight.

Enthusiastic you.

Yeah, you can do it.

I can do it.

Of course you can.

Of course I can.

This is going to happen.

Sheila again, trailed by Jef.

"…it's been playing up, and I think it's to do with the valve at the top. Because it's not been right since—"

They fuss and meddle with it a bit, alternately taking the mask and trying it at their own noses.

Sheila looks down at me. "Sorry about this. How are you doing? Can't clear your lungs properly?" I shake my head. "It's all right. I'll get the other one if we can't… Oh, wait, oh, there we go."

Jef passes me the mask. Triangle of rubbery plastic over my nose and mouth.

"There now," says Sheila. "Hold that to your face, OK? Don't worry, it'll pass, it'll pass. I want you to concentrate on getting your breathing down, to slow down, so it's more comfortable, OK? Breathe normally there, don't try any great gulps, and just take in the oxygen. It's going to help you."

Jef gives me a small smile and leaves.

"There we go," says Sheila. "Keep it on your nose and mouth, all right? You need to make sure you've got a good bit of oxygen going into your system."

Through the door, I hear the woman in the next room has started up her groans again.

Uhhh.

"Oh, hello," says Sheila. "Old Faithful's started up again." She smiles at me.

"I'm…I'm sorry," I say. "Causing all this bother."

"You're all right," she says, thrusting her hands into her tunic pockets and balancing absently on one foot like a young girl. "I've got to earn my wages somehow, haven't I? OK, I'm just going to look in on her now. Keep that mask on until you're feeling better. I've reset your buzzer, but press it again if you want anything, OK? Don't hesitate. That's what it's there for."

Come on now, baby.

What have you got to say to me?

What would you say?

Think calm. Get yourself into a good state of mind, and it'll come. Easy.

Easy. Ease.

Diaphragm

"Right, well, if you're going to persist in showing the capabilities of juniors, I'd better treat you like juniors. Who can spell *diaphragm* for me?"

Mr. Miller stands at the front of the class in his weird blue blazer with its six gold buttons and those ever-present musty trousers.

"What sort of blazer's that?" mutters Mal to me and Kelvin. "It's like it's from the nineteenth century or something. Who does he think he is? King Dickface the Turd?"

Kelvin and I crease up laughing. Dickface the Turd.

"Kelvin!" says Miller. "Well done. You've just volunteered to spell it out on the board. Come up here."

Kelvin reluctantly leaves his lab stool with a wooden creak and shuffles up to the front.

I look at Mal and do an eye roll. "What is it about Kelvin that makes him Miller's whipping boy?"

"OK," says Miller, handing him the chalk. "Off you go. Oh, and I forgot to mention. Anyone who gets it wrong gets a detention."

A prickle of suppressed outrage crosses the class.

"Kelvin?"

Already resigned to his fate, Kelvin fumbles the chalk, drops it, picks it up, and then tries to hold it like a pencil.

D.

Miller places the eraser on the board next to Kelvin's tremulous and malformed letter *D*. Kelvin looks up at him, questioningly. "Carry on," says Miller. "It's going very well so far."

Chuckles from around the room.

I.

"Excellent!" Miller cries sarcastically.

A. Kelvin pauses, and Miller's head shifts fractionally, sensing the kill.

R.

"Nope!" Miller whips the board eraser across Kelvin's efforts, knocking his hand away and flicking the chalk across the room into a table of girls.

"Detention for Kelvin, and the chalk's landed with you. Up you come." He points a knobby finger at one of the girls. She gathers up the chalk and tries to brush its mark off her sweater, before replacing Kelvin beside Miller.

Kelvin dumps himself back on his stool beside me.

D, she writes.

"Good—"

Y.

Miller pauses awhile before mugging around to the rest of the class. Then he wipes her away and picks the chalk up himself.

"*D, I, A, PEEEEE, H, R, A, GEEEEE, M*. Anyone who gets that wrong after I've spelled it out so plainly will deserve the detention they get, OK?"

Spirits broken, we mumble our assent.

"Right, now, as you'll hopefully remember from last year, the diaphragm is a membrane, just here in your chest, and when you breathe, you are using your muscles to pull on that diaphragm, and in pulling, it draws the air in through your nose and throat and into your *lungs*, which enables you to *breathe*." Miller scrawls *breathe* tetchily out onto the blackboard and underlines the final *e* about eight times. "Now, *that* is exactly what you *can't* do…" He picks up the large book that has been sitting on the bench in front of him all this while. "Can't do…" He struggles to find the page, and an adventurous few begin to giggle. "If your lungs look like *this*."

He cracks the book open at a double page that is completely taken up with a photo of a pair of lungs, branched through with black, like burned cheese on toast.

One of the girls pipes up: "Ah, sir, that's nasty."

"And that," concludes Miller with a self-satisfied flourish, "is *exactly* what is currently growing inside one of you."

A sudden hush. He paces the room, bearing the chalk eraser

before him, in his usual manner of dramatic pause, loving it. Loving it.

But what can he mean? What can he mean?

"The only question is, which one of you currently has this growing inside them?"

From the left three-quarter pocket of his big blue blazer, he teases out a pack of cigarettes and wields it between thumb and index finger in front of the class.

"Which one of you is missing a nearly full packet of these from this morning's session?"

We sit aghast. I look at Mal.

A pack of twenty Embassy No. 1.

He sits there impassive, watching with absolute innocence as his cigarettes are dropped with a light pat back on the desk, and Miller takes up his favored place, leaning against the slender edge of the blackboard.

"Well, there they are," he says. "Whoever wants to come up and collect them may do so now." His eyes seem to settle on Mal, before the bell for the next lesson rings off down the corridor, but nobody moves.

An impossible, unnatural silence descends as the game of chicken settles in. Outside, the corridors begin to fill and churn with kids making their way slowly to their next lessons, with maximum noise.

"I know," says Miller, "you think I'm going to let you go."

Shimmering silhouettes of students' heads begin to imprint themselves on the frosted wire glass of the classroom door.

"I know you think I'm going to have to let in the next class. But I don't have to do anything."

Mal looks at me, and I look at him, and an idea begins to form.

Miller makes his way slowly over to the door and opens it. His presence immediately hushes all activity out in the corridor. He slowly fixes the door shut and returns his attention to us.

"I have let classes stand out there for the full fifty minutes before today, and I'd be willing to do it again now. So." He sits down and once more picks up the packet of cigarettes. "So."

Miller loves to have his enemies, and he'll be even more triumphant to get the new kid. I'm sure he's been zeroing in on Mal ever since Mal started sitting near me. And he seems all right, Mal. He's got a lot about him. Miller's just a twisted, bitter old has-been. Everyone hates him, and he knows it.

I don't look at Mal. I raise my hand, and it takes Miller a while to see it. Some of the girls see it, but they're too scared to draw Miller's attention to it.

"Sir," I say.

Miller swivels his eyes first and then turns his head to face me. "Yes."

I want to say this without fear.

"They're mine."

The class finally drains out and down the corridor, and Mal takes hold of my heavy schoolbag and shifts it to the next class ahead of me.

Noted.

Miller is already carefully maneuvering himself between the

desks and discarded chairs in my direction. I know what his response is going to be. Not anger, but sympathy. Annoyance, yes, a longer detention, no doubt, but sympathy because of my home situation, and him not wanting to step over the line.

The classroom door clicks shut behind him, and he softly begins to speak.

"I must say, I'm disappointed…"

"What did Miller actually say, then?" asks Mal, sticking two rolling papers together meticulously, the zips on the sleeves of his leather jacket jangling as an accompaniment. He lays the papers on his bag while he roots around in his coat pocket for his pouch and tin.

I'm sitting on the floor at the end of his bed, sucking on the thank-you beer he bought me. I'm a bit pissed.

"Well, I thought he was going to start going on about my dad and about cancer and all of that stuff. But he didn't really go there. He started talking about how he'd fallen in with a group of friends who'd got him to smoke a cigarette once, but that he hadn't liked it, and it had made him sick, and he didn't know why people ever did it."

Mal laughs dirtily at the ceiling. "That tells you all you need to know about him, doesn't it? Made him *sick*? I bet he gets home and whips himself every night after work."

"Ha! Yeah." I begin whipping myself with an imaginary lash. "*I must not let anyone spell diaphragm wrong.*"

Mal cracks up satisfyingly. "*I must not glance down the girls' tops and rub one out in the staff toilet at break time.*"

"Wet break," I say.

Mal laughs and points at me. "You're a funny lad!"

I laugh myself and bask in the glory. Try desperately to think of something else funny to back it up with, but nothing comes.

Kelvin's still standing, leaning against the door frame and nursing his can of Coke. He laughs a gurgly laugh. "*I must not ever let anyone get away with anything!*"

The laughter expires, and Mal sets about twisting and mashing up the machine-made cigarette, emptying its contents into the fresh flat paper, before crumbling gear carefully and fairly up and down it.

"So what's this about your dad then?" says Mal.

"Oh, he died of cancer when I was six."

"Ah, man, really?"

"Yeah, that's kind of why I did it, because I knew he wouldn't want to push it too far."

"Ah, mate," says Kelvin, frowning. "That's well low."

"What?"

"It's well sick, using your dad like that."

"Is it?"

"No, it's not, man; it's genius," says Mal, compacting the mix and rolling the loaded skin back and forth in his fingertips.

"Ah, no, not my style," says Kelvin, crouching down in the doorway and eyeing the joint with increasing nervousness.

"The dad thing makes you untouchable. And, you know, it's a shitty thing to happen to anyone, so if you can make it work for you, I think that's a smart thing to do. It's not like you haven't earned it, is it?"

Mal dabs a piece of cardboard from the cigarette packet into the skin as a roach.

"So what about you then?" Kelvin asks Mal. "What made your dad and mum come down here?"

"The old man got reassigned to a new parish."

"Your old man's a vicar?" says Kelvin.

Mal doesn't answer but pulls a sarcastic face, like the question is beneath contempt.

"Wow, that must be really interesting," says Kelvin.

"Yeah? Why's that then?"

"I don't know," says Kelvin, a little unsettled. "All the confessions he'll get to hear or whatever."

"Sounds like you already know all there is to know about it."

"What do you mean?"

"Confession is just Catholics, I think," I say quietly.

"Oh. Is that different from…" He peters out.

"So have you moved around a lot then?" I ask.

"Yeah, following the old man's mission," Mal says moodily. He looks up at me. "Do you want to swap dads?"

I meet his gaze briefly.

This is Mal all over. He's not afraid to go there.

I laugh ruefully. "No, you're all right."

"And now from the glorious north down to this shit hole," he says, stretching and yawning.

"Do you miss being up there, then?" says Kelvin.

Just when I think he couldn't ask a dumber question.

I'm definitely a bit pissed.

"I'll miss the parties," says Mal.

"What did you get for your exams?" asks Kelvin.

"Eleven A's."

"Bullshit."

"Yep."

"*Eleven?*"

"Yeah."

"Fucking hell!" Kelvin looks at me with moronic enthusiasm. "I only got one A, and I only did ten exams."

Mal shrugs, making his leather jacket creak. "It's not hard to get all A's if all you want to do is get all A's… Just learn how they want you to learn, predict how they're going to ask the questions. It's no big secret, is it? But I'm like, fuck it. Not interested. Don't want no tests no more."

"But you're doing your A levels."

"No tests no more."

"Are you going to quit then?"

"I haven't decided. I was thinking about getting a place in town maybe, get out of here. Start up a few things. I've got some ideas."

Mal runs the paper along his tongue tip and seals it shut. Mal, master joiner. Never too tight. Meticulous mix.

He draws out his Zippo from his jeans pocket.

Flick, flick, and flame.

"Right, now, who wants this?"

He passes it to Kelvin, who pauses just long enough to look uncomfortable before taking it at fingertips' length. He begins to suck on the end. A bit of smoke in his mouth, quickly blown out.

"No, man, come on. Stop fucking about," says Mal.

"What?"

"You're not doing it right." He lifts the joint back off him. "Now," he says, invoking his most imperious Mr. Miller impression, "if you remember your diaphragm, which is this membrane at the bottom of your chest here"—he jabs Kelvin in the chest—"you need to pull down on it to draw the smoke"—he takes a deep toke, holds, and exhales—"into your lungs and out. Into your lungs and out."

Poor Kelvin. It's so obvious he's never done this before. I watch carefully as Mal shows him how it's done. I've only smoked a couple of Laura's cigarettes, but I think I'll get away with it.

Everything we do is glacially slow.

Seriously, I'm not sitting on this beanbag anymore. I'm properly flat on the floor, and my head is planted where I'd been sitting. I can hear all the little beans inside tumbling over each other: delicately, impossibly light.

I look over at Mal and squint. Blink a bit to see if I can make more sense of it, somehow.

Kelvin's standing again, looking down on us from the doorway.

"Listen," says Kelvin, "I'm going to go, all right? I've got—"

"You not want any of this?" says Mal, holding up the second joint.

"Nah, thanks, man. I've got my own at home. I'm going to go and...got stuff to do." He looks at me. "Are you coming?"

"No. I don't want to," I say. "I feel too nice here."

This is so nice. I'm exquisitely comfortable.

"I'm never going to move again," says Mal. "I just want to be sucked into the sofa."

He starts giggling goofily, and I start retching laughs.

We sit there with the TV turned off for another lovely long age. It doesn't matter. It's an impossible distance away.

"Well, I'm going to go, I think," says Kelvin. I look over at the doorway, and he's *still there*. I thought he'd gone *ages* ago.

No one's going to try to talk him into staying. No one should have to talk anyone around to anything.

It's getting to the point with Kelvin where—I don't know—I just don't say anything in case it makes him talk more. I don't want talk, just want to say *shhh*. But that seems to make him anxious, which makes him jabber.

"I'll see you around," says Kelvin.

"Bye, Kelv."

Three's a bad, bad number for friends. The two gang up on the one; it's always the way. Two's company, three's a political situation. Just make sure you're one of the two.

It's good he's gone.

I feel a bit bad, but it's good for everyone.

"Knock-knock," says Sheila, knock-knocking on my door frame. "How are we doing? Oh, that's much better. Your breathing sounds a lot easier now, doesn't it? Come on, let's get that mask off you, so we can see how you do without it."

She pries the mask from me, and I stretch my clammy face, run my fingers over my cheeks to feel for mask marks.

"There we go. I'll leave it here for you, OK?"

"OK."

"I'll get Dr. Sood to come in and have a look at you in the morning, see if there's anything else we can do to make it a bit easier for you."

"OK."

She unclips my chart from the end of the bed, draws a pen out of her white-piped pocket, and begins to gnaw unsanitarily on the lid. "What are we going to do with you, eh?"

"I don't know. Listen, Sheila—can you make it so that I don't get any more visitors? I don't…I don't want to see anyone."

She looks up at me, over the top of the clipboard.

"Are you going to tell me what this is all about then?"

"What?"

"Well, when one of my people gets into a lather about a simple little trip around the garden, I like to try to get a handle on why that might possibly be."

She peers at me intently with her bottomless black irises.

"Just…good old family baggage."

"Was that your brother then?"

"Kelvin? Ah, no, no. He's playing the servant to my sister."

"Things…a little bit tricky back there?"

"Little bit."

She frowns and looks back down at my notes.

"Things with your sister?"

"Little bit."

She bats the clipboard flat against her chest. "Tricky enough that you want to sever all ties?"

I close my eyes and sigh. "Look, I know what you're getting at. But it's for the best. We've said all we've got to say to each other."

"It's not for me to judge, Ivo. You'll know better than me, I'm sure." She slots the clipboard back in place, repockets the pen, and comes around to half sit at the end of the bed.

"Let me take you through what I'm thinking," she says. "What I'm thinking is, here is a man, he's not well, and he's clearly not happy. Now, it's none of my business, but I'm here for a reason. If you don't want to see anyone, that's up to you. Whatever you want, that's what I do."

"Right."

"But you've got to know, if you refuse all visitors, that *means* something to us. That sends us a message. Dr. Sood will come in here in the morning, and he and I will have a chat about all the cases, and he'll look at your notes, and he'll say, *Oh, refused all visitors*, and he'll draw certain conclusions from that."

"Yeah, I know."

"It's just my job to let you know that. I mean, there are a lot of things we offer, to help people out when they're having dark thoughts. I can arrange one of our counselors to come along and have a chat at any time."

"No. No thanks."

"Just so long as you know I'm here to help. I'm here to help you get what you need."

"It is. It's what I want."

She smiles at me and holds up her hands. "OK," she says. "OK. I'll see what I can do. Just do me a favor: don't close yourself off completely. Any fool can be unhappy. Cutting yourself off from absolutely everyone… Well, it's very tempting, I know, but sometimes it's not for the best. Sometimes you've got to try a little bit, so you can feel better."

I frown at the wall fractionally. It sounds like the sort of thing you'd say. I can hear you saying it.

"I don't want to see anyone," I say in a measured tone.

"OK, lovey. I'll put the word in on reception."

I look up at her and nod. "Thank you."

"Your wish is my command." She smiles, standing and brushing imagined crumbs from her trousers. "But listen, Ivo. You can be as grumpy as you like with me; I'll keep on coming back. Just…just don't leave anything unsaid to the people who matter. It only takes a few words to change your world."

It's quieter in here today. Something's not quite right—people's rhythms are different. Sheila's not dropped in as many times, and when she has, she's been giving off different signals. Busy, busy. I've been thinking she's avoiding me because I was short with her. She's very businesslike.

But I'm starting to realize it's not me on their minds. The signals beyond my doorway, out there in the corridor, they're starting to become clear.

The breathing from Old Faithful next door has become more labored. It's lost its body. Sounds like a kazoo, exhaustedly huffed.

Hzzzzzzzzz, hzzzzzzzzz, hzzzzzzzzz.

It's constant, but weary. Weary clown.

Is that a rattle? Is that what they call a death rattle?

Hzzzzzzzzz.

Death rattle, deathbed—all these words accumulated from somewhere. Sometime. All the experiences from all the bedside farewells across the centuries. All point here, to these sounds, these feelings, these signals in here now.

Sheila has a respectful professionalism about her. She keeps conversation to a minimum, and her serious face only looks in on me from time to time to deliver medicine or adjust the blinds. Her amiable meanderings have straightened out into a purposeful efficiency. It makes it all so quiet, like a subdued Sunday. I'm only aware of the swish of her trousers and an occasional ankle click to mark her advance on a target.

Hzzzzzzzzz.

Old Faithful's husband was camped out in the visitors' waiting room all last night. Square-looking unfashionable Japanese man, roughly of retirement age, but still dressed in a crumpled work shirt and tie. He wanders aimlessly, waiting, eking out the time. The kind of walk you see people pacing out on train platforms when there's no train. Waiting, waiting. The walk of the dead.

Hzzzzzzzzz.

He walks past my doorway once more, glances in. I try to catch his eye to give a reassuring smile. I don't know why. There's nothing I can do to reassure him. Perhaps I mean: *This is going to happen, and you'll be all right.*

He returns my smile with a nod. Good, that's good.

He moves on.

I look out of the window once more, to the magnolia tree. There's no robin so far today. But look at it. I could gaze at it forever, in late bloom as it is. I like them when they're a little tighter, getting ready to reveal themselves. Better suited to a Japanese garden maybe, all clean lines. But beautiful, beautiful.

Hzzzzzzzzz.

"All the nurses here are very nice ladies." I look up. Mr. Old Faithful has stopped on his way back past my doorway.

"Sorry?"

"All the nurses here are very nice ladies." He ventures in.

"Yes, yes," I say. "The best."

"They have looked after my daughter and me very well. They have a good understanding of the stresses. They are very supportive."

I nod and smile.

"Are you being looked after well?" he asks.

"Yes, yes. They are very good here. Can't do enough for you. Whatever you ask for."

"Yes," he says. "Yes."

Then his face collapses almost comically, his nostrils flare, and his mouth tightens.

I don't know what to do.

"Sorry, sorry," he says. He looks to leave, but he's nowhere to go, so he stays where he is, forced to compose himself. "Sorry, sorry. It's hard. I'm here, you know, with my daughter, and we're just watching her mother slip away. I don't know what I'm going to do. A father is a very poor substitute for a mother."

"That's really sad," I say. "I'm really sorry."

"I'm sorry, I'm sorry," he says. "You understand."

"I do."

"This cancer is a very awful disease," he says. "It's evil. It's hard to believe that there's no more they can do. We thought she was getting better. She had been given the all clear. So we allowed ourselves to hope. She started to regain weight. She started to look a bit more like she used to look. But the cancer came back. You can't ever drop your guard. I worked too hard. We didn't have enough time to enjoy ourselves. When we realized what was happening, she wasn't well enough to enjoy herself. I worked too hard."

I want to help this man, but I honestly don't know what to say.

His daughter appears at the door with two mugs.

"Papa?" she murmurs in a barely audible undertone. She can see he has been crying and comes over to him. She proffers the mug and looks shyly over at me. I nod and purse my lips, indicating…something.

He accepts the mug and takes a couple of attempts to get the correct number of fingers through the unfamiliar handle. A teacup man. "Sorry, I was just—" He looks over at me. "This is my daughter, Amber."

"Hello," I say.

"Hiya," she says.

She looks brilliant. Rich black hair with a deep blue streak. Eyeliner, in the same way that I remember you wearing it. The *swash*. I struggle to meet her with the right sort of look. Beautiful, clear, lively eyes. Part Japanese, part not. Striking.

What am I? Flirting?

It's all I know how to do. A reflex action. She's exactly like you were. Confident. Confident enough to say "hiya," to look me in the eye.

She can't be eighteen. Less than half my age.

"Are you both coping?" I ask. "As much as you can, at least?"

"Once you know what to expect each day, it's better," says Amber, throwing a look at her dad. "You get a routine."

"Yeah. Routines are good. Uncertainty is almost the worst thing," I say.

"It's rubbish," she says. "But the nurses here…I mean, they've been brilliant. We're so lucky. She could have been in the hospital, and we didn't want that. This is nicer than the hospital. We trust them with…with my mum."

Even from the way she's standing, I can see she's the one in charge. Only a teenager, but she's carrying her dad along with her. As she talks he looks disconsolately out of the window at the tree and the lawn beyond.

"Anyway, you shouldn't be asking us how we are," she says. "How are you feeling?"

"Oh, it's much easier to worry about others," I say. "Every time I see a doctor, my first question is always *How are you?* I worry that they're too overworked to see me. I worry about Sheila. Have you met Sheila?"

"I love Sheila," says Amber. "She's amazing. Always there. Knows exactly the right thing to say. Things seem to be a bit more cheery after you've seen Sheila."

For her age, Amber seems so mature. OK, so there's the blue

hair, and her eyes, her beautiful artfully painted eyes, and her clothes hung and slung about her. Statementy. Like any teenager. But a grown woman's mind.

I want to say to her, *Listen, you're too young to be in a place like this.* But I can't, can I? *You're too young to lose your mum.* Society will decide: *You are too young.* Society will tut into the silence of the drawing room and say, *It's a crying shame.*

I want to comfort her.

But she won't take that from me.

Let it go.

Let her go.

E

Eyes

"What are you doing?" says Dad.

"Nothing," I say.

Even aged four I know not to admit I'm pretending to be car indicators with my eyes.

Embarrassing.

I'm holding the bull's eye with the very tips of my latex-gloved fingers, but I can still feel the refrigerated coolness, the slippery deadness that might somehow come alive. I'm leaning as far away from it as I can, and I'm pressing at it with my scalpel, but it *won't go in*, a *scalpel*, a fucking shitting crappy blunt school scalpel, and it won't shitting fucking puncture the cold and slippery surface, and Kelvin says give it here, and he takes the scalpel off me and I shrink away as he stabs and it squeakily dodges, and he *stabs* and it bursts and flicks inky black juice at his face. He blinks and flinches and reaches for his eyes with his wrist, flashing the scalpel around near his other eye.

"Oh, my—fucking *hell*! That's—*fuck*!"

But that's… No, that's wrong. That's not my eyes, is it? That's just eyes.

What should it be? Should it be things my eyes have *seen*, or ways in which my eyes have *been* seen?

"How's my star patient doing today?"

Sheila's head appears at the doorway, and I look up at her, give her a smile.

"Oh dear," she says. "That smile didn't quite reach your eyes, lovey." And she's in.

"Didn't it?"

"No. You're going to have to try harder than that to keep me happy, I'm afraid."

I give her a big sarcastic smile, all the way up to the eyes and beyond. She laughs. She seems more relaxed now. More time for me. Perhaps Old Faithful's condition has eased.

"Nice try. How are you keeping?"

"Fine."

"You finished that A to Z yet?"

"Heh, no hope."

"No hope? Well, that doesn't sound too good. Tell me what you're up to."

"*E*. I was just thinking about eyes, actually."

"Well, the eyes will tell you whether someone's smile is genuine or not."

"Oh yeah?"

"Yeah. They're a dead giveaway," she says, tapping her nose and winking.

"My mum used to stare straight into my eyes to see if I was lying."

"Ha! Yeah! *Look me in the eye and tell me honestly!* I used to say that to my boys all the time."

I feel a sudden surge of affection for this woman, now tucking my feet back among the sheets, who has tenderly and patiently and unquestioningly cared for me. She's a natural mother. Maybe that's what these care workers are. Natural mothers, all. And sort of innocent with it. Innocent, but having seen everything there is to see.

"And there are cultures where you're not supposed to look people in the eye, aren't there?" she adds. "Kings and queens—if you looked straight at them, they'd have your head chopped off."

"Yeah."

"Maybe they didn't want you to know if they were lying or not," she says simply before disappearing out of the room for a moment. It's a statement that chimes true in the silence.

She comes back cradling a steaming mug. "We used to have a rule," she says, with relish. "A rule about flirting with your eyes when we were out in the clubs. I used to be ever so good at it. You'd look at a fella for four seconds, and then you'd look away for four seconds. And then you'd look back at him for four seconds, and if he was still looking, you knew he fancied you. I got ever so good at it!"

I shake my head and smile a smile that I'm sure this time reaches my eyes. There's a sweet dimple that's come out on her cheek, I notice. I can see her now, the mischievous young thing she must have been, still alive and well, just a little softer at the edges.

"I know," she says. "I'm terrible, aren't I?"

"Well, you've got to use what you've got."

"That's right! Use it while you've got it. Mind you, I haven't had it for a long time."

She squares a look at me before realizing how this sounds and raises her hand to cover her mouth before disappearing quickly through the doorway. Out in the corridor I hear her cluck: "I'm being inappropriate with the guests!"

Glance across to the stage, your vivid blue eyes are looking at me. I catch them for just long enough to see you switch them away.

Did I imagine that? Your eyes, lit sharp in the surrounding dark, looking over the top of the microphone as you sing, looking across the back room of the Queen's Head at me.

You look up again now. I look away.

Embarrassing.

You might think I fancy you. I wasn't *looking* looking.

Look again.

The *swash*, the calligraphy of the eyeliner. Eyeliner makes whites pure white. You draw good eyes.

You look away, look down, faint sense of shyness as your hair drops across your brow, and you check that your fingertips are pressing the right frets as you shift your hand along the neck of your electric guitar. You check too as your sneakered foot switches on the guitar pedal, and the chords now begin to throb around the room, written across us in sound shaped by those same fingertips that deftly flicked out your eyeliner.

I feel it. I can feel it like that.

I am an eyes man.

That's it: that's what I should have said when Becca was going on and on all those years ago about whether I was a bum man or a boobs man or whatever. I should have looked her squarely in the eye and said with all confidence and conviction: "I'm an eyes man."

Was it love at first sight?

People used to ask us this, didn't they?

You'd say, "Yyyeah… Sort of…"

I'd feel a bit put out when you said that.

Anyway, is it a worse love, if it's not love at first sight?

I look behind me at Becca and Laura, being bumped and shouldered by an unusually enthusiastic crowd for a Thursday night at the Queen's. Becca's smiling and clapping and looking at me and nodding.

"Is that your new housemate?" I say.

Becca is dancing deep within herself and nods and smiles without taking her eyes from the stage. "She moved in after Christmas."

"Is she a mature student?"

"Trainee nurse."

I return my gaze to you, and you're checking back behind you at your amp and glancing across to the semi-interested soundman to your right, before engaging again with the microphone and singing, eyes closed, settling into a rich harmony with your simple distorted chords. I can't quite make out the words, but the effect is mesmerizing.

Your eyes open again, and again you're looking over at me, and as your chord diminishes, your solemn face gradually warms into a smile, and I'm thinking, you're smiling at me. Jesus, you're smiling at *me*.

You're too good to be smiling at me.

But it only dawns on me now that, no. No, no: all this time you've been looking over at Becca, because you *live with* Becca. And it's so *obvious* that this is what you were doing. You don't know *me*.

Becca leans in to talk directly into my ear. "Isn't her voice beautiful?"

I smile and nod. When I thought you were looking at me and you weren't, it felt like the first bit of good, the first glimmer of something…I don't know.

My phone buzzes, and I push my hand in my pocket and pluck it out. Mal. Again. Wanting to sort out a meet-up for later. I wonder about sending him to voice mail, but I don't want him to know I'm deliberately saying no. I hold it and watch the name until it stops and the screen dips dark again.

I slot the phone back in the right pocket. Always the right.

In the left, I pat the fold of ten twenties. Two hundred to go out and get absolutely hammered tonight.

Mal will have the gear by now. The two hundred's as good as spent.

But I just… I don't really want to do it. I mean, I'll do it, but I'm not into it.

Frowning to myself as your next song sets in, I'm thinking, I've given up on myself. Without having realized, I'd given up on the idea that anyone might find me remotely appealing.

What would I be able to say if you asked me about myself? Well, I could tell you I'm on a final warning at a job I've stalled in at the local garden center because of repeatedly coming in two hours late and being too wasted to get through the word "chrysanthemums" on a Sunday morning. I've got a sickie lined up for tomorrow. What? Yes, I live with my mum, technically, apart from the nights when I live at my sister's to get fucked up with my mate.

This is not me. It's not who I set out to be. How did I become this total moron I'm playing?

There aren't many times when all things fall away and you start to see yourself for what you are, but that's what I'm feeling now. The shimmering sound from your amp burns the deadwood in my brain, and I'm thinking: I can do this. If I can just…just break away from what Mal's waiting for on the other end of the phone, I can have the confidence to say no to Mal. No, no. I know I said I'd go out and get smashed again, but I don't want to go out tonight. I'm doing all this for no reason. Everything I've been doing for…for *years*, I've been doing for no reason.

I want to press reset in my head, and I don't want to…I don't want to do this anymore.

Is…is that all right?

I don't know.

My spongy brain blooms in all directions at the possibilities. Whatever it is you've got to get you up there on that stage, that's what I know I want.

You finish your final tune, lay your guitar carefully in its case, and pick your way over to us, thanking and smiling at people who offer congratulations.

"Oh, hiya!" you cry. "I'm so pleased you made it down!"

"I brought a few friends," says Becca. "Everyone, this is Mia."

You make your greetings and kind words, and I manage to chip in an insignificant "well done," which you modestly acknowledge.

Becca invites you to come and sit with us, but I've clocked before anyone else that there aren't going to be enough seats. Instinct makes me stand, and I weigh up the options. I think, if I just go—go to the bar maybe—then you'll have somewhere to settle.

"I'm off to get a round in," I say. "Here you go. Sit here, if you like."

"No, no," you say, with a soft northern accent I hadn't quite imagined. "Let me… I'm sure I can get a stool or something from somewhere." You look around for any vacancies.

I offer to fetch a spare chair on my way back from the bar. You smile up at me, and I don't know where to look, so I look away. Look back, and you've looked away.

"What's everyone having?"

I look at you directly with a look that means you're included too.

"Um, I'll have an orange juice, please? If I can buy you one back."

"Orange juice? Nothing stronger? I have just been paid…"

Oh, your eyes. That killer feline cut. Are they blue, actually? I thought they were blue, but they might be green. They're sort of a mixture. Really striking. I'm definitely an eyes man.

Becca wants a snakebite and black for old times' sake, and Laura settles for a white wine because red wine stains whitened teeth.

I take myself away and jockey for position at the bar, creasing my twenty-pound note unnaturally lengthwise, the better to jab at the bartender.

What was it? OJ, snakebite, white wine, Beamish.

I chance a look back over at the table, but your eyes aren't on me. I can see you watching Becca animatedly explain something, while Laura pouts and nods. Oh God, I bet Laura's off on her relationship anxieties with Mal. She just has to go over it and over it, and it never changes.

My pocket buzzes again, and it's Mal. It's always Mal.

I could tell him. I could tell him now, I don't want to go. I don't want—

The two hundred—no, the remaining one eighty—burns a hole in my pocket. No choice.

OJ, snakebite, white wine, Beamish.

Hurry up, hurry up.

"Yes, mate?"

"Orange juice, a pint of Beamish, a snakebite and black, and a white wine, please, mate."

Four drinks. It's an awkward number to carry back from the bar. As the bartender lines them up in front of me, I hand over the cash and weigh up the differently shaped and sized glasses. Do a couple of test huddles to see whether I'm going to be able to manage them all at once. Nope. Not a hope.

Finally I opt for dunking fingers and thumbs into mine, Laura's, and Becca's with one hand, and carrying yours normally in the other.

Laura is not impressed.

"Ugh, Jesus!"

"'Scuse fingers," I say.

"Some sort of tray?" you suggest.

"Would have been an option," I say, and genuinely wish I'd been sharp enough to ask for one.

There's still no spare chair, so I settle the glasses and crouch between you and Becca. You make to move, but I gesture that you should stay seated.

"All right, come on, share," you say, patting the seat beside your thigh. "You can get half a bum on there."

We sit slightly back-to-back in a halfway sort of way. Sustained contact.

"So what do you do then," you say, "seeing as you're evidently making enough to splash the cash?"

"Well, that's me wiped out for the night," I say, the one eighty making a neat but blatant rectangle on the thigh of my jeans.

"Has it? Oh dear! Well, don't worry. I'll buy you one back," you say. "So how do you know Becca?"

I explain.

"Oh, I see. Ah, I bet all you boys are madly in love with her, aren't you?"

"Ah, she's lovely," I say, ultracarefully moderating my tone. "Not my type, though."

"No? I'd have thought she was everyone's type."

I shrug. "I'm not everyone then, I suppose."

Do you hold my gaze for a second longer than normal? I'm sure—

At this moment Becca leans across the table. "Cheers, ears!"

"Cheers!" I say and turn to you. "To a really good gig."

We all strike glasses, but you pull me up short.

"No, no, you're not doing it right. You've got to maintain eye contact when you're clinking glasses," you say.

"Oh, is that what you're supposed to do?" asks Becca.

"Wasn't I?" I say.

"No, come on. Do it again," you say. "Cheers!"

"Cheeeers—" I say and malcoordinatedly proffer my glass. "This is hard. I should be looking at the glass."

"Nope, then it doesn't count," you say. "Try again. Cheers!"

"Cheeeer—"

The glasses knock together: *t-tinggg*.

"OK?" I say.

You scrunch your nose up. "Well, technically it needs to be a cleaner *ding*."

I try again, looking deep into your eyes. "*Cheers.*"

Tinggg.

"Perfect!" you cry, and grin at me.

"It's the spontaneity, I think, that really made it special," I say.

Definitely a lingering look there. *Definitely*.

My phone, trapped between us, buzzes once more in my pocket. You jump.

"What's that?"

"Oh, sorry," I say, hopping up from my half of the chair. "I keep…I keep getting calls." I look down at Mal's flashing name and cry, "Leave me alone!" rather weakly at the screen.

Feeble. *Feeble*.

I look down at you, and you're watching me with amusement. "You must be very popular."

And still, your look sustains.

I don't know what it is about you, but for the first time in… in years?…I can feel a little of the anxiety beginning to slip away. I'm able to keep your gaze. And it's only now I realize how unconfident I've become lately.

My phone ceases vibrating.

I say, "You have lovely eyes."

There it is. I have said it. Matter-of-fact.

"Well, thank you," you say, a little taken aback. "That's a sweet thing to say."

No! It's a terrible thing to say! Everyone will have said this to you!

But you smile.

And I smile too.

"Ivo?" calls Laura.

"What?" I look up at her, and she's holding out her phone.

"Mal wants you."

And I can't stay. I can't fucking stay.

"I'm really sorry," I say. "It's been lovely to meet you, but I've got to—"

"Ivo..." Laura's shaking her phone at me.

"Tell him I know," I snap at her.

"Oh, right," you say disappointedly. You look instinctively away, and I can feel the disconnect.

"You coming?" says Becca to me, as she gathers up her bag and coat.

"Yeah, yeah," I say, trying hard to think of some way to pick up again on what we just had. "Hey, listen—I know we've only known each other for about three minutes, but would you maybe fancy coming out for a drink with me at some point? Unless..."

"Oh," you say, surprised. "Well, yeah, yeah. That would be nice."

"Brilliant. I'll get your number off Becca maybe, and—" My phone starts again. "I've got to go. I'll ring you, OK?"

"OK."

I stumble my way across the pub, trying to answer my phone and catch up with Laura and Becca.

"Y'all right, our kid?" says Mal on the end of the line. "Where've you been? I've been ringing for ages."

I feel a tug on my arm, and I turn around to see you holding on to my sleeve. I mouth "What?" at you.

"Sorry," you say. "I was forgetting… I'm going home tomorrow. I mean home home, back to my mum's up in the Lakes for Easter."

"Ah, shit."

"You what?" says Mal.

"But, you know, after then perhaps?" you say.

"Yes, definitely," I say.

"Here, let me get a pen, and I'll write down my mum's land-line. Maybe give me a call there?"

You root around in your bag while Mal's voice in my ear demands to know what's going on.

"Just hold on," I say to him testily.

"Here you go," you say, pulling out an old pen. "Have you got some paper?"

"Write it on here," I say, offering the back of my hand.

You twist my wrist around with your palm and write the numbers out nice and clear and render a very professional-looking treble clef at the end.

"So you remember who it was in the morning." You smile.

Ears
‾‾‾‾

Ears. I haven't thought about this for years.

It's you again: it's you, just after that Easter, on the railway station platform, surrounded by all those people.

Hours we've spent, talking on the phone this holiday. And it's been so comfortable and warm, talking about anything and everything, how you missed your mum all term, but five minutes was enough to drive you crazy. And we've got the tragic dad stories out of the way too. And it feels—it feels *right* with you. I've told the dad story a thousand times, and I always find people embarrassingly backpedaling. I constantly have to reassure them everything is fine and so on and so on. But when you told me about your dad, I was struck by how matter-of-fact you were.

"Yeah, my dad left—what, back when I was fifteen? He was a drinker. Still is, I think. And he couldn't give my mum what she needed. I mean, for years they stuck at it, but it was never going to work. They were a real mismatch."

"Oh, right."

"I don't blame him for it, though—he's had some rough times, made some bad choices. But it doesn't make him a bad man."

"No, I suppose not."

"I don't see that much of him, because I think it sends him off the rails a bit. I think he feels bad, and I don't want to cause that. It's sad. But, you know, I don't let it define me."

I was almost able to hear your shrug on the phone. So I

embarked on the thousand-and-first version of my dad story and sort of found myself mimicking your matter-of-fact tone. It felt for the first time like I was telling it in a way that I wanted to tell it.

So now I know: I don't have to be Laura about it. I don't have to amp up the melodrama, because it's a thing that has happened. It was sad, and it remains sad. No one's going to take that away, for good or bad.

You called it sad-dad top trumps. "Ah, dead dad beats nonviolent alcoholic every time."

After weeks of talking almost every night until the early hours, I can't believe we've only met once before.

You said, "How are you going to recognize me at the train station?"

"Of course I'll be able to recognize you."

"Ahhh, yes, it'll be my lovely eyes." Teasing me for what I said on our only actual meeting. "I'll fix them on you like a gorgon and draw you across the station concourse."

"Nooo—actually, it'd be your enormous, deformed ears."

You gasped and slammed down the phone. As a joke. I think.

Now I've managed to work out which train is going to be yours, and after the anxious eight extra minutes' wait, my limbs tingling with the anticipation, it has flashed up as "arrived" on the board, and I'm beginning to worry that I genuinely might not recognize you. And if I don't recognize you immediately, you're totally going to read it in my face, and that will be the end of everything.

As the passengers begin to flow through, first in small numbers, but now in an unmanageable surge, my eyes flit around for the sight of you. The sight of something familiar. Something I might be able to recall from that night three weeks ago.

I'm wondering whether I've built all this up too much. And of course I have. I mean, face-to-face there might be nothing between us, no chemistry, no low pub lighting to give a bit of atmosphere. Just the flattened dabs of black chewing gum on the platform, the squat coffee shop, offering the same old coffee since 1989, only this time in a cardboard cup with a plastic lid, exactly not quite like the posh coffee chains.

Still no sign. I look behind me, half expecting to see you leaning against a wall, looking at me and tapping your foot in disappointment.

When it all comes down to it, what the hell am I doing, leaving myself open to all this?

But no, look: there you are. Bobbing along the platform, already looking at me, already smiling, half hidden behind a disordered group of students. *That's* you. I totally would have recognized you. And nestled unselfconsciously in your hair, a pair of pink bunny ears bounce over your face like exclamation marks.

"Hello!" you say, dropping your bag when you finally reach me and giving me a kiss on the cheek and an enthusiastic hug.

"Hello," I say, and all of my anxiety melts away with the warmth and ease of our greeting.

"It's so lovely to see you finally," you say.

"Yeah! You too," I say. "So, what's with the ears?"

You frown and look at me noncomprehendingly.

"Ears?"

Aha. I get you.

"Oh, nothing," I say.

"Right," you say airily. "So, are we getting the bus then?"

You turn and bend down to pick up your bag.

A fluffy white bunny tail, elasticked to the back of your jeans.

No, I'm not going to mention it.

I've got a laugh smoldering in my chest all the way to the bus depot.

❧

Urgent electric siren now sears my ears and seizes my brain, jolts me awake, and my heart pound-pounds and the sweat starts to prickle and emerge out onto the surface of my skin.

What's…?

I look around for some sign about what I should do. What should I do?

The siren settles in, oppressive on my ears, redrawing the shape of my skull with each regular blare.

It's punctuated now by the sound of urgent footsteps.

I see Sheila flash past my doorway and stop a short way along the corridor.

Then a male voice, buried among the echoes. Jef, I think. I can't make out the words.

"No," replies Sheila. "Yes, but it's been opened. Have you got the key?"

Another Jefish sound from off down the corridor, and I see Sheila relax and stroll back up toward my room.

She notices me and stops half in and half out of my doorway.

"Sorry about this," she calls, keeping an eye up the corridor. "People are always pushing on the alarmed door. It says it *right there*: 'Alarmed door.' What do they think's going to happen?"

"I haven't seen anyone around," I say.

"No." She sighs, without surprise. "It's a bloody nuisance. Everything's on electrics. They say to you, Oh, it's going to be a big improvement on what you had before, and the next thing you know the whole bloody place has been improved out of all usefulness."

She keeps an eye out the door and rolls her eyes to Jef as he strides past, flipping a small bunch of keys in and out of his hand.

The door is slammed shut, its echo rolling down the corridor, and the blare stops dead, leaving the ultrasonic imprint in my ears, and my heart racing.

Was it you who sent a gust of wind to open the alarmed door and assault my ears?

Sometimes I could be persuaded.

Calm now, calm.

Hzzzzzzzzz.

Ah, there. Old Faithful.

"Thanks, lovey," Sheila says to Jef as he comes back past.

"All right," he says.

"It won't be long before they're putting the respirators on the same circuit as the coffee machine," she says, coming fully into the room. "And we'll have a double-shot latte and a side order of dead resident."

She dumps herself in the visitors' seat and strains to lift her foot up to her other thigh, pushing her finger inside her shoe to ease an ache.

"I'm sorry," she says wearily. "I probably shouldn't be talking like that to you, should I?"

I smile, more troubled by the presence of her foot. "Don't worry about it. It's good to see you care."

"Well, I do care. This is supposed to be a place of peace and tranquillity. But you still have to deal with all the efficiencies and management brainwaves like anywhere else. If you can't escape the red tape here, you can't escape it anywhere, can you?"

F

Feet

Lying on the sofa, I cannot bring myself to speak.

Mum comes and lifts my legs and drops them back across her lap as she sits on the seat beside me.

A cartoon is on TV with the sound down, but I'm not watching it.

I can see she's found my card. Or the rattly collection of macaroni, sugar paper, and glue that the stand-in teacher sent us all home with. Mum must have dug it out of the bin.

Happy Father's Day.

Mum rubs my feet, carefully avoiding the ticklish areas. She looks sometimes across at my face.

"Takeout tonight, kiddo?"

I can't answer.

Looking down at my foot, she says, "Looks like it's just you and me then, foot. How are you feeling? Are you feeling sad?"

After a short pause, my foot nods sadly.

"And how about you," she says, collecting up my other foot, "are you sad too?"

It too is sad.

"Oh dear," she says. "Oh dear." And she sits there, considering, while I clutch a cushion to my belly and look at the screen.

Long silence. Long, long silence, full of cartoon noises. Bullets and boings.

"I tell you what," she says, addressing my big toe, "let's have a talk about what you've done today. Let's talk about your shoes. What shoes have you been in today?"

My foot thinks for a while and looks across the room, toward the door.

"Your Hi-Tec Silver Shadows?" she says. "Are they your favorite shoes?"

Foot nods.

"And what about you?" she asks the other foot. "Have you been wearing Hi-Tec Silver Shadows?"

The other foot nods too.

"Of course you have. It'd be silly to wear something else, wouldn't it? Then you'd be in odd shoes. Did you like wearing your Hi-Tec Silver Shadows?"

The left foot nods yes, and the right foot shakes no.

"Er…"

I say, "They like them, but one rubbed a bit."

She leans in to my feet. "Who's that?" she whispers, gesturing up toward my head.

Both feet shrug.

☙

"Do you have tingly feet at all?"

Dr. Rhys.

"Do you have tingly feet?"

"Mmm...sometimes? Maybe?"

"Yes, you see, that's not normal. With diabetes that could indicate the onset of nerve damage. Which can mean you get sores that don't heal and become infected, and then we might have to amputate. I've got four people in this district who have a cupboard full of useless left shoes as we speak."

☙

This is it. This is good.

I'm walking. I've left my bed and I'm walking down the corridor and it was my idea.

I'm so rubbish at having the idea myself. I have to imagine what you would say to me. What would you say? You'd say:

Imagine yourself there. Then you'll recognize it when you get there.

I'm walking, I'm walking.

I'm doing something with my life.

And it's good. Good to keep the feet moving.

Got my blanket on my back, your arms around me.

It's nice. Take it slowly.

One foot in front of the other.

Push, slip my way through the fire doors. They chunk shut behind me.

It gets the circulation going. Gets the brain going. Gets the thoughts, the ideas going. It's good; it's positive. Something as simple as things to look at, new things to take in. Makes you look more kindly on the world.

Wish I'd done it earlier.

The coffee machine, there it is. The Café Matic 2. There's a big stack of mugs beside it. All different. The staff brings them in. *I Love London. Phantom of the Opera. A Room of One's Own… Virginia Woolf.*

Steady, now. It's nice to go at a glacial pace. Keep near the wall.

I glance in on the room to my left. There's an old lady on the bed. A younger woman looks up at me from the visitors' chair, and I'm gone.

Around the corner now. Bulletin board up on the right, pinned every inch over with flyers and leaflets. The papers at the bottom lift and flutter in the convection of the heater beneath.

Convection current. Another concept Mr. Miller taught us in science. Will I never be rid of that man's influence?

St. Leonard's Church Fete—£430 raised for the hospice. Not a bad sum. Or is it? It's hard to tell. *Huge thanks to all.* Yeah, thanks.

Palliative Care in the Home. We all want to be where we feel most comfortable. Familiar surroundings. Not my home. *With family and friends.* Not my family. Or my friends.

Cancer, Sex, and Sexuality. Everyone is different. There is no such thing as a normal sex life. You may still have needs and desires even if you are very ill.

Massage. Karen Eklund. Swedish masseuse. Twice weekly sessions in the Baurice Hartson room. Sessions last approx. 50 mins. Write your name below for a consultation. No pen provided.

Reflexology, Bowen Therapy, and Reiki. Heal yourself.

Time to move on.

Laughter now colors in the corridor from the room at the far end. Audience laughter. And a voice. Familiar voice. By the time the sounds travel down the corridor to me, the words gather shimmer from the walls and the floor, so they are buried amidst the avalanche of sound, of gloss paint and vinyl. They talk of the corridor. They talk to me of pastel wallpaper and detergent. Shiny floor. Easy to clean. Health-inspector fresh.

I squeak along the corridor toward the sound, and the words grow more distinct.

"*So what about the Budget then, eh? Terrible, wasn't it?*"

The Budget. Ugh, noise. Outside noise. Noise of a world carrying on without me.

"*But you wouldn't want to be chancellor, would you? No. You wouldn't want to be chancellor.*"

Everything in me wants to turn back to my room, to get back into bed.

"Can you imagine? Cutting all those public healthcare budgets. You wouldn't dare fall ill, would you?"

No, come on, come on.

"...well, I'm sorry, Chancellor, all these health cuts, you know? I can't afford to give you anything for constipation. You'll have to stay full of crap."

In the TV room the television's broadcasting to an audience of empty chairs. Screen light switches upholstery now blue, now yellow, now white, now blue. I've gotten this far. I might as well sit and watch for a bit. I select the chair next to the big trunk of toys, pick a Rubik's Cube off the top, rotate it uselessly in my hands.

"So what's the answer, eh? You're so good at budgets, I suggest you go back to number eleven and work it out with a pencil. Yes?"

There is loud laughter now, and I wince at the noise. They turn it up higher and higher these days.

"That'll help him budge it, won't it, eh?"

Laughter.

Amber appears at the doorway, carrying two empty coffee mugs. I look up at her and smile.

"Hiya."

She peers at me from behind her hair, and I think for a moment that she's not going to acknowledge me, but she does, tentatively stepping in and looking at the screen.

"On coffee duty?"

She doesn't reply but looks down at the mugs in her hands.

"I've come to get myself a bit of culture."

"Oh, him. Yeah. I don't really like him."

"They always turn the audience up so loud."

She smiles politely. Ugh. Such an old-man thing to say.

We're not such different ages. Twenty years. Twenty-two, -three. I just want to say to her, *I understand you. I get what it is you're trying to say. With your deep blue streak of hair and the way you dress.* I mean, I want to turn to her and say, *You, me, friends, yeah? Same, yeah?*

But no. No, no.

You can't cling on to things like that.

"Sorry to be a pain," I say, "but if you're off to the machine, would you mind getting me a cup of tea? I'd go myself, but—"

She clears her throat. "Sure," she says. "Milk and sugar?"

She disappears.

I flick through the channels for something a bit less full-on. News, news, panel show. What would Amber want to watch? I end up on one of the music channels and leave it at that. Turn it down to background.

She returns bearing two mugs. Deep red and deep blue. One says *Humph* on the side, and one says *Albert*.

"Humph," she says.

"Thanks very much." I take it from her.

She retreats a few seats away and sits cross-legged, cradling the cup against her lips, propping her elbows on her knees. Green-and-black-striped tights.

"Have you got stuff to keep you busy out there?" I ask. "All the waiting. It's draining."

"I've got some books. But it's not really the best place to read. I can't concentrate."

"No, it's hardly surprising, is it? You want to try playing Sheila's game."

"What's that, then?"

"Well, what you do, you go through the alphabet and think of a part of the body for each letter. Then you think of a story about that body part, like, say what is the best thing your fingers have ever done. The moment in your whole life when they were best used."

My explanation grinds to a halt, and I think she must wonder what the hell I'm talking about.

"Adrenaline," she says brightly. "I'd start with *A* for *adrenaline*."

"Why adrenaline?"

"It motivates you and keeps you safe. It makes people do amazing things, like become superhuman. Do you know there was a woman who managed to actually heave up a car that was crushing her child?"

"No, really?"

"Yeah, in America. I read about it—it was the adrenaline in her arms."

"That makes my Adam's apple story feel a bit inadequate," I say. "But that's what you get for working in a garden center all your life." I look at her, and I don't see a light go on. "Garden of Eden," I say. "Adam's apple."

"Which garden center did you work at?"

"You know the one down the road from here? At the junction?"

"I know. We go out to the café there sometimes."

"Oh, yeah. Good cakes."

"Yeah! *Great* cakes!"

We gaze at the TV screen for a while, and begin to get drawn in by its conversation-sapping magnetism. I try to think of something to say about adrenaline. I can only think of it as an antidote to drug overdose.

"I love your blanket," I hear her say. I look, and she's reaching over to touch the edge of it.

"Oh, thanks," I say, smiling. "It was made for me."

"Wow. It's gorgeous. Can I have a look?" She turns a corner. "It's a got a beautiful tension in the stitches. I'm looking to do textile design at college. I've always loved it."

"Here," I say, handing it to her. "It's really heavy." I can't keep the pride from my face.

Amber interrogates the blanket with confident, intelligent fingers. Funny how a slight difference in movement or poise can tell you about a person's talents. "Look at this." She holds the blanket up to herself, talking to herself almost. "The hexagons. Really unusual. It must have taken forever."

"She went for hexagons because they're a bit more gentle, I think, than squares."

"Who was it who made it?"

I hesitate a moment, unwilling to admit to ever having had a girlfriend, in case—in case *what*? Amber might be *interested*?

Jesus.

"My girlfriend," I say. "Ex."

Amber looks up at me with sudden sympathy.

"She could do a lot better than me," I say, to deflect any questions.

"It's beautiful-quality wool, must have cost a fortune."

"Yeah?"

"Yeah, totally. She definitely must have thought you were worth some trouble."

"Heh. Yeah." I smile, and then my face must fall a little, because Amber looks concerned.

"Are you OK? Sorry, I don't mean to—"

"I always used to get roped into her big schemes. Always some plan to carry out some random creative act somewhere. She used to do yarn bombs. Is that a known thing in textiles, yarn bombs?"

"No… What's that?"

"She used to plan to go to these places in town at four in the morning and decorate them with crochet hearts or daffodils or whatever else it was she was making."

"Oh wow, that sounds amazing."

"Yeah, little snowflakes at Christmas, little chicks in the spring. Just random acts of kindness, but executed to an insanely high standard. She was totally meticulous about it."

"And you had to trail along after her?"

"Yeah, well, I never wanted to look at it like that. People used to say to me, 'Oh God, I bet you hate getting up in the morning, don't you?' But I never wanted to be the person who hated getting up in the morning. It was hard, but it was never bad. It was really, really good. Maybe that's how proper projects should be."

"Didn't the crochet just get swiped?"

"Oh yeah, they were inhaled. But that's absolutely not a reason not to do it. People will be how they're going to be. You'll never be able to control that."

"Yeah…" Amber looks unconvinced.

She hands me back the blanket, and I pat its thick form. It looks like a flag they fold up at military funerals.

"Would she come and visit you? Even though she's an ex?"

The question takes me by surprise.

"No," I say. "No."

Fingers

"What's this? It looks like a bumhole!"

Mal jabs a finger through one of the holes in the stitching of the blanket, and his fingernail raps the wood of the pub table beneath. The burned-down roll-up pinched between his knuckles drops a flake of ash.

"Mal! Fucksake."

I flap at him.

He withdraws and snorts me a chastised smile.

I see it straightaway. Where his finger touched the blanket there's a grubby mark. I look quickly up at you, but you haven't seen it—you're busy battling back the bags and wrapping that are sliding off the seat beside you.

I'm not going to point it out. It's my birthday and my present, so I'm not going to take the rap for screwing it up. It'll probably scrub out anyway. I might have a try in a bit.

"Oh, look at that. It's gorgeous," says Laura, reaching across and turning over the edge to look at the back. "You *made* this?"

"Yes," you say, finally karate-chopping the discarded wrapping paper into cooperation.

"For him?"

You look at me and break into a warm smile. "Yes."

"Do you know what?" I say. "I think it's the first time anyone's ever made anything for me."

"That's why I wanted to make it," you say. "It's made with love."

I'm ashamed to realize I dart my eyes around to see if anyone's registering their amusement at the word "love." Becca is whispering something in Mal's ear and laughing. He laughs too. A nice, private little joke.

"Ah, Ivo, you always get the best stuff!" says Laura. "How do you always manage to land on your feet? How many stitches are in this?"

"Ouu, I don't know," you say. "About…fifty, sixty thousand?"

"You're mad," says Laura. "Sixty thousand stitches? For him?"

"Is that mad?" you say, straightening the blanket, checking for imperfections, tutting when you find a loose end.

"I don't know where you find the time for everything you do. You're like a cottage industry or something, with all the guitar playing and songwriting and crochet as well as training to be a nurse."

"Ah, you can find the time for the right person," you say. "He's worth it."

"Well, I'm glad you think so," says Laura, pulling an incredulous face. "I don't think there's anyone on the planet I'd do this for. Or I haven't met him yet, anyway."

I catch a brief cloud cross Mal's face as she says this.

"I've enjoyed it. I had all those bus trips to work, and I used to fill up any quiet moments on night shift: I could pick it up and work on it, and it made me feel like we were together." You look up at me. "Think of it as an apology, if you like, for being away on nights all those weeks. This blanket is made up of all those hours when I was thinking of you, and when I wanted to be back with you."

"Aww," says Laura, turning to me. "That's lovely."

"And whenever I got stuck with anything, there were a lot of the older patients who still had all their crochet skills—I learned hundreds of little techniques."

"Do you love it?" Laura asks me.

Your eyes switch slightly shyly to me, and the pressure of expectation immediately swells.

"Yeah, it's really… I like it a lot." I feel myself scratching around for the kinds of words I want to be using, now the whole pub seems to be watching. "It's really…really *heavy*." I weigh it, impressed, in my hands.

"It's only a blanket. All you want to know is, is it warm?" says Mal. "Is it going to keep those frail little knees from knocking together or not?"

Maybe there's a twitch in my DNA, a switch flicked in my middle, but I look at Mal now, and I think what a child he seems. How puerile can he get? Surely he can do better than that.

I know I can.

"It's brilliant," I say deliberately and decisively. "I love it." And fuck you, Mal.

"Well," you say, turning to me, "as far as I'm concerned it's just something someone thought enough about you to spend a lot of time making. And that's what I wanted to do for you," you say. "Happy birthday."

I'm touched. I'm genuinely touched.

"Well, here you go anyway, fella," says Mal, reaching around inside a plastic bag he's got with him. "Happy birthday, yeah?" He lands a packet of twenty-four Kit Kats on the blanket and a packet of twenty Benson & Hedges on top of that.

I look up, and he's primed and ready for my laughter.

"Aw, what's not to love about that," you say semiquietly. "Perfect for a diabetic."

"Cheers anyway, fella," says Mal, raising his glass and encouraging others to do the same.

Then, he says, "Sorry, Mia, I forgot you weren't drinking."

"I'm not not drinking," you say. "I just haven't got a drink."

"Oh, right. I thought because of your dad and everything."

"What about him?"

"Being an—sorry, was I not supposed to say?—an alcoholic?"

"Mal!" cries Laura.

"What?" says Mal, raising his hands in fake innocence.

You look at me, and I shake my head like I don't know how he found out.

"What's this?" you say.

Ah, shit, you've found Mal's fingermark.

You glare up at Mal straightaway.

"This took me eight months. Mind what you're prodding it with, OK?"

"I don't get it," you say. Your computer table and all your books are juddering as you stomp up and down the carpet of your room. "I don't understand what kind of special code they want me to crack to gain entrance to their little clique."

"Will you sit down?" I say. I'm lying widthwise on your bed, my head propped up on a big cushion. "You're making me tense."

You sit on the edge of the bed, leaning forward.

"It's hard," I say, "but we've all known each other for years. I think they get a bit... I don't know, a bit lazy when new people come along."

"It's been nine months now we've been seeing each other. That's a bit more deliberate than lazy. I mean, what's the deal with Mal? He deliberately made that mark on the blanket."

"No, it wasn't deliberate. I saw him do it. It was an accident."

"Yeah, well, he wasn't too apologetic about it, was he? He was openly taking the piss. Why do you hang around with such a bunch of piss takers?"

"I don't know."

"Seriously, they just leech off each other. Anything that doesn't fall in with their little world view gets stamped on immediately."

"I'm not like that."

You sigh and slump back on your bed. "No, I know you're not. I don't know how you managed to escape it."

"They don't know anything about you. They don't know the real you at all. It'll just take time."

"Becca's supposed to know me, but she's too busy being fawned over by everyone, all latching on to her."

"Ah, no, Becca's all right."

"Oh, she's lovely, but she'd never stand up for you. And what's the deal with her and Mal, whispering like schoolkids?"

"No deal. They've just known each other a long time."

"Yeah, I wouldn't be surprised if there was something there, you know. I don't know why Laura puts up with him."

"I don't know why you put up with me," I say, offering you a Kit Kat.

Actually: green fingers. It was my mum who said that to me. She said, "You'll have green fingers."

She was struggling to push the old hooded lawnmower up and down the lawn on a Saturday. Saturdays always made her sad. Sadderdays. It was something Dad should have been doing.

She said to me, "We'll have to set aside a little piece of the garden for you to call your own. You'll have green fingers like your dad."

Slight twitch of a frown on my face. It presented a bad image of rotting green fingers deep underground.

Maybe she noticed—I don't know—but she quickly said, "That's what they say if you love gardening. You've got green fingers. Have you never heard that?"

I shook my head.

She set me aside a little patch I could tend and look after all by myself. I grew sunflowers that first year, and the patch was soon allowed to stretch to the size of a full bed, an odd hodge-podge of annuals and perennials, herbs and vegetables. Within a few years the whole lot was mine, and my mum could confine herself to enjoying it around her on warm summer evenings.

It was the least I could do.

Funny what small things it takes to set your life on a par-ticular course.

God, look at my face.

I've got a triangle where the oxygen mask has pressed around my nose and mouth.

I steady myself with my hands on either side of the bathroom's sink and peer through the bad lighting into the mirror.

My face is *yellow*. Dark gray under the sunken eyes.

I slowly move my head around, checking out the angles, watch the pupils fixed stock-still, compensating for the rotating of my head.

I've always done this, since I was a kid. Always pondered the fact that you can only ever see your face from one place, from your own eyes. I will never see myself looking away.

Not without a camera.

Jesus, though. I look more and more like my dad.

There's a face that's imprinted on my memory. Dad. It's the *movement* of a face that stays with me. The *way* he smiled. The way he laughed.

From all those years ago, it's still as strong, that blueprint.

Face

"All right there, little man?"

There it is: the familiar face. Familiar old Dad smile.

"Something up?"

I look at him and twiddle the end of his bedcover. Comb my fingers through the tassels.

"C'mon," he says. "Tell your old dad."

I peer up at him. "I'm not allowed to bother you."

He considers me a moment, and I can see his face breaking into a little laugh. Not completely his usual laugh.

"Who said that? Did Mum say that?"

I nod.

"Ah, well, she's very tired," he says. "But what you should do is be a good boy for her, OK?"

Nod.

"But don't worry about me. You can play me up all you like."

I look at him, curious.

"Are you going to die?"

He frowns, and again it's familiar, that deep groove straight down between his eyebrows. After a brief pause, he holds his hand out to me. I take it and roll myself up gratefully in his arm and end up looking away from him. Away from the frown. I feel him stroke the hair on the top of my head.

His voice comes to me now.

"It looks like it, little man. I'm really sorry."

I say, "That's OK." I have a strong sense that I don't want him to worry about me.

"Will you look after your mum for me?"

"Yeah."

"And your sister."

"Yeah."

"And then I'll look after you, OK?"

"Yeah."

"I'm sorry we haven't started work on that pond of yours yet."

"That's all right. I don't mind."

"Well, just keep it in mind. And you might be able to start it yourself when you're old enough. When your mum says it's OK. OK?"

"OK."

"Just make sure you work slowly and carefully. It's not a race. If you go a bit wrong, all you have to do is keep calm and put it right, yeah?"

"Yeah."

"What you don't get right, you can always put right. Don't be afraid to change your mind."

The words don't mean much to me, but I hear the click of his lips behind me as they stretch into his familiar old warm smile. He's happy he's told me this. That makes me happy.

What you don't get right, you can always put right.

But I couldn't, Dad.

I tried to put it right, but it just kept drifting wrong.

Every night I would say to myself, *I will not go out tonight. I will not get stoned tonight.*

But every night I would fail.

I wish I could have asked you what I should do then, Dad.

I wish I could have asked what I should do when every instinct in my body was urging me to do what I wasn't supposed to do.

And then I'll look after you, OK?

I'm imagining his smile.

The ghost.

Just thinking of that smile now, the calming, comforting movements of his face, it brings out actual physical reactions in my body. It makes my heart lighter. It makes my shoulders instinctively spread and settle.

The ghost exists: my body has seen it, and shaped it.

"Hiya."

I look up suddenly, and the elastic on the oxygen mask plucks my stubble, makes me flinch and frown. Standing awkwardly in the doorway is Amber.

"Oh, hello…"

And ah, no, she's caught me here in my mask. Ah, shit. I didn't want that. Old man, old man.

"Sorry about that," I say, hooking the mask back on the canister. "I'm trying out the laughing gas."

"Can I come in?"

"Yeah, yeah, of course," I say. "Have a seat—if you've got time."

She heads for the visitors' seat and plants herself down, still in her coat. When you're a kid you don't think to take off your coat. You just put up with the uncomfortableness.

I realize quickly when she doesn't say anything that she hasn't come here for any particular purpose. She just wants to hang out. She looks tired, but she's clearly together enough to put on a public face. Matte scarlet lipstick to offset the shimmering blue streak in her hair, still troubled to put on the eyeliner.

"Oh, hey," she says, reaching down and rooting around in her bag. "I've got something I wanted to show you."

"Oh yeah?"

"I went into college this morning, to try to stay in touch and let them know what's going on—"

"Good thinking."

"—and I was talking to my tutor, and I've managed to start up with this."

She retrieves a small, curiously familiar little shape. A scrap of oatmeal-colored crochet, slung over a hook and attached to a small ball of wool. "I wanted to try to…try to get my stitches to be even slightly as good as you've got on your blanket there."

I take the shape from her and turn it about in my hands. It's so comforting, the fledgling idea, the work in progress.

"Oh, wow, yeah. It's really good," I say. "Lovely tension." I nod at her, impressed.

"It's good, when you've got so much going on in your head, to have something for your hands to do. Something to focus on."

It's lovely, just these few seconds, she's there, open-faced, setting her cares aside, completely immersed in what she's showing me. And for a few seconds, I'm swept there too.

"So," I say, handing back the crochet, "how are things?"

She takes it from me and looks down at it, kind of smiling. "Yep, pretty bad."

"Yeah?"

"I've been trying to make some preparations. Organizing whatever bits of the funeral I can, trying to get all that sorted. Quite a lot to learn and do. Dad just sort of… He can't do it."

I find myself lowering my eyes to allow her to swallow down another spoonful of sorrow in some sort of privacy.

"It's just… I don't know," she says. "It's really hard, not knowing how to do this stuff."

"Yeah."

"I try to get to sleep at night, but my mind's turning over and over. You know: what if I forget to do something, what if I forget to sign the right bit of paper, what if the coffin's wrong, what if it's not what she wants. What if the food doesn't arrive for the after party. And it's all… She's not even gone yet. I don't know when all of this is supposed to kick into action. It could be tomorrow; it could be weeks away."

"And your dad's not…doing anything?"

She takes in a great breath and makes an effort to pull herself together.

"Sorry, sorry," she says, and laughs. "You don't need all this."

"No, no, don't apologize."

She purses her mouth, does a little gulp.

I can feel my breath getting shorter. I hung up that oxygen mask too soon. It's no good. I'm going to have to take another hit. I sit myself up with difficulty.

"Sorry, can I do anything?" says Amber, standing. She makes to shift the pillows to prop me up better. "Or…should I…leave?"

I accept the mask from her, inexpertly rake the elastic over my head. I look up at her and frown, and she looks a bit shocked.

"Sorry," I say, muted in plastic.

"No, no."

"Looks worse than it is."

Resigned, I adjust the mask in its place and let it settle in, settle me.

She sits once more and just waits for me to reacclimatize. Look at her, her eyes are so tired and puffy.

"I'm really sorry to see someone like you going through all this," I say.

She raises her eyebrows. I wonder for a moment if she's going to cry, but she simply exhales and says, "Yeah. It's a bit shit. I just don't want her to be in pain anymore."

"They won't let her be in pain. Not really."

"That's all that matters. But…it feels so wrong…wanting it to be over."

"No, no. Not wrong."

She stares across the room, a lost expression in her eyes.

"I mean, she's been amazing. These last few weeks I think she's been trying to protect me from knowing how bad she was. Didn't want me to worry. It's such a selfless thought, you know?"

"Sheila told me she thought your mum was an absolutely lovely lady. Kind and uncomplaining. She really seems to like her."

"When Mum told me the cancer had come back, she actually said sorry." Amber breathes a quick, quiet little laugh. "I thought, how can you say sorry for something like that? But she said to me, 'I'm sorry to mess up your studies and make you worry.' I think she liked to reduce it to a few little things she could be sorry about."

"It's a lot to take on," I say. "She'd want you to take such care of yourself, wouldn't she?"

Amber purses her lips again and looks down.

"I know what it's like," I say. "Mind racing. Feeling trapped. Maybe…if you just…stick to the small stuff. Practical stuff."

"Yeah."

"Forget what-ifs. What-ifs aren't yours to control."

"No, no."

"If you sort all the practical stuff, the big stuff tends to get done too."

"Yeah," she says, frowning down at herself.

"What's on this afternoon's agenda?"

"I've got to sort out flowers, and what readings there are going to be, the music. I don't know what she liked. It feels like I don't know anything about her, even the smallest thing."

She looks so lost. She's too young. She needs a dad.

She needs her mum.

"And there's nothing your dad can do to help?"

"He doesn't know anything. He didn't know her. He spent all his time off at work and… He wouldn't be any use."

I can feel her anger simmering away, barely beneath the surface.

"Do you mind if I say something?"

"No, go on."

"Making all the decisions, it's too much. I know it might seem easier—"

"It is."

"But it's not." I lift the mask from my face, hold it in my hand a moment. "I mean, say you set everything up, you have the funeral you think she wanted… What about after? You're left angry at your dad because you let him drift through it."

Amber glares down at her little scrap of crochet, turning it around and about.

"You've got to plug him into this."

She looks up and tautens her mouth.

"And it's not…it's not fair…to ask you to do this, but…he needs guiding through it."

I'm sure she's listening to me.

"He's got, what, twenty-five years' worth of life with your mum?"

"Yeah."

"Quarter of a century. That's a lot to ignore."

"Yeah," she says reluctantly.

"Even tiny little choices. Like, what music did he and she like? What"—another pull on the oxygen—"what were they like before you were born?"

"Yeah." I can see her eyes mulling over the possibilities.

"Ask him: get three possible readings. Even if he says he can't. Give him a day to do it. And you can decide between you, yeah?"

"Only he won't know any readings."

"But then he has to go and ask his friends. His friends who knew your mum. It'll be his task. You just set him off."

"Yeah, yeah." This seems to ease her brow a little.

"You might be surprised. It's a great…it's a great opportunity. For everyone to remember her. In ways you might not have thought of."

❧

"Hallo, lovey!" says Sheila, waggling a bunch of lunch cards as she breezes into my room. "Have you chosen your lunch yet?"

"Mmm, yes. Could I try a bit of the cod, please? No promises."

"Oh, right," she says, swiping up my card and looking it up and down. "Bit more adventurous today?"

"Yeah, something like that. I've just had Amber come to see me. We had a chat."

"So I saw. How's she doing?"

"She's a sweet girl. So much on her plate."

"Hasn't she? But she's got her head screwed on. A real smasher. One of the lovely things about this job, you get to see the real good in people."

"Yeah. Sad to see her so young, though."

Sheila bites the edge of the lunch cards. It dawns on me that she must see worse. Much, much worse. "Still," she says, "I'm really proud of you for taking the time to try a bit of mixing. I told you it's a tonic, didn't I, meeting a few different people?"

"Yeah. Yeah, it's been nice."

"It's good to have visitors now and again. Where are you up to on your A to Z? You'll nearly have it finished by now, I should think."

"I'm on *G*."

"*G*? Blimey, talk about taking your time. What have you got for *G* then?" she says, frowning out the window. "There's gut, groin…"

"Gonads."

"Oh my God, it's all the rude stuff, isn't it?"

"We used to have a game at school called Gonad."

"Oh, right?"

"You know, that age where you think every vaguely anatomical word is a swear word."

"Little boys, they're awful for it. Terrible gigglers."

"Yeah, well, we used to think *gonad* was this majorly sophisticated swear word, and we had this game where we had to shout it out in class. Well, someone would say it quietly, then the next person would have to say it a bit louder, and the next one even louder, you know."

"Oh, right. So we know what kind of a little boy you were then."

G

Gut

"I'm getting a gut," I say, looking sadly into your bedroom mirror. "I never thought I'd get a gut."

"You haven't got a gut."

"I have. Look, it's there."

"Where?"

"*There.*"

"That's a stomach."

"It's a gut."

"Look, I'm a nurse. I'm practically qualified. It's a stomach. You're as neurotic as your sister, do you know that?"

"No, I'm not."

You hold up the iron and blow a dismissive cloud of steam at me, before dumping it back down on the ironing board and continuing to nose around the buttons of your uniform.

I turn and indulge myself in another look at my ugliness. I was always proud when I was a teenager to be able to hitch up my T-shirt and see—well, never quite a six-pack, but at least a pure, taut line from belt buckle to breastbone. I could suck it in and make a cave. See myself as a skeleton. Is vanity so bad? I just want to look my best and stay that way forever.

You finish with the iron and hang your uniform over the wardrobe door before taking your familiar position before the mirror.

"What's the matter?"

"I hate getting older."

"Well, twenty-eight." You tut. "Ten years past your prime."

"I hate being diabetic. It makes me feel old."

"Old's got nothing to do with it. And you're not fat."

"It's not like I wanted to have diabetes," I say, jiggling my love handles and then smoothing them with flat palms, as if that's going to get rid of them. "But then part of me used to think it was quite nice to have a *thing*. Is that bad?"

You do a kind of Gallic shrug with your mouth. "Everyone wants a bit of attention once in a while."

"Yeah, but I used to play up to it really badly. I mean, *really* badly. I wouldn't eat properly, and I'd miss out on shots, even if I was feeling ropy."

You say nothing, draw your fingertips through your hair, and glance up at me in the mirror.

"It started to feel like, the more tired I felt, the happier I was. And the thinner the better. You can get to enjoy that stuff."

"But you're not doing that now, though, are you?" you say, turning and looking directly at me. "You're not missing shots now?"

"No." Mostly no.

"Because I've already watched my dad destroy his life, and I don't intend to watch my boyfriend do it too."

"*Look*," I say, grabbing my gut and tugging it at you. "Does it look like it?"

"You're not fat! You're man-shaped." You come over and lay your hands under my shirt. "I love your tummy. I love you."

"Yeah, well." I'm unconvinced.

"Anyway," you say, slapping my bum and sitting down to pull on a pair of tights, "stop being so down on yourself." You shimmy your thumbs upward to distribute the denier and snap the elastic at the waistband. "If you're getting fat anywhere, it's in your head. Why don't you go out tonight? Go do something. You haven't been out with your mates for ages."

I dump myself down on the bed and wrinkle my nose.

"I don't fancy it."

"Give Mal a ring. He'll be glad to see you. He thinks I'm the queen bitch from hell, so he'll be pleased I've let you off the leash for five minutes."

"No, he doesn't."

"He does, because you haven't been in touch with him, and he thinks that's because I won't let you."

"I don't know. It'd be nice if it was just pubbing and chatting, or going to a gig or whatever, but there's always the clubbing afterward. I can't be bothered, you know?"

You take your uniform off its hanger and begin buttoning it on.

"Oh, that reminds me: Do you want me to pick up a walker for you while I'm at work, Grandpa?"

"I *am* getting old. And fat."

"Right, that's it. You're going out. I don't want you hanging around, just waiting for me to get home. That's not what we're about." You pick up my phone and scroll through it. "There we go," you say, pressing the screen.

Mal Sampson. Calling…

H

Hair

One thing that stays with me about Mum's last weeks is how simply getting her hair washed and done would make her perk up no end. So heartening to see. Now I know how she feels. Jackie sorted me out with fresh pillowcases this morning, and now my hair feels shamefully greasy in contrast. My scalp's itchy, and I'm sure I must be leaving a stain on the starchy linen. I can't remember the last time I gave it a proper wash with shampoo. But I can't just ask for a hairdresser to come in and do it, can I? I'd feel like one of the old ladies.

My whole life I've been trying to avoid having embarrassing hair. I always thought I could avoid being like those old pictures of my dad from before I was born where he had the 'stache and the sideburns with tinted thick-framed glasses and his receding hairline. I would honestly think to myself: How could anyone ever get caught out like that? I would never, ever make that mistake.

And there have been moments in my life when, if I say so myself, I have got it absolutely right. I remember a time, sitting in the car on the way to school, looking in the rearview mirror, and I'd got my curtain hairdo absolutely perfect—it was exactly the right length, with precisely the right curve to the curtains, just clean enough, but not so clean as to be fluffy, with maybe a couple of artfully stray strands of hair breaking the line to say, Hey, I didn't have to work too hard at this. It was one of the few occasions I've prayed in the utmost seriousness to God: *Please, please let this perfect hairstyle be perfect forever so Helen Worthington will have no choice but to love me for eternity.*

There it is again: all I've ever wanted to do is just look my best and stay that way forever. If God existed, I'd be a forty-year-old man with a fourteen-year-old's hairstyle.

And then there was Mal. Mal, of course, the new kid at school, fresh blood, fresh meat, fresh hair. Long on top and shaved underneath at the time. I thought it was the coolest thing I'd seen. So I started growing out my curtains almost straightaway.

I vaguely knew even then it was kind of a crushy thing to do. But it happens all the time, doesn't it? Every generation of young lads herds through the same town-center streets, aping each other's hairdos, just like my dad did, I suppose.

❦

I'm sitting on the floor of Laura's apartment, watching Mal play the PlayStation in his dressing gown, and my head is being licked coldly sideways by Laura's rhythmical brushstrokes.

I can't believe I'm going ahead and dyeing my hair. This isn't me. This isn't the sort of thing I do. It's sort of brilliant, sort of scary. God, I'm such a child, even at twenty-two. Such a child.

Mal's sitting there with his hair already brushed and cooking.

"Hold still, for God's sake," says Laura.

"It hurts."

"Oh, give it a rest," she says. "This is what women have to put up with all the time. Hold *still*. It's supposed to be even all over."

"Have you ever done this before?" I ask Mal, trying to keep the fizz out of my voice. "Does it ever go wrong?"

"How wrong can it go? If you think of some of the kids at school who used to do it."

I'm a bit pissed.

Is Mal pissed? Sitting there in front of the TV, game controller in hand, he doesn't seem pissed. He doesn't seem bothered at all.

Laura's definitely completely pissed. But she's the only one who knows how to do this, so hopefully she'll keep it together. The front room now stinks of the bleach or ammonia or whatever it is she's slathered on our scalps.

"Right, that's you done," she says, and stumbles off out of the room and into the bathroom.

I say, "I can't believe we're doing this." As it comes out of my mouth, it feels like the sort of thing Kelvin would say. Squealingly naive.

Mal's game crashes to a conclusion, and he hands me the control.

"Ahhh, it's good. You should try anything once."

"Dyeing hair—it's something other people do."

"You reckon?"

"Yeah. It feels like there are too many parts of my brain saying, 'I'm going to look like a real dick.'"

"Who cares if you do? It'll grow out in a fortnight. No one should ever worry about looking like a dick for a fortnight."

I edge my character along a narrow ridge and hop into the go-kart for the trip down the hill.

"I'm not like that, though," I say. "I never ever say, 'I want to do this, so I'm going to go ahead and do it, and I don't care what anyone thinks.' You've got that; I haven't."

"Yes you have, you moron. You absolutely have. You and me, we're pretty much the same dude," says Mal. "We both get things done, maybe just using our different special powers."

"I don't. I never do."

My kart rattles over rough ground, but I'm quick enough with the joystick to get past the tricky bit that normally sends me flying.

"Yeah, man, that was one of the first things that I noticed about you, when you… You remember when Mr. Miller found that pack of my cigarettes?"

"Oh God, yeah."

"I just could not believe you'd take the hit for that. And I thought, man, he doesn't even know me. I'd better stick around with this lad; he really doesn't give a shit, you know? He can really go there."

"Yeah?"

"Anyone who can…fucking"—he ducks instinctively as my kart passes under the low branches—"use their dead dad just to get one over on their science teacher, well, they're someone who doesn't give a shit about what anyone thinks, aren't they? Someone who's prepared to go there. You're a Machiavellian type, I reckon."

I've heard the words he's said, but I'm only slowly piecing them together in my mind to make sense of them.

Feels sort of…nice?…to be thought so shrewd.

My go-kart pings off the edge of the cliff and drops into the abyss.

I hand him the control. "Is your head a bit hot?"

"A bit. That's probably normal."

"Where's Laura?"

A graphic retch and cough leaks out from the bathroom, followed by a protracted series of spits.

"I think she went for a little lie-down."

A whole hour later, with my head stinging, she's blearily washing the bleach out, and my dreams of a platinum-blond cut like the Russian Action Man thunder into the bath with it.

Orange-yellow at the back, bright yellow at the front. And

dark patches all around the back top where she hadn't brushed it in properly.

It'll grow out in a fortnight; it'll grow out in a fortnight.

Something wakes me again now. I look up from my pillow, and it's still dark. Sheila hasn't been in, I don't think.

As I concentrate on the rectangle of light beyond the foot of my bed, I can hear a low regular noise. Old Faithful's breathing has changed. Maybe they've switched her medication again. The kazoo sound is still there, but it's like she's gently huffing through it, a more thoughtful sound. A peaceful sound. I prefer it to what she was doing before.

I am lost in a world of regular hums, distant beeping, the periodic reheating of the coffee machine in the corridor, and that steady kazoo. I don't know how long it has been. Is Amber wandering around out there? No sign.

Knuckles knock-knock on wood. Rap through the static atmosphere. I glance up at my doorway, but there's no one. A moment later, I hear a murmur next door, and a murmur in response. The tones of a woman's voice, Sheila's voice, hushed, and the lower tones of a man. Mr. Old Faithful.

Slight metallic clink of a chair leg, and something knocks against the thin partition between my room and hers. It makes me start, makes my heart briefly beat a little faster. For a while there's a sense of movement out there in the corridor. Diligent attendants move to and fro, and now a nurse passes my doorway.

Sheila pads past too and glances in at me.

I've no idea whether she can see if I'm awake. Maybe she's trying to read my eyes in the darkness. See if there's a glint off an eyeball. I narrow my eyes, narrow the chances. I don't want her to see that I'm awake. I don't know why. I don't want to encroach on this. Don't want to be a witness. All I feel is the rhythmic thrum of my heartbeat between the sheets. Can she see me breathing? Sheila drops her look and moves on. Still the kazoo keeps time, though it's gained an edge of intensity.

There's a lot of pacing going on out there. No one's staying anywhere for long.

Slow figures drift past my doorway, closing in on Old Faithful.

Slow spirits.

Come to take her away.

Tender noises from next door.

Gentle huff. Pause.

Gentle huff from Old Faithful. Periodically pausing.

Her own heart, slowing.

I don't want to be here. I don't want to be here for this.

Hands

Yes, there again, my dad's hands, kneading and rubbing my calf to work out the cramp.

Or walking to school with Laura…

"Mum said you had to hold my hand over the road."

"Hold your own hand," she says callously.

Oh. I'm on my own.

I don't know why, but I flush hot and feel empty in my tummy, and a surge of hot tears boils up. I try to fight them back, I do. I don't want her to think I'm getting in the way. I know she doesn't want to because she wants to look good in front of Danny Refoy and his mates. But Mum *said*. This is what she *said* we had to do.

The thunder in her glare as she snatches up my hand and drags me across the road.

You took my hand for the first time after our second date—our first proper date after your Easter trip back to the Lakes—walking away from the Blue Plate Café.

I looked down at you questioningly.

"What?" you said, holding up my hand. "You weren't using it, were you?"

"No, no, be my guest."

All that anxiety about whether it had gone well, about whether we might kiss—gone. I kissed you onto your bus back to your digs.

I didn't want to let go, once you'd set the seal.

I waited too. While the engine idled and the driver checked

his watch, I waited, and when he finally hissed the door shut and pulled away, I waved you out of sight.

Then I floated off into town to meet Mal.

Was this love?

It felt like love.

The kazoo next door pauses, stays paused. One more murmur from beyond: "Do you think that's it?"

And the kazoo begins again.

No more murmur. It was not it.

Hands, hands.

Your hand in mine.

My hand in yours.

Our hands.

So lovely, so simple to be able to take ownership of someone's hand.

Palms pulsing together.

"Have you noticed," I say, "you're normally the one who says 'I love you' first? Then I say it."

"I hadn't noticed."

"I never think the second means as much."

"So I'm winning, would you say?"

"It doesn't mean I'm not thinking it. I always feel a bit defeated when I have to follow up with 'I love you too.' It's like the sequel to a film: *I Love You* and *I Love You Too*. You know the second one's always going to be a predictable reworking of the first."

You laugh. "Well," you say, "it's just like this noise that drops out of my mouth. Sometimes I think it's down to things as simple as luh-luh being nice to say. You say luh-luh, and it feels nice with your tongue and it creates a resonance in your head that feels nice. Nice vibration. And that's got to be a good thing."

"Bluh blah bloo."

"Yeah! Exactly that. Bluh blah bloo."

"Bluh blah bloo too."

And the kazoo pauses once more.

Silence.

Soft breathing of the fans of the machines fills in the emptiness.

And that's it.

No more from Old Faithful.

And still no more.

And still.

Heart still.

I hear a strangled sniff, a man's voice. Mr. Old Faithful.

Newborn widower.

The coffee machine rasps into life once more, works up through its steady crescendo of warming the water, reaches its peak and ceases.

And Amber. Amber must be out there too.

Mumless.

Muttering now from next door. Mr. Old Faithful, I think, and Sheila. Sheila's tones sound kind and concise. A nurse I've not seen before emerges, and then Sheila herself appears, leading Mr. Old Faithful and Amber too. None of them looks in, but they walk past my doorway and troop into a room across the corridor. Its door clicks rudely shut.

It's just me out here now.

Me and Old Faithful, on either side of the partition.

The lately living and the due-to-be-dead.

I'm here.

I'm still here.

I'm still awake.

I'm thinking nothing.

What is there to think?

The latch sounds again, and the door draws open. Sheila passes my doorway and disappears into Old Faithful's room once more.

She speaks, softly but clearly, and I can make out her words. "Hello, lovey," she says. "I'm going to take your wedding ring now, OK? Just going to give it to your husband for safekeeping. I'll be as gentle as I can."

There is no response.

Till death us do part.

There it is.

Love ends at death.

Does it?

Heart

"Why do you think people link love to their hearts?" I say.

You look up at me in the orange streetlight, push your hair inaccurately back from your face with your mitten. "What do you mean?"

"Or, like, why is your head supposed to be so sensible?"

"Mmm. I don't know. Come on, let's tie a few of these to the bike rack."

I reach into the bag and try once again through my gloves to untangle one of the crochet hearts.

You've plunged into the activity as usual, mittens now off and gleeful. I don't know how you do it. How can you stay so buoyant when it's so insanely cold?

I've got to say, it's only reluctantly that I draw my gloves off too, and immediately I can't feel my fingers. I take up the heart and begin to tie its two specially loosened threads around the nearest part of the bike rack. By the time I've finished one, you've tied on five, and we both step back and admire our handiwork.

"They are having an impact, aren't they?" you say anxiously.

"Yeah," I say. "They look great."

They do, they do. I thrust my hands rapidly back into my gloves.

"I was worried they'd be a bit small and look a bit random, but they're just right. They look like they've been thought about."

"Yeah."

"Come on, let's finish this off and head over to the church-yard. Almost halfway done."

Almost half? I look down into the jute bag, which now holds about thirty crochet hearts. My own heart sinks. It's as much as I can do to prevent a childish whimper escaping my throat.

Come on, come on. I want a new response. I just…I need a response that's going to help you finish this.

"Hey, come on," I hear myself saying. "Let's go over to King's Walk. There's a tree on the corner that looks out over the whole town. Let's hang a bunch in the branches; I think they'll look great."

There. I've launched those ambitious words into the air between us to convince myself as much as you. The hug you give me as we set off is return enough.

"Hey," you say. "Then we could go back and have pancakes for breakfast, couldn't we? I'll make you pancakes for being my amazing helper."

"With bacon and maple syrup?"

As we make our way along King's Walk, the sun splits the hori-zon and strikes the landscape through with a clean, clear light.

Come on now, come on. I wouldn't be seeing this view on any other day. It's almost worth the cold, and there is satisfaction to be had from hard work. It's not all lying back and letting it all come to you, like so many bacon-and-maple-syrup pancakes.

"You OK, gorgeous boy?" you ask, linking your arm in mine.

"Yeah," I say, trying to walk less like a frozen robot. And yeah, I am.

You look at me fondly and say, "This is all a terrible waste of time and effort; you do know that, don't you?"

"You reckon?"

"I don't know why you tolerate me. It's sixteen below zero."

"Is it? I hadn't noticed."

You laugh. "And you're tying hearts to trees and lampposts to please a whole lot of people you've never met."

"Well, I think, if I ignore the cold and the earliness, it's… probably what I'd choose to be doing? If I had the imagination."

"Ah, you do! I'd never thought of putting anything up on King's Walk. I think it's a tremendous idea. Very creative."

"Yeah?"

"Yeah. And I love how kind you are about it, and really patient with my silly ideas. I don't know too many men who'd put up with that."

So simple, to nudge me with a little appreciation, but I can actually feel my heart growing warmer as you say this. Even at sixteen below zero. It's my mini furnace. Yes, yes, yes, it's agonizingly cold. And yes, yes, I'd much, much rather be in bed.

But I'd much, much, much rather you had someone to do this with. And I'll be pleased it was me.

"Well," I say, "what else was I going to do with these redundant early hours? More meaningless sleep? Come on."

God, I'm so easily manipulated.

We've stopped where the path curves back on itself as the town drops away spectacularly into the valley and the river wriggles off into the distance. The usual breath of traffic has yet to start up, and so far only one or two chimney pots are beginning to spill their early morning smoke. I hand you the jute bag and launch myself at the lowest bough of the target tree, hoist myself up onto it.

"Careful!" you call. "It'll be frosty."

"I used to do this all the time when I was a kid." I successfully cover up my mild surprise at how much effort it takes to get me up there today. It's been a few years. "Pass me up a bunch."

You pass me up ten hearts, and I bite off my gloves before starting to tie them among the twigs.

"Lovely," you say, directing me from place to place. "They're going to look amazing here."

"Here you go," I say, and I inchworm my way along the next bough up, which stretches out over the speared iron railings and hangs over the section where the land tumbles away down to the road below. "I'll put one here, and no one will know how on earth it got so far out over the road."

"Careful," you say. "If you kill yourself over a yarn bomb, I'm going to feel bad."

Just as I find myself a prime spot for tying, I recognize my fingertips starting to tingle, and I realize my limbs have drained of all energy. I'm feeling properly wobbly. Insulin wobbly.

Hypo time. Shit.

I take a quick glance back along the distance I've traveled, make a quick calculation about how to get back, but—not easy. I'd better just... The uncertainty in my body is transferred into the bough, which I'm sure is shivering beneath me. My mind flits through its tick boxes, and of course: early morning, no breakfast. I look down at you and smile confidently, but your look of concern is not diluted.

"Are you OK?"

"Yep, yeah," I say. I could black out here. I need to get back. If I blacked out I'd drop like a stone and tumble down to the road fifty feet below. I edge back a bit, with the pretense of looking for a better place. Edge back, edge back.

My fingertips are fumbling the fraying thread as I try to tie a simple bow, and it keeps misbehaving—if there's any...thing that makes me believe in a God it's the way...fucking inanimate objects...behave when you really—real—what?

There's a sudden deep, thick silence, and gravity shifts and sweeps around me until I'm punched solidly in the lower third back of my body, with a hump and crackle from the pavement, and all I know is my head is in the gutter with all the leaf mold and bird shit and dried-up Friday night piss, probably.

And there's you, looking down on me.

"Oh my God, are you all right?"

"Yeah, yeah," I say, scrambling to my feet and trying to ride out the dizziness.

"Stop. Sit down a bit. You really banged your arm. Come and sit on this bench."

I consent to sit.

"Sorry," I say. "My fingers froze, and I lost my grip."

"I'm so sorry," you say, mortified. "Have you got any pain? How's your arm?"

"Fine, fine. No damage done. Look," I say, pointing up at the tree. "Looks good?"

"It looks fantastic," you say, squeezing my arm and inadvertently hurting it. "In the morning, everyone in town's going to see these little hearts dangling all over the place and think, 'What kind of mad person would be bothered to put those out there?'" You look at my face for the laugh, but you can see something's wrong. "Are you sure you're OK?"

"Yeah, yeah. I just need some food."

"Let's be getting back. I've got some cookies in my pocket here. Have a couple of those."

"What are you doing carrying cookies around with you?" I say, tearing into the packet.

"Oh, I don't know. I imagined I'd probably need them one day. Come on then, let's go home and get those pancakes sorted."

We stroll arm in aching arm back along King's Walk as the town is flushed through with the onset of morning, and my heart is pounding, and I'm resisting the dizziness with all my might.

I only have to get back to yours. That's not far, down into the valley and over the bridge, but then uphill and into the terraces.

But no, no. Not *too* far.

As I amble, I catch sight behind me of the result of our labors: a cluster of colorful hearts, hanging happily in the tree, dancing and fluttering in the early-morning breeze.

Worth it, yes.

What's…? What's the time?

It's light. Afternoon light.

They must have left me to sleep through the day.

I was awake all night.

I look up, and I'm surprised to see, crackling at the doorway to my room, loaded with blowsy colorful flowers, Amber.

"Oh, hello!"

"Hiya." She gives me a weary smile. "She's gone."

"Amber, I'm so sorry."

"She went last night."

"Come in, come in."

"We've just come to collect a few of her things. Hospital bag and nightie, slippers. We're going to take them home and… I don't know, wash them or something."

She looks up at me and smiles.

"How are you?"

"I'm…I'm doing OK at the moment, thanks. It's a relief mostly, I think. She's…she did *so well*. I'm *so* proud of her."

I nod, smile.

She looks down in her lap and seems to see what she's carrying. "I brought you some flowers."

"Ah, man, how have you found time to do that?"

"I wanted to go have a look at some flowers for Mum, and I thought you'd like some to brighten up your day."

"Ah, wow, they're lovely." She hands me the wrap of about twenty stems. "Man, just amazing. *Ranunculus*, absolutely my favorite. How did you know?"

"You said you used to work at the garden center up by the junction."

"Are these from there?" I turn the tag over and see the familiar old logo.

"I went out there this morning and mentioned you, and they said they thought you'd like these best."

I'm stunned.

"I know you don't want many visitors, so you can't get many flowers or anything. So I wanted to let you know I've been thinking about you, and I'm really, like, really thankful to you. And all the people you used to work with are thinking of you as well."

I catch my breath, rattle, and there's nothing else I can say.

What can I say?

She is golden.

"Twenty-two years I worked there," I say.

"I hope you don't mind," she says. "It seemed like…it seemed like a thing to do."

"Just…thank you."

She gathers up the flowers and sets about arranging them neatly in my water jug. I watch her, amused. Not sure Sheila's going to like the smattering of rebellion.

"What?" says Amber, turning and seeing my look. "I'm improvising."

"You go for it."

While she finishes her little act of vandalism, I straighten myself in the bed and try to slap my face into some kind of being. With permission, Amber rinses her fingertips in the bathroom and flicks the excess onto the floor on her way back to the visitors' chair.

"I…I wanted to tell you," she says, "I didn't exactly go to the garden center just to get flowers."

"No?"

"Not at first. I wanted to…I wanted to see if I could find her." She gestures at my blanket. "Your girlfriend, who crocheted your blanket. You spoke so warmly about her, and you seemed so much in love, I wanted…I wanted to see if I could get you to see her again." I feel absolutely still. Absolutely calm.

"I asked the man there if he knew her, and where I might find her. He told me. She…she died, didn't she?"

Silence.

"Yes," I say. "She did." I look down at my blanket, settle a couple of the stitches.

"I'm sorry," she says. "I didn't want to know and then pretend I didn't."

"No. I wouldn't want you to."

She looks up at me and smiles. "I cried in front of the man."

A warm ache rises through my chest as I picture it.

"Oh, Amber, I'm…I'm really sorry. I should have told you."

"No," she says, "no, no… I shouldn't have… It was a dumb thing to try to do."

I shake my head slowly. "A lovely thing."

"It just made me feel so *sad* for you." She sniffs. "I'm sorry. That's probably not what you want to hear, is it? It's just…everything's really on the surface for me at the moment." She half laughs.

"It is sad. The saddest."

"When…when did she die?"

"Ten years ago, now."

"What happened?"

And there it is again. I might have asked the same question before I learned all the questions you're never supposed to ask.

What's that in your throat?

My chest swells again as the question washes over me like a sluice of icy water.

"I'm sorry," she says. "I didn't mean to intrude."

"No, no," I say. "I—"

"It seems so *unfair*. From the way you were talking about her—everything—she seemed like…she seemed incredibly special."

"Yeah," I say, absently cupping my arm through the blanket.

"I don't know if I could ever be that special to anyone."

"Oh, you will."

She laughs quietly to herself, evidently weighing up her invisible options. "I don't think I'd know where to begin."

"Just be. Just be yourself."

She looks down at her knees, and I feel like I know exactly what she's thinking.

"There are people around, people who make you feel energetic," I say. "And there are people who are just"—I reach around for the right amount of contempt—"they suck the fun out of everything. They're fun *suck*holes."

"Yeah." She smiles, looking up.

"Well, you give energy. Look at you. You're going through the worst you'll ever go through now, and you're still being creative. That's *life*."

Amber purses her lips and looks to the floor.

"Surround yourself with as many people like that as you can— that's what I think. Energy givers. Life livers. People who make you feel most like yourself."

"That was how my mum used to be, before she got ill. Really playful, creative, really fun."

"Yeah?"

"I'm worried," she says, looking up at me now with tears in her eyes, "that I'm only going to remember the little frail woman in that big bed and…that's not my mum at all. That's not how I want to remember her."

I set down my mask and look into her tearful eyes.

"Give it time," I say. "I promise it will change."

"Knock-knock…"

A singsongy voice. A kind voice.

Who's…?

"Are you awake?"

Mmm?

Sheila. Her face looking down at me now. Look at her mascara. Thick. A bit much today.

"Hello, lovey," she says gently. "You awake, are you?"

"Mmm?"

"I'm sorry to wake you, but there's someone who wants to say hello, and I wondered if you wanted to see her."

Amber? Is it Amber back?

"What day is it?"

"Still Saturday."

"What's the time?"

"Half past eleven."

I take a moment to clear my throat, try to pull my thoughts into some sort of order. Sheila has drawn away and is talking softly out in the corridor. There's a mutter and a shuffle.

"Say to come in," I say. "Let her in."

And so she appears in the doorway: Laura.

She's heavily fortified with makeup, like a caricature of what I remember from all those years ago. It's a mask to meet me with/ But the wrinkles and folds still encroach like bindweed, around her eyes and neck. Everything she's been resisting over the years. Age creeps up on all of us.

"Hiya," she says, before her mask creases and she crumples into tears.

Ah, shit.

"Aw, come now," says Sheila, plucking up a tissue and hurrying over to her. "Come on, let's get you a chair, eh?" She reaches for my visitors' chair and draws it safely away to the foot of the bed, where Laura allows herself to be settled.

"I'm sorry," says Laura, slowly pulling herself together. "I swore I wouldn't cry."

"There's no shame in crying," says Sheila. "We all cry, don't we? Everybody cries."

"Yeah." Laura blinks, little girl, trying to be brave. "I'm sorry," she says again, finally able to focus on me, and then, "Hello."

"Hello."

She has only fleetingly met my gaze; she's spending a lot of time looking around on the floor, checking, checking her sitting position, checking the leg of the chair isn't nudging the base-board, checking behind her for…for whatever.

"Now, you've got your coffee," says Sheila. "How about you?" she says, looking over at me. "Can I get you anything? How's your water?"

I shake my head—nothing for me. No water. No visitors. I said *no* visitors.

"All right," says Sheila, retreating. "Make yourself at home, and I'll see you later."

She exits the room and shuts the door quietly behind her.

Alone together. The shock of her being here at all has quickly given way to…to what? I don't know. I'm casting around to feel something, but I wonder if I feel nothing.

"So, how are you?" says Laura, finally looking at me properly and frowning.

"Never better," I say, and immediately wish I hadn't, as she begins to cry again.

"I'm sorry, Ivo. I'm sorry. I just…I was so worried about coming here, but seeing you there like that, in your bed, I feel so stupid about all the years we've let slip."

There it is, the last time Laura and I saw each other, a per-functory good-bye in the parking lot of the Yew Tree as the tires of other mourners' cars tugged at the gravel around us. Job done, Mum safely in the soil. All organized by me, down to the buffet. Seven years. A lifetime ago.

"It's such a *waste*, you know? Don't you think what a waste of time all this has been?"

And now I'm the one who can't meet her gaze. You see, face-to-face, I can't back up what I've said so often in my mind. This is bigger than both of us, so should we just give each other up? Abandon hope? "Yeah," I say. "A real waste."

She hops out of her seat and comes over and gives me a strong, deep hug. I'm not sure I want it, but I let it happen, and somewhere deep, deep in there, beneath the makeup and jangle of the great gesture, there's warmth, there's goodness.

"I'm so glad," she says, releasing me from her grasp and sinking back into her seat. "I'm so glad I came. I was scared to come. I knew you wouldn't want to see me. But I thought, screw it, you know, whatever's gone on, whatever rights and wrongs, you're my brother, and I'm your sister, and that should *mean* something."

"I'm…yeah. I'm glad you came too," I say with a dilute smile.

"I wasn't going to come, but Kelvin…he said we should both act like adults, so I agreed to come with him."

"Oh yeah? Is he here?"

"He's parking the car. I think he's going to wait a few minutes to see if we start tearing each other's hair out."

"No, well, that was never going to happen, was it?"

"No, I've just had mine done, so…" She dabs at the edges of her hair, and I sort of do a little singular snort laugh. Funny. She's funny. And how easily we fall back on those years of practice about how we slot together. The rhythms of a person, they become ingrained. These are the Laura patterns I've known all my life. It feels… It does, it feels nice, all this. It feels like me and Laura. Feels like home.

"I got you some grapes," she says, reaching down and drawing out a brown paper bag. "Sorry, it looks a bit feeble now. I would have got you something else, but—"

"Fine, it's fine," I say. "What do you buy for the man who has…you know."

Her face tightens into a frown. "Kidney failure?"

I look at her and let go another laugh and break out into a gurgling cough. "That's not quite what I meant."

She sits and watches me while I cough, and I think she might be a bit shocked.

"What would Mum say if she could see us now, eh?" I say.

"She'd say, *Shoes up, bags up, coats up*." The old clarion call of Mum as she came in the front door to find we'd wrecked the house on our return from school.

"You sound just like her, you know."

"Oh, don't. Mal always used to say—"

My face must drop, because she stops suddenly and looks me directly in the eye, her mouth still open, like gasping.

"I don't want to talk about Mal," I say flatly. I reach across to unhook the oxygen mask from the top of the oxygen canister— its elastic straps come free at the second attempt. I lay it by me, more for something to do than because I'm short of breath.

"Look, Ivo, I've wanted to talk to you about everything since Mum's funeral," she says, working two fingers at her temple and closing her eyes. "I thought it might bring us together. I really meant to talk with you, but you never—"

She croaks as she reaches out for words, but none come.

"You're my sister," I say. The words emerge ultraquiet. "It is supposed to mean something. You weren't there. For me."

"I didn't—"

"You went with him. The one time I needed you to stand by me and support me, you made your choice. You disappeared off with him."

"I wanted to support you. I did. But I had to make a choice."

"You weren't there for Mum either, when she needed you."

"I couldn't do it. There was no way," she says, with real desperation. "You and her were always close, but I didn't have that with her. She hated me some days."

"She never hated you."

"Some days."

I look away. I don't know what I remember from those days.

My heart is pounding. It's pounding, pounding. All the meaning of the last decade and more hangs in the air between us, undivined.

"There were years…six years he was in prison. I was on my own," she says. "You wouldn't see me, would you? You wouldn't see anyone."

"I saw Mum."

"Mum was scared to talk to you about anything that might upset you. She thought she'd push you away. But the few times I talked to her, she just said she wanted us all to be together again."

"Yeah, I know." I know, I know.

"But it didn't happen, did it? She never got to see that happen. And that's not all my fault."

A great burning swell of acid regret rises now. I'm so sorry, Mum. I could have tried harder. I should have done better.

The tension breaks, and we sit there in silence awhile. After everything, I don't want to blame her for stuff that's not her fault.

"I'm not blameless," I say quietly. "I never claimed I was blameless."

"No, nor me," she says. "Poor Mum."

"Poor Mum."

And so very easily Laura tips once more into tears. Thick, wet silence, and there's nothing I can do. I'm just going to have to let the arc rise, rise, and slowly crest and descend, slowly, slowly descend again until she comes back to earth.

"Er…hello."

I look up at the doorway, and there he is. Kelvin himself.

"Oh, hello," mumbles Laura, working at her nostril with a tissue. "Come in."

Kelvin glances over at me. I look away. He shuffles a meter or so inside the door, technically in. Look at him, loving the job of chauffeuring Laura around. Designed to be a lackey for her. In the hope that maybe one day she'll fall into his arms.

"So how are we doing?" he says with a falsely light air.

"We're…talking," says Laura. "When I can stop bursting into tears."

Kelvin roots around in his wax jacket pocket for a clean tissue. "Here you go."

Laura takes it… Sense of some intimacy between them? I don't know. What do I know? It's been ten years. None of my business.

"Have you asked him?" Kelvin says to Laura.

She shakes her head.

"What?" I say.

"I brought her here for a reason, mate. I know you didn't want to see her, and I'll take the blame for that. But there's a reason."

"A few of us… Well, we've been supporting Mal these last few years," says Laura. She looks up at the ceiling and exhales again with the effort of everything. "Giving him help and support through prison. We did a lot of visiting, helped prepare him for coming home. But he's struggled. He has struggled."

Kelvin nods sagely.

"He's got himself a bit of a habit—drugs, you know. Impossible to avoid in prison; they're everywhere. So he leans heavily on me and his dad and mum. He can't really hold down a job yet. But we try to understand, and we can put up with all that. And"— she smiles now, with some kind of pride—"it's working. It's definitely working, because he's been starting to get himself sorted, and…well, there's been some real hope for him. But…" She looks down at her knees and stops midflow.

"There's the thing with you, Ivo," says Kelvin.

"It's there, every day," says Laura. "It's a big knot."

"All he wants to do," says Kelvin, "is have the chance of setting the record straight."

Laura leans forward and puts a hand on my bedcover. I feel the vibration. "Just to have five minutes of your time. You were like the brother he never had. He really used to look up to you. He still does."

I ignore the obvious clichés and bullshit; it's as much as I can do to hold in a laugh. We fall to an awkward silence, but no: I don't want to let it settle in.

"I can't see him," I say.

Their heads both do the same: lift to some kind of internal music. Some preagreed strategy.

"I can't. I can't do that. I can't see him."

Kelvin contemplates me a moment and draws in a great and steadying breath. "Listen, mate," he says, "I know you don't want to hear it, but he's up to the eyeballs in regret. He knows he's done wrong, and he's full of remorse about it. And he's…he's got no way of getting rid of it."

I turn away. Look out of the window. Look at the magnolia tree.

Laura peers up at me nervously. One of her eyelids sticks shut briefly. "You wouldn't even have to say anything. You could maybe let him say what he has to say, and he'll go."

"No," I say. "No."

"Please…five minutes, I swear that's all it would need. Please just give him five minutes of your time."

I draw myself up and cough at the effort, but I need to get up the presence to combat this. Finally, finally, something inside me breaks. "When is it, right, when is it that this will just fucking leave me alone?"

Silence.

The two of them, there, looking at me.

"When is it that you can say, now, here, that what happened was wrong? What happened was wrong, and there's no going back?"

"Mal's gone missing," says Laura.

Silence.

Kelvin stares pointedly at the floor.

"Missing?"

"He's been gone over a week. Ten days."

"We've had a word with the Missing Persons people," says Kelvin in a low voice. "We're supposed to try to think of a way to solve as many of the problems he was having as possible. Hopefully let him see that home is worth valuing, and he's not coming back to the same unchanged mess."

I look down at my hands, colorless and cold. I begin to rub them firmly together to give them life.

"And all of it, the whole lot of it, points to you. The situation with you. We want to arrange some contact between you, if that's agreeable to you, and if—"

"We think he might try to come here," says Laura. "He knows he needs to…to sort things out while he's still got time. While you have time."

"Here? He doesn't know where I am."

"He does," says Laura, in a small voice. "I told him. Before he left."

"But—"

Surely, surely they wouldn't let someone in here if I didn't want to see them? But they let Laura in, didn't they? My heart begins to thunder in my chest, and all the strength sweeps out of my limbs. Surely this is a place of rest. "Get Sheila," I say. "Tell Sheila I won't see him in here."

"Please, just—"

"Get Sheila."

❧

Sheila returns to my room in a flap.

"Have they gone?" I ask.

"Yes, yes, they've gone."

"*No* visitors."

"I'm so sorry. I thought you knew it was your sister. I thought you were a bit more open to seeing people because you said let her in."

"I thought it was… No, no. *No* visitors."

"I'm sorry, that was my mistake." She looks shocked. "Who is this person, anyway? The one you don't want to see?"

"It's her boyfriend. He wants to see me. But I don't want to see him, all right?"

"Right… Well, we do ask everyone to check in at reception, so—"

"Is there anything more you can do? Securitywise?"

"OK," she says, retrieving a sizable set of keys from her uniform pocket. "Here's what we'll do." Calming voice. Professional voice. "Before anything else, we're going to take a while and calm it down and see if we can take it one step at a time. Is that OK?"

There's a familiar tone. That's a you tone. A keep-it-in-perspective tone. She's saying come on, come on, don't let the paranoia leak into everything.

"We're all in a dither here, aren't we? So if it's OK with you, I want to spend some time on this."

"Yeah."

"So, first things first: I'm going to get you a bit of something to calm you down a touch, all right? Take the edge off."

"No, you're not listening—"

"I am, lovey. I'm hearing every word you say. And I just want to take the edge off so we can talk about things calmly and do the right thing, first time."

Her eyes stay fixed on me as her head gently nods up and down.

"OK," I say. "OK."

"I'll be back in five. Max."

She leaves the room, picking through her keys for the meds cupboard.

I lie down on the bed, on my side, fetal. Need to focus, focus. Press my head down firmly to feel something. Man, punched deep in the pillow, it honestly actually *pounds*. Every pulse a hammer blow, each blow muting my hearing, recovering enough in time to be muted again. My heart connected to my head. It's pressure, isn't it? It's making me scrunch my eyes up tight— tight, like *tight*—and that stops the pound-pound, by making it one long pound for a few moments. It's my heart; it's the pulses pulsing, pulse pound, and it will not stop. It's my heart beating the blood around me, and it just will not stop. I want a stop.

I've got my fists up clenched, clutching the bedsheets around my jaw. Beneath the sheets, the agitation. It's all rest; restless rest. My feet shifting in the sheets. Right forward, left back; left forward, right back. My only relief, to offset the hell in my head: marching through the linen like a slumbering foot soldier. Now that's the only sound, the soft *shiff, shiff,* and the occasional *zip* of a toenail scratching against the cotton.

It's the morphine. That's it, isn't it? That's why Mal's going to come here: it's a fucking bursting bank of clinical morphine, diamorphine. I'm not joking, I'm not joking; that's the only outcome. He's got Kelvin and Laura wrapped around his little finger, and they think he wants to be forgiven. He doesn't want to be forgiven. He—

And the pain and realization shoots down my neck and penetrates deep into my back, so deep as to come out the front into my chest, like getting kicked in the kidneys, jars out the breastbone, and blooms up through my chest, tight. Nausea blooms and churns within.

The door sucks shut in the corridor, and I look up at my doorway with a start.

It's Sheila, finally.

"OK," she says. "I've got a sedative here, just to get us back on an even keel."

I sit up and look at her, and she must read my mind.

"Do you trust me?" she says.

I nod.

She hands me a pill and a beaker of water, and I take it.

"Now," she says, sitting lightly on the arm of the visitors' chair, "are you able to tell me a little bit about this?"

"About what?"

"About the visitor you don't want to see. It helps if I know what I'm looking for."

"It's a man. His name's Malachy Sampson."

"And why does he want to see you?"

"We used to be friends. He's been seeing my sister."

"OK."

"But he's dangerous. He's properly bad news. He's not long out of prison. So, what you were saying about the store full of drugs and needles…?"

She starts to show the right amount of unease. I'm getting through to her, and it's beginning to encroach on her responsibilities. "OK, well, that's helpful for me to know, at least."

"He could do this. I'm sure that's what he's after, and I think he's going to try to come and *get* me."

I know how this sounds.

Her face softens in exactly the way I hoped it wouldn't.

"He's going to think I put him in prison. He's going to wonder why I didn't fight to keep him out—"

"Listen," she says. "I'll look into this, and I'll make sure we do everything we need to do to keep you feeling safe and secure."

"Thank you," I say, looking up at her.

"But I know what you're like, Ivo. You're the type of person who's got this worry-shaped hole in the middle of your head. And it doesn't matter what's going on; it doesn't matter what I do to make things better—you're going to fill it with whatever's in front of you at the time. You're not the first to do this, and I daresay you won't be the last. So do yourself a favor and keep yourself occupied, all right? It'll help, I promise."

I

Intestine

Yeah, now it comes up.

Intestine.

I could do a whole A to Z of my life's worth of intestinal misery. What have I ever done to be cursed with a body that deals with any level of stress with a punch straight to the gut?

Three nights I threw up when I moved to secondary school. I didn't know where any of the classrooms were; I had all new lessons, and I'd been warned these were all going to be much more difficult; I had to wear a new uniform—all that stuff, like a putrefying knot in my belly.

My first day at the garden center, aged eighteen, I threw up in the break room at the sheer amount of new information they were giving me about how to operate the tills. Within a fortnight I was even doing returns and refunds without having to think about it. It's easy, it's *easy*. But my intestines had to have their moment.

It's like something has not been worth doing if I haven't thrown up in contemplating it.

⁂

"Poor love," you say, stroking my back as my stomach muscles spasm again and I am subjected to another involuntary heave of fetid breath and spittle. "Come here..." You hand me a pat of tissue and a tall glass of fresh water. I swill out my mouth and spit down the toilet. Flush it away.

I slip on your dressing gown and look down.

"It makes my arms look really long."

"It's pretty. Come on, back to bed."

I shuffle across the landing, trying hard, trying very hard not to shuffle. It's all in the mind. I need to stride purposefully, pretend I am coping absolutely fine with your announcement of going away.

I'll shuffle.

Honestly, who throws up at the merest tiniest little upheaval like their girlfriend going away? I'm an absolute lily.

"Here you go," you say, placing the sick bowl on the floor beside the bed and climbing in beside me. "What does this mean for the insulin you've injected? You'd just eaten—does it mean you've got to eat something else to soak up the excess?"

I frown and cough to clear my throat. "Oh, I don't know. I've got a leaflet somewhere about sick days. I think it's fine. I'll test in a while and see from that."

"OK. As long as you've got that covered."

"Covered," I say, snapping my fingers and winking at you in a funky gesture of all-rightness.

"Listen," you say, "Ivo. I've decided. I'm not going to go on this work transfer."

"No, Mia. No, you can't—"

"It's three months away. It's too much. Especially, you know, if I'm not sure I… Well, I don't even know if I want to do nursing anymore."

"What? Why not?"

Your face grows unexpectedly sullen, and you hug your knees through the duvet.

"I don't know. It's just… I've not met anyone who I can relate to. Everyone seems happy to do the robotic thing, treat all the patients like units." You rake your hand down your face, pummel your eye sockets with the heels of your hands. "I mean, I feel terrible saying it, because here I am, I've spent all this money, and you're being amazingly patient about the whole thing, and I feel like I'm wasting your time."

I gaze at you, trying to digest everything this means.

"I keep thinking this is not what I went into nursing for. I wanted to make a difference for people, to treat people like humans. But if I ever say anything like that to any of the other students, they look at me like I'm insane. It's so tiring. More tiring than the actual work."

Now it's my turn to stroke your back.

"I just feel like I've been so naive about it."

"Listen, I don't think you've been naive."

"I've been really naive."

"OK, you've been really naive. But all this stuff—at least it's going to show you what you don't want to do."

"But I don't want to spend three months away from you, feeling like a leper."

"You're not a leper, just because everyone else treats you like one. That's their problem."

"But three months of it."

"It's not forever," I say. "Look, sleep on it. But I don't want you to ditch your career just because I'm a walking nervous breakdown. It's not fair on either of us."

You pull in and arrange your limbs around me, delicately avoiding my stomach.

"I'll sleep on it."

"Good."

"If I go, are you going to be sick for the whole three months?"

"I'll be fine. I'll work. I'll watch TV."

"You'll use the time to do something amazing and creative, I know it."

"Yeah…I don't know about that."

Ffff—fuck it: press the buzzer.

Push the button to the click.

Fffff—Jesus, the *pain* of it.

Ahhh. Ssssssurges.

Is this it? What if this is it? This could be it. This is definitely it.

No, no, ridiculous*sss*.

Oh, all I can think of is you. I love you, I love you, I love you, if this is the last thing I think, I'm so, so sorry, and I love you.

Calmness. Positive thinking. Put it in context. Concentrate yourself away from pain. Walk away from it.

It's not pain; it's sensation. It's—

Owowowow. It's making me almost *laugh* with pain.

No, not laugh.

Sheila appears quickly at the door.

"What's the matter, Ivo? Are you uncomfortable?"

"Yes, yes, pain…just here…"

"Down here, is it?" She lays her hand flat on my lower belly, gently, gently.

"Mm*ff*."

"Mmm-hmm." She steps back and checks my chart. "When did you last pop to the bathroom?"

"Mmm—two days."

I wince again as another surge of pain flashes across my middle.

"OK, OK, lovey. Now, I want you to keep calm, OK? We're going to get this all under control. Do you trust me?"

"Yeah."

"Dr. Sood's in this afternoon, so I'm going to fetch him to take a view."

As I watch her leave, anxiety seizes my stomach, and the pain lashes back, another whipcrack. I don't want to be alone—I don't want to be alone if this is it.

It's unbearable.

Positive thoughts.

Come on, come on. Think it through, carefully, calmly, calm, calm.

Is it pain anyway? Am I weak? How would I know? Maybe it's not pain. Maybe I've never been in real pain. Maybe only the pain I've seen in other people has been the real thing, and I've only ever imitated their sucking of the teeth and wincing and cringing and sighing and huffing.

No, no. Calm it. I'm not in pain. Not real pain.

If I were dying, it would be the worst pain imaginable, surely. Is this the worst pain imaginable? No, it is not. What shall we call this? We could call it taken-abackness. It's like when my knee clicks, or…or when my coat pocket catches on a door handle as I'm passing through and I might say "ow," and I give off many of the signals of having been in pain. But it's not pain, is it? It's just being taken aback. Surprised.

And anyway, they don't let you feel pain these days. They give you drugs. Like they gave Old Faithful drugs. They don't let you feel the pain.

Thank God.

Ffff*ff.* "Yeah, he's in here."

Sheila enters the room all businesslike, Dr. Sood in tow.

"Good afternoon," says Sood. "How are things with you today? I gather you've been in a little discomfort?"

"Severe headaches," says Sheila, "shortness of breath, anxiety over…a number of personal matters. And sharp abdominal pains."

"Mmm." He cocks his head to one side. "How's your vision?"

"Light hurts."

"Breathing is still troubling you, yes?"

"I cough a lot."

Nice Dr. Sood. He's calming in a rapid sort of manner. He talks in an efficient, quick, and minimal way. His mouth clicks form an integral part of his speech pattern. To the point, but kindly enough.

He turns to Sheila. "Any general feeling of panic, of distress, or anything like this?"

"We've been using oxygen for a few days," says Sheila. "Regular shortness of breath."

"Any improvements?"

"Nothing substantial."

This seems to push him into some kind of decision.

"Hmm. I'm wondering whether we should be administering relief for these symptoms. We can take care of the pain here in your abdomen. But we also have to consider any sort of panicky anxieties you have been experiencing. We could be administering a morphine solution, which should take care of the worst of it and give you a little more space within yourself to control these symptoms better."

"Morphine? I'm not ready for that, am I?" I look at Sheila. "I don't think I'm that bad."

"Well, one of the things we are watching in a case like yours is the contamination of the bloodstream with toxins such as potassium. Do you understand? And the buildup of toxins often leads to an increase in anxiety and irritation in the patient, and, well, if the symptoms are as we believe them to be, then you might find that a mild solution can help you—"

"No, thank you. No."

I'm surely not far gone enough for morphine, am I?

No, no. I'm not dead yet.

"I just need a little something to…take the edge off." I look up at Sheila hopefully. "Just a little something."

"Well, as I say, we can get you some relief for your abdominal pains, which we can probably put down to a spot of trapped wind in your intestine. Sharp, sudden pain."

As he says it, another flash of pain darts its way through my belly.

"Trapped wind? Seriously, it's—*ffff*—it's really, really bad. I'm sweating here. I'm sweating. It's—*ffff*…"

"It can get like that, honestly," says Sheila. "And it's to be expected. I'm going to get you something to relieve that, OK?"

"OK. Yes, please."

"And you do not want the morphine solution?" says Sood.

"No. No, thanks."

"May I ask why?"

"I don't want to go there. I…I don't want to."

"Addiction is not an issue, if that's what you're worried about. It's entirely up to you and how you would like to handle your symptoms, but just so long as you are aware of the options available to you. I'd like to register with you the fact that I think a solution of morphine would help you along, ease your symptoms to a point where you'll be in a good deal fairer fettle than you are now. So I'd like you to bear it in mind going forward."

The two of them depart, Sheila with a little wink, Sood off to the patient he had come to see in the first place. I'm left here with his final words in mind. Going forward.

Going forward?

To what?

Tell me this is not trapped wind. Trapped wind can't be this bad. It can't. Old Faithful's dead, and I'm here wriggling around with trapped wind. I really hope it isn't trapped wind.

No, I really hope it is trapped wind.

Sheila returns alone, rotating a small, rattly white box around and about in her hands, trying to find the best way of opening it.

"Here we go now. Don't worry. It's nothing we haven't seen before. Fact of life, isn't it? We've got some suppositories here, joy of joys. They'll encourage the muscles in your lower intestine to start working a bit to try to help you go to the toilet, all right?"

"Right."

"Would you like to pop this in yourself? I mean, I can—"

"No, no, fine. I'll do it."

"Here you go. If you head over to the toilet, unwrap it, pop it in pointy end first, and wash your hands after."

She helps me down from my bed and across the room—and I need it.

I need the help.

Jesus.

I try to take in a breath but fail. Cough more, but stop short in pain.

"Oh, you're all right, lovey. Not at the end of your tether yet, OK? You're doing very well. Now, you might want to run it under the tap a bit first. I'll be standing out here, so give me a shout if you need me, won't you? Don't be embarrassed. Easier said than done, I know."

I shuffle into the tiny bathroom and turn to face the mirror. My eyes have yellowing whites, red around the rim.

This is it. Another intestinal episode. The day I thought I was going to die, and it was just a tummy ache.

I am pathetic.

Sheila takes me by the arm as I emerge from the toilet and bears me over to the bed. An old man.

"There you go," she says tenderly. She fetches me a small paper cup of pills and pours me a glass of water. I throat the pills and shift them with water, shake my head to persuade them down. "That's it," she says and smiles. I sit back on my pillows, which she fluffs up behind me. She picks up your blanket from the end of the bed.

My blanket.

"Here you go, lovey." She drapes it around my shoulders. It feels heavy and comforting, like a hug. "Just imagine those pills working their way up to your head and spreading their magic. And that suppository freeing things up in the opposite direction."

"Yeah, yeah. Thanks."

"Now bear in mind you might be taken a bit by surprise at how suddenly it works, all right? So I've left a pan by your bed in case you don't make it. And I don't want you getting all anxious about that. It's there to be used, so use it if you need it, OK?"

"OK."

She looks at me and tuts to herself. "Listen, lovey, I'm not here to twist your arm, but are you sure you're doing the right thing about the morphine solution? It's really very mild, and I don't want to see you distressed. There's absolutely no need for that."

"I'm fine," I say. "I need to stop being pathetic. Get my mind under control."

"Well, that's what the morphine would do—give you a bit of space upstairs."

"Like you say, let it go, get a bit of perspective. I can do this. Mind over matter. Just—are you sure, are you totally sure there'll be no visitors?"

"Everyone's aware; all the checks are in place. I've left strict instructions with Jackie to make sure everyone signs in at reception, all right, lovey?"

"All right. Thank you."

"Only…do me a favor. If you want the morphine, go ahead and take it. You don't get extra points for style in this game."

"No, I know."

"Now, have you got everything? How are you progressing on your alphabet?"

"I'm up to the letter *I*."

"*I*? Well, it's staring you in the face, isn't it?"

"I've thought about intestines."

"No—insulin."

"God. Is that an acceptable part of the body?"

"Yes! It's a hormone, isn't it? The main thing I remember about it is that it's produced in your pancreas by the *islets of Langerhans*." She draws her arms out wide in a romantic gesture. "It might be my favoritely named part of the body, the *islets of Langerhans*... *And* it comes under *I*. How about that?"

I'm not convinced.

"It's interesting, though, isn't it, all the different hormones and potions your body is able to produce, just like that? Amazing, really. That's what medieval doctors used to think: your whole body was governed by humors. And if they got out of whack, you'd get ill. It's not that far off what actually happens with your insulin."

"Yeah."

"And it makes you think, in a thousand years' time, they'll be thinking, *What? They used to inject people? In their veins? Seems barbaric.*"

Insulin

OK then, OK. Insulin. Another *I*. The *I* that defines me. Who would ever think that something as tedious as insulin was ever going to be their biggest enemy? No one. People go through life thinking everything's going to be fine… No one can be on guard against everything. It's a slippery slope. So do what I did and be on guard against nothing. Another slippery slope.

Here we go: life is a snowcapped mountain, and all you've got to do is choose which direction your slippery slope is going to take. I say choose the sunny side.

They always told me there was nothing I'd done wrong to stop my body's natural flow of insulin. Not like some people who could never gain control of their weight in these high-sugar, high-fat days. But thinking about it, I don't think the Mars bar and the pint of Coke I used to have for breakfast every morning in the school holidays will have helped. That must have been a major trauma for the old islets of Langerhans to cope with. Brilliant times, though, at home with Laura while Mum was at work.

I remember saying to her, "Does Coca-Cola really have cocaine in it?"

"Yeah! Yeah, it does. Like a Mars bar has bits of the planet Mars in it."

Then, at nineteen, the insulin dwindled, and that was more or less that.

My pee started smelling like Candy Hearts.

I couldn't keep the weight on.

So I got my diagnosis, and the doctor gave me my little pouch with everything in it: the blood sugar tester and the injector pen and the insulin and—

Me, my body; my body, me. I'm all the same but *not*. I didn't *want* it to happen like that. I am my *mind*. Not my body. But it was like my body wouldn't let my mind get away with it.

Mum's still in her work coat, sitting next to me on the sofa. I'm trying to watch the TV, but she's flipping noisily through *Diabetes* magazine, which she's insisted on subscribing to. I think she thinks I'm going to have a look at it, but I look at the cover and it leaves me feeling tired. Static smiling people of mixed ethnicity. They're happy because they have diabetes in common. Ha ha ha.

"You've got to stay on top of it though, kiddo," she's saying. "People go blind," she says. "They lose feet."

I look her directly in the eye, and I don't know why, but I start to laugh.

"What?" she says, starting to laugh herself. "It's not funny. This is serious!"

"I don't know. It's…it's funny for some reason," I say. "Losing feet. Seriously, Mum, don't worry about it. I can look after myself."

Every night after that, she would say, "Have you got your insulin?"

"Yeah."

And if not: "What would you do without me, eh?"

These early evening preloading sessions around Mal's are getting out of hand. I've landed back in the habit with you away on your work placements, because there's nothing else for me to do. But when you're actually in-town-but-impossibly-busy, I sometimes think I'd rather be watching TV in bed while you revise at the desk. But you won't have any of it. I only come over to Mal's out of something like politeness. Politeness to you and to him.

"Now," says Mal, "what have I got here?" He roots around in his jacket pocket and retrieves a twisted little plastic bag. "Here, man, look." He jiggles it enticingly and grins.

"Fucking hell, what is that?"

"What do you think it is?"

I look closer, at the powder, and I don't want to say it in case I sound stupid.

"*H*," he says.

Mal's car.

It's the best option.

I clamber and collapse into the back on the driver's side. Mal swings the front seat down, locks me in. Claustrophobia quickly starts to squeeze my chest. I need to get out; I want to get out. But all exits are blocked. Becca has settled in beside me, and Laura in front of her. Surrounded on all sides with the windows steaming up. No way of opening them. No way out the back.

C'mon, put your seat belt on.

Under way, rubber rumbling on the asphalt through town as Mal manhandles the gears upward, we're all thrust backward and forward as his feet push the pedals, side to side on the say-so of his hands. I'm fumbling for the seat belt, but I can't focus. I can't… get… I don't know what's the lack of insulin and what's the drug, but I'm coming down now; it's all starting to feel more familiar. Worse than familiar. Yank again at the seat belt but the safety lock's locked. It's too awkward, too hard to do. I'm going to leave it off.

Straight orange wash of streetlights replenished on Mal's seat back, wiped out over his headrest, banished by the black, over and over in rapid rhythm.

Are you good to drive?

Yeah, I'm good to drive.

You're sure?

Yeah, I'm sure.

I try a little look across the seat to Becca, and she smiles at me, takes up my hand. I want to tell her we have to have a plan, we have to get our story straight, because you're not on placement this time, you're home, studying the night away, and I need to have an explanation. But I can't herd my feline thoughts. Becca has my hand. She's stroking it reassuringly, tenderly. It's nice, it's nice.

Out again on the street, your street, and I'm being walked along the pavement—a long, straight terrace street stretching off into the distance, and I'm measuring out my paces along the pavement, slab by slab. Tiny ups and downs, wobbly wonky. I've Laura and Becca on either side, and they're supporting, and there's no… Where's Mal?

Jangle now as Becca retrieves her keys for the front door. Laura's at my other arm, but I can feel her becoming softer, more uncertain. Less and less support. The front door unjams and judders, rattling the knocker familiarly beneath the mail slot.

"You'll be all right from here, won't you?"

Words from Laura to my right, and now her presence drains away, leaks off back down the street, back off to…to Mal?

And now it's your room, and it's you. Urgent, attentive, professional.

I look up at you as you tend to me, your forehead frowning, your eyes precise.

"I'm so sorry."

Unscary daylight. The safe, spacey morning-after wooziness. And you're being so gentle and kind.

I don't deserve any of it. Look at you, you're shattered.

"Can you remember what happened?" you say, climbing in at the foot of the bed, giving me a bit of room. "Becca was a bit hazy on details."

"Just fucking stupid," I say. "I forgot my insulin, didn't I? I left it there on your desk. And I was in the club and, you know, I felt a bit weird, and I knew I was having this hyper. I thought I could ride it out."

"So you forgot your insulin…and that's it?"

"So stupid," I say.

"So why did Becca bring you back? I thought you were out with Mal and Laura?"

There's a significant edge to your tone, and I feel you holding my glance a little too straight. You're scanning, scanning.

"Oh, yeah," I say with a wash of unfocused guilt. "No, Becca was there too. Mal and Laura and Becca."

The events of last night are captured only as still images, swelling sounds. It remains aching in my limbs and squealing in my ears and my soul. Tired but alert. Remnants of trippiness in the head.

"Are you all right?" you ask. The fatal question.

"Yep, yeah. I'm fine," I say.

"You sure?"

"Absolutely." I smile. Sort of.

Maybe if I vented everything, maybe it would all work out OK. I can actually feel the tip of my tongue tensing against the top of my mouth to say…to say what?

You've tipped your head to listen, eyebrows expectant.

Launch.

"Listen," I say, "I wanted to tell you…"

And straightaway your face grows concerned. You look away, fearful.

Bad start, bad start. Start more gently.

"It's OK, it's OK," I say. "It's nothing major. Don't worry. But it's just…it's something I want to feel that I can talk freely with you about."

"Drugs?" you say, looking up at me swiftly and directly. "I'm not blind. Your pupils were like dinner plates."

"I'm sorry."

You look at me a moment and reflect. "You don't have to apologize to me. I'm not your mum," you say. "Why didn't you tell me before?"

"Well, I don't know. It's not something you can easily talk about, you know? And then…I don't know. I got scared because…" Again I hesitate.

"Because what?"

"Well, there's your dad and all the stuff you went through with him. And then there's the fact that you're a nurse and everything." I quickly add this on at the end, because your face falls at the mention of your dad.

"The fact that you can't take your insulin properly," you say. "That's what the nurse is unhappy about."

"Yeah, well."

I'm relieved to see some of the anxiety has passed from your face. I think maybe you thought my big revelation was going to be about Becca after all.

"Listen," you say, "I'm not a fun killer, and I absolutely refuse to be the one who's telling you what to do. Don't paint me like that, Ivo, because we won't survive that."

"I know."

"But you've *got* to look after yourself. You're not like Mal and all the others—you're just not. You're not in your body, and you're not in your mind either."

As I sit there, the scale of all the lies expands around me. Lies to myself, I suppose. But now that you're here, and you care, they've become lies to you. Missing insulin jabs since I was twenty—maybe one a day, every day. And the drugs too—not just pills. Do I need to declare it all? What can I get away with? I feel like I want to tell you everything but…would that be poisoning it for no reason?

"What's the matter?" you say.

"It wasn't only last night. There's been a few nights. Quite a lot of nights."

"I don't doubt." You shrug. "Do I want to know?"

"On and off since…well, before you and I were together. On and off."

"And while we've been together?"

"The odd weekend…you know, when I was stuck at home and you were off on night shift or on placement."

"So, what, more pills?"

I breathe out unsteadily.

"Pills. Some acid." I wince. I hear the clicks of the corners of my mouth. "A little bit of powder."

"Powder? Well, what, cocaine? Or—"

"Cocaine, yes."

"Shit, Ivo. *Cocaine?* I never thought it was anything like that."

I sit meekly, while you frown and drill your eyes into the middle of the bed between us, trying to work it all out.

"So, cocaine then," you say.

Oh, don't ask. Please don't ask.

"That's it? You've not done…anything else."

It's not a question. I can't answer. It's not a question.

"*Heroin?*" you say, and your shock tops out. "Jesus, Ivo, I just don't know who you *are*. *Heroin?*"

You fling the covers off and start tearing clothes from your closet, wrenching on your jeans.

"Mia," I say. "Mia, listen—"

"I don't want to hear it. You *promised* me you'd look after yourself, Ivo. You *promised.*"

"Nothing's changed. Nothing."

You try to pull on a sock while standing, but stumble and have to sit down. The mattress bounds beneath me as you do.

"I know you don't want to hear me, Mia, but I'm the same man."

You pull on your shoes, tugging at the tongue and aggressively driving in your heel.

"I just…I get *bored*, all right?" I say. "Bored and *lonely*. You're the one who's working all the hours."

"So, what, you're saying it's *my* fault?"

"No, no, I'm not saying that—"

"You want me to give up nursing and come hold your hand, is that it?"

I close my eyes. Stop now. Absorb all the tension in the room. No point, no point. I will not snap back.

"But it's *so stupid*," you say. "You're diabetic! What do you think you're going to say when the doctors start asking you about your history?"

Silence.

"What if you end up needing a kidney transplant one day? Because that's what happens. They'll put you at the bottom of every list. They probably won't even bother putting you *on* the list. Jesus, who *are* you?"

"I wanted you to know," I say. "I've done it like three times. Ever. And I'm not going to do it anymore. It's stopped."

Well, there it is. There you have it: me.

All of me.

"Are you going to say something?" I say.

"I don't have anything to say," you say.

And you leave.

I pick up the gun and point it at the customer's fertilizer, watch the red laser dance across the bar code. It beeps.

"That's fifty-four eighty-six in total, please," I say, the automatic words feeling good in my mouth. Trusty script. "If you'd like to put your card in the machine. And type in your PIN."

The old guy squints down at the keypad and thumbs in his number. It's 1593. We wait, and I look across at Laura, Mal, and Becca as they stand awkwardly nearby. I cannot *believe* I've had to get them to come in. I cannot believe I forgot to bring my insulin with me to work.

The printer blurts and chops out the receipts, and I pair them up with the card and hand them back to the old guy, who takes them and trundles his heavy cart away.

"You can't work twenty-four hours a day," says Laura, stepping forward once more.

"I'm not," I say in a quiet voice. "I just want to keep busy. Keep occupied. Get paid." I can barely bring myself to speak at a normal volume these days. I slot the laser gun back into its holster.

"Have you spoken to her?"

"We've talked on the phone a couple of times."

"And what did she say?"

"She says she's got her exams to get through and she doesn't want to jeopardize them. She doesn't want to see me."

"So do you reckon that's it then?"

"Sounds like it, doesn't it?" says Mal.

"I don't know," I say, miserably. "I'd say like 99.9 percent certain."

Another customer wanders up, and Laura, Mal, and Becca step back once more, wave her through.

Work is good. They've been good at giving me extra hours here, and once you've been in the job long enough, colleagues start to recognize the patterns. Someone suddenly wants extra hours, no-questions-asked, you oblige.

I'm grateful.

"I don't see what the big deal is," says Laura, when the coast's clear. "Why's she looking to control everything you do anyway?"

"It's not like that," I say. "It's more complicated than that."

"Well, why?" she says.

"It's not something I can really talk about. It's a private thing."

"Come on, you can tell us. It's not like we're going to tell her. You won't say anything, will you, Becca?"

Becca shrugs. "Nothing to do with me."

"It's a basic trust thing, isn't it? Look, her dad was an alcoholic, and it kind of screwed up her family, and—"

"But that's totally different," says Laura. "You're not an alcoholic, are you? I don't see why you should be the one who has to pay for whatever mistakes her dad's made in his life."

I close my eyes and try not to boil up at Laura. But it's hard, it's hard. She will not read the signs. I don't want to talk about it. I pray for another customer.

"And anyway, has she never made a single mistake in her life?"

"She's a nice girl," says Becca. "But, you know, maybe she's not quite the right one for you, Ivo. Going out at four in the morning, decorating the town. It's a bit…" She wrinkles her nose.

I can't answer this. I'm struck silent; the thick sort of silence where I'm trying to hide the fact that I'm choking back the tears. I clear my throat noisily and find myself exhaling like a horse. I smile broadly and mirthlessly at Becca.

Becca's brow knits in sympathy, and she puts her hand on my hand and squeezes it.

"Tough times," she says.

I nod, tight-lipped.

"Seriously, Ivo, you're better off out of it, if you ask me," says Laura. "People like Mia… I mean, she's a lovely girl and everything, but she makes you be someone you're not, maybe to fit in with what she's doing, you know? You need to make sure you're doing what *you* want to do."

A smile, a nod, and it's Becca who finally reads me right.

"Come on," she says to Laura. "I want to buy some cut flowers."

"Over the other side, by the aquatics," I say.

They move away, but Mal hangs around and watches another couple of customers drift through the checkout.

"So where're you going to go?" he asks. "Back to your mum's full-time?"

"Ah, I don't know," I say, feeling a bit foolish now to be so low.

"Listen, I was thinking," he says, "between you and me, I'm going to be getting my own place soon, I reckon."

"Really? What about Laura?"

"Laura's place has always belonged to her, and I've always meant to get my own place; I just never got around to it. C'mon, what do you reckon? We could move in together. Get a bigger place, if we pool resources."

My absolute instinct is no. I'm still hooked on the idea of you and me: you and me living together, and if I move in with him, that's like saying good-bye forever. Like it's never going to be OK again.

"Listen," he says, "I don't want to say the wrong thing, but"—he reaches over and tugs the laser gun out of its holster, starts targeting things with its dancing beam—"well, there's nothing in this world that's *all* bad, you know? There's different choices now."

"Yeah." A dead yeah.

"We'd be able to do what we wanted. We could hire a big TV, get a new console. Have tourneys, man. Have a bit of a smoke, you know, get the pizzas in, beers. Get Kelvin around, maybe."

"I'll have a think, man, yeah?"

"OK, yeah. I'm going to look into it meantime."

"Yeah…yeah, all right."

The light flicks on outside. The garden is flung into being once again.

Or was it just me opening my eyes?

I can't be sure. I can't be sure.

"Are you OK, lovey?" Sheila's in at the door in a second.

"Ugh." I knuckle my eyes. "I don't want to be the kind of person who complains about lights—"

"I know, I know. I'm so sorry. We've got the contractors coming in again tomorrow or the next day, and they're staying until they've ironed out the problem."

I frown and scratch at my bristly face. "Were you waiting out in the corridor?"

"You what?"

"You came straight in."

"Oh yeah, I'm keeping vigil outside your room every minute of the day, sweetheart. And it's only a coincidence that's where we keep the cookies."

J

Jugular

"There's a way," says Mal. "There's definitely a way you can kill someone. If you know the right pressure points."

He grabs Kelvin at the base of the neck. "It's to do with the jugular."

Kelvin's like, "Ow! Get off!" He squirms to get away.

Mal keeps a grip. "It's around here somewhere."

Kelvin seriously thinks he might actually die. "Get off!" Definite note of panic in his voice.

Mal lets go, and Kelvin hops out of reach and twists to inspect himself.

"Fucking hell, look at that!" Red fingertip marks now begin to take hold around Kelvin's neck and shoulder.

"See?" says Mal. "It's somewhere around there."

The door unsticks again, and Sheila's footsteps return.

"Well, well," she says.

"What?"

"It was nothing to worry about. It was a visitor. It was that man who was here before with your sister."

"Kelvin?"

"That's right."

"I don't want to see him."

"Don't worry. I sent him away. I don't think he was too surprised. He didn't put up much resistance."

I hide my face in my hands. "I don't need this. I don't need it."

"Now come on, there's nothing to be worried about. Honestly, there isn't."

She comes and sits down, and I'm a little surprised when she takes up my hand and holds it. Dimly wonder whether they're supposed to do that sort of thing anymore. It feels nice. She strokes the back of my hand tenderly, and the assortment of rings she has on her fingers clink reassuringly. Reminds me of a gypsy. Sharp twinkle in the eye.

"This panicking's not going to do you any good," she says gently. "You've said it yourself, haven't you? You know it's true."

I nod. Frown and try to keep my anxiety down.

Everything's so close to the surface now.

"Sheila, can I say something to you?"

"Anything you like, lovey. Anything at all."

I sniff and catch my breath, exactly like a little child who wants his mum.

"I can't let it go," I say.

"What do you mean?"

"I try to let it go, all these *things*, these anxious *things*. But I *can't*. They just keep coming back to me."

She strokes my hand tenderly.

"It's invading. Even playing this stupid game, it's like it's invading me—it feels like every body part brings it back to me. Every part of me wants to tell the same story. It feels like maybe, maybe it's *meant* to be that way."

Insane to even think it.

Embarrassing.

But it's possible to think it might be true.

Sheila looks at me, unembarrassed, and with calm collectedness. "I know. I know, lovey. I know. I can see it. And is there no way you want to talk about these things? Share the problems? I'm all ears."

She puts her fingers behind her lobes and dinks them out sideways.

Silly.

Silly woman.

"Listen," she says, "I hate to be the bearer of bad news, but I ought to tell you these accumulated problems would benefit from... Well, if you're still dead set against the morphine solution..."

"Ah, I don't know anymore."

"Or if you didn't want to go there, at least a little bit of massage, and maybe some gentle exercise."

"Mmm."

"Nothing too strenuous, just something to take your mind off things. And we've got a woman who'll come and do that for you—Karen. You'll like her; she's lovely. I can book you in for one, if you like? I'd like to see you up and about more, please."

"Mmm."

"Or there's a Reiki healer? Some of our residents get a lot from that; the woman comes in and realigns your chakras for you."

She does an admirable job of saying it seriously, though I suspect at the center she thinks it's nonsense. I shake my head. No, no.

"No, I didn't think that would be quite your bag, somehow." I give her a smile. "Honestly. You've got to help yourself as much as you can, and I'm not saying that because I don't want to do it myself. I can do whatever you want. But you've got to help yourself."

"Mmm."

"Promise me you'll at least think about it."

"OK."

"Promise?"

"Promise."

Kidneys

I've put off making this call for as long as I can.

I must have picked up the phone fifty times today and put it down without pressing a single digit.

Now I've pressed them all, and it's ringing.

It's six weeks and four days since we split up, and we've spoken—what?—four times? And each of those calls has stuttered to a halt in the end. You need space. You don't know if it's worth it. At any rate, you need to concentrate. You don't know if it's even possible to keep a relationship going and get through what you're trying to get through.

"So many of the other women on the course have split up from their partners," you said. "I sometimes wonder if nursing and a private life mix at all."

And in each of our halting conversations, with a leaden heart and closed throat, I've said, "Can you tell me absolutely that there's no hope of anything happening at all? Ever?"

And that's what's left those long static silences. You haven't been able to kill it completely.

There has always been that finest thread of hope.

The finest thread, which I'm about to snap forever.

"Hello?"

Heartbreaking warmth in your voice when you pick up. You're showing a guarded pleasure from seeing my name light up on your phone.

"Hello," I say simply. And then I realize I've not really thought this through. What can I say? "I'm…I'm sorry for ringing you."

"No, it's nice to hear from you."

"How are you doing?"

"Ah, not brilliant, if I'm honest. I've got my final exam coming up, so I'm flat-out busy and completely stressed. It's a bit of a classic deadly combination."

"It's never-ending," I say.

"But it's good to have a break. I was quite hoping you might call."

Oh, don't be nice to me. Don't. I don't need hope now, when I'm about to throw the whole thing away.

"Look," I say, "I…I wanted to say something, but I don't really know…"

"OK…"

"I've got some…some shit news from the doctor's."

"Oh no, what?"

Think quickly. I need to get this out there quicker—because you think I might be dying now, and I don't know… I don't know if I *am* dying or something—

"I've been trying to get to grips with a few things since…you know, lately…and I've been for a bunch of checkups. I've been referred to the renal consultant."

"Oh my God."

"I had the appointment this morning."

"And what—"

"He says I've got high levels of…creatinine? In my blood."

Silence. I think for a moment you might hang up.

I think you might say *Serves you right*.

I think you might say *I told you so*.

You say, "Shit."

"He says there are signs of kidney failure."

"Fuck."

"Yeah."

"Why didn't you *tell* me? I could have come along with you. What—"

"I'm sorry for phoning you. I just… I've been such a dick. You're the only person I know who I could talk to about it. And you're a nurse, so I thought you might know something."

You sigh heavily, and you sound much more shocked than I thought you would. The tiny ember of hope still glows in the middle of all this suffocating ash.

"I don't know. I don't know," you say. "Is it a stable result? Did they test a full day's samples?"

"He was talking about Stage 2 kidney failure."

"Ivo, why didn't you say anything? You must have been beside yourself."

"I didn't think you'd want to know. You said you don't need to watch someone else fuck themselves up."

"How could you think that?"

"Kidney failure. Exactly what you said."

"I would never turn you away like that," you say. "Come on, you know that."

I heave an exhausted sigh. "I don't know if I do anymore."

"Listen," you say, slotting into a practical gear, "I've got a whole load of notes about renal care. Let me dig them out. I might be able to find some pamphlets I can send you that explain it all."

"Thank you," I say, touched that you might care. "I'm… I'm really—"

"Sorry, yeah," you say.

⌘

"OK, lovey, here we go." Sheila's got a bottle and a spoon. "Nothing to it. What I'm going to do is measure out an amount in here"—she waves the spoon—"and then you'll take that as you might some cough medicine, OK?"

I'm scared. I want you. I want your arms around me. Where's my blanket? I want my blanket. Should I ask now?

"And you'll start to feel the benefits more or less straightaway. All right? So by the time the local news comes on TV, you should be feeling more together."

"They should give this to everyone who watches the local news." Weak smile.

Sheila laughs.

I want you—I want you to tell me. Am I doing the right thing? If I take this, I'm not coming back.

Fetch my blanket. It's in the cupboard, isn't it?

I want to ask Sheila. I should ask her. I'm not sure about this. But you can't even ask doctors, can you? They're not allowed to tell you what to do. You've got to decide for yourself.

Your health in your hands.

But I'm not the one who's been through seven years of medical school.

"I don't know," I say to her.

"What's that, lovey?"

"I don't know if I want to. Do…do you think I should?"

"Yeah." She smiles. "I'd take anything that's going."

Oh. She is allowed to tell me what to do. Is she?

"I just…I don't want to get addicted. I know, it's stupid. But…I've been addicted, sort of. I mean, why does it have to be down to me? You've got all"—breathe—"all these people who are supposed to help you and…and all they say is, 'I don't know. What do you think?'"

She pauses a moment and sits down in my visitors' chair, unhurried, offering all the time I need.

"Listen. No one's going to make you do anything you don't want to do. I'm not. Dr. Sood's not. But I've seen a lot of people go through what you're going through. Every day. I don't want you to do it the hard way."

"No."

"And it's only a light solution, OK? It will ease the anxiety. It will ease the symptoms. It'll stop you worrying. Give you a bit of space in your head."

"Right."

"So let's pause a moment, OK? Let me get your blanket for you."

"Yeah."

"In here, is it?"

"Yeah."

She fetches it from the cupboard and helps me draw it around my shoulders. I hook my fingers through the knots.

"I tell you what. I'll make you a deal. You take this now, and I'd say by late this evening the effects will have worn off. So, I promise to come back to you this evening, and if you don't want it, you won't have it ever again, and that is my absolute solemn promise, OK?"

"OK."

OK.

"Are you ready?"

She takes up the bottle, carefully charges the spoon, and proffers it.

"Down the hatch."

Down the hatch.

Tighten fingers, clutch through crochet. Feel the knots.

"Now a sip of tea. It'll take the taste away. There."

Sip.

Cup rings back into saucer.

"All right?"

"Right."

"OK."

"Is there anything else I can get for you? Your wish is my command."

"No. Thank you."

Lips

Your lips. The most delicious kisses.

    Oh, when I remember your lips.

    Lying back here now, I long to think of them, but…I can't.

    The perfect pout…

    I'm scared to even begin.

    Can't even bring myself to think, to think of the kiss…

    No.

Think about it differently. Lips. What was that first kiss?

    The first ones were Grandma and Granddad. Granddad's was always over-slobbery and beery. Laura used to hate it. I remember every time she would *cringe* on the way in. I used to quite like the smell of stale beer. Quite fruity.

But I shrank away from Grandma's kisses. She had thin, dry lips, cold and without resistance, like the kiss of a ghost. But the worst bit was there must have been this one-off piece of stubble or something on her top lip, a little to the left of center—it must have been where she regularly plucked out a hair because every time I had to kiss her good-bye I would be pricked by it, like a little electric shock.

I can't believe how she put up with me writhing to get away from her, whining, *There's a spike on her lip! It hurts!*

What must the older generations put up with?

First serious girl kiss: Nicola Peterson.

Aged fourteen, out in the middle of the school playing fields, far away from anyone.

The *lunge* that girl used to make. The first thing I would see would be this great wide chasm of a pie hole launching itself at me like it knew what it was doing. For a while I thought maybe it was me who was getting it wrong. I didn't know, did I? Because no one really teaches you how to kiss; where would you start? You have to make it up as you go along.

Her kisses *frightened* me. That's not right, is it?

Kelvin thought it was hilarious, but he'd never kissed anyone.

There were four or five in between, all bases reached, virginity merrily dispensed with, but it really was you who taught me to go back and love kissing.

No.

No—I *can't*. I *can't* unlock it. It's too… I'm scared to. It might release it all again, just be too much. Too, too much.

Here comes the cavalry.

I venture into my mum's bedroom, where I'm not really allowed, and find her sitting on the edge of her bed, gazing into her mirror, a collection of makeup shrapnel slithering in beside her on the comforter.

Twenty minutes since Laura slammed the front door behind her and left the house shivering, Mum still seems sad.

She sees me—"Hiya, kiddo"—and her mouth automatically straightens into a smile, but for once she can't sustain it, even though I smile back.

She is very sad.

She unclicks her lipstick lid, twirls out the waxy stick, and aims it at her mouth. But before she sets it to her lips, she sighs and lets her hand drop back into her lap.

It's on instinct that I step forward and reach for the lipstick myself. She lets me have it.

Delicious smell. One of my favorite smells.

I reach up toward her mouth, and she turns her face toward me to oblige. I begin to apply, top lip, and then bottom lip, in vague imitation of what I've seen her do more or less every morning of my childhood. And like more or less every drawing of my childhood, I go over the edges.

And I know I've gone over the edges, so I keep going. And Mum keeps her face there. She keeps it there until I've drawn a big smiley lipstick face almost all the way up and out to her ears. As I apply the lipstick, the skin of her cheeks is stretched out sideways, and I worry it might be painful, but she doesn't move, and I need no more encouragement than that.

When I have untwirled the wax and slipped and clicked the lid back into place, she turns and looks at herself in the mirror.

She smiles, a small smile in the middle of my great big one.

It's still possible to smile when you're crying.

In the unfamiliar pitch-black, lips press themselves passionately to mine. Not like yours. Different from yours. They open, and my lips open, open together, drive deeper; a tongue pushes between m—

No. No. I can't think of this.

"Are you all right, lovey?"

Sheila, doorway.

Her voice is like… It's like listening to the radio when I'm falling asleep.

Somehow clearer, more acute.

"How are you bearing up?" She's speaking slowly too.

"Yeah," I say, "good."

"Well, I'll check in on you in a little while, see how you're going on. You've got your button if you need me."

I look at the button. There it is, snaking across my bed. Friendly.

"I've got my button."

"OK, lovey."

She's not there anymore.

Is this working? I think the morphine might be working.

It's gentle. I feel gentle.

It's like sitting in the back of the car, the voices and the radio around me, swirling and stirring me to sleep.

m

Muscles

"Our concern is over muscle wastage," the consultant mutters to your mum.

Plastic mask marks your face.

Bedbound, the ventilator breathes out, you breathe in; clicks; in, you breathe out.

A ventilator is not a part of the body. It absolutely is not.

Brain branded.

We've been sitting with you for two days now. The ventilator breathes out, you breathe in; clicks; in, you breathe out.

"We have to hope that she is going to be able to breathe unaided before long. The concern is that, with the ventilator doing all the work, the muscles she uses to breathe will become too weak to work on their own."

No—*no*.

Bitter, evil memory.

That's where poor Amber will be now. Her brain will be branded with the memory of her mum, lying there in the bed. Like the blinding blink trails of a dark sun, repeating on her retina.

It took me over a year to blink away those final moments of you, even for a little while.

Nose

That Crayola crayon in my first year of primary school.

That's why I remember that.

After wearing it down to something the size of a pea, I stuck it up my nose and was surprised to find it stayed there. I distinctly remember not being able to pincer it out with my thumb and forefinger. It just went farther up.

I didn't panic.

I sat there, looking at my rectangular cat drawing, a deep scrunch of my nose every few seconds. Even then I knew I should act as if nothing had happened. And there was no way I was going to go ask for help. I basically selected another color and carried on coloring, and sat with the pea-size crayon up my nostril for half the afternoon.

Then the brainwave: I could try squeezing my nose from above the crayon, and it might come out like that.

Squeeze. Pop. Rattle.

I looked down, and there it was on the desk.

Maybe this moment of simple harmony between my thoughts and my actions—that is, the reflection upon and the execution of how to remove a crayon from myself without needing to go ask a grown-up—was the absolute high point of mental achievement in my entire life.

Eyes open suddenly. Why?

Daylight. Daytime.

At the window, sliced through with strip-lit reflections, a man's face is staring in.

Unkempt, unshaven.

The face of a man in a maroon jacket, some yellow detail on the top pocket—?

Then he's gone. Wh—?

I don't know what if—

He was definitely—

Push the button. Push now. Push to the click.

My heart leaps to racing. Beat, beating, beating in me.

Footsteps in the corridor. Sheila.

"Yes, lovey, are you all right?"

"There." I jab my finger at the window.

"What's that?"

"There—*there*. There was a face."

She finally wanders her way over to the window and levers it open.

There *was* a face, definitely.

I wasn't imagining it. Not a hallucination—if this was a hallucination, it was the most solid—no. Sheila's—I know she is—she's going to turn and tell me there's no one there.

"Oy!" Her voice sounds washed out, projected over the lawn outside. She barks a few demands, and there he is again: the man, drifting in from the right. He's explaining himself to her with a hint of dumb petulance.

Who the hell is it?

I can't make him out.

He's looking at Sheila like a scolded schoolboy. All I can hear is the placatory ascent and descent of the tones of his explanation. Tones that say he didn't know he was doing a wrong thing, that it wasn't his fault he was doing a wrong thing, that it was someone else's fault and he was only following orders, and why was it a wrong thing anyway?

Sheila's voice is calmer. But still matronly. I catch a few bits. "Patients in here…very serious condition…how would you like it?" Phrases that have their own signature tone.

The man beats a sheepish retreat, and Sheila fixes the window back shut.

"Bloody useless, aren't they?" she says. "It's the NRG maintenance guys again. I've told them they have to come straight to reception, but they think they own the place now. Are you all right?"

"Not really, no," I say, grasping for my oxygen mask.

"Sorry about that," she says, coming to assist.

"Anyone could get in. It could have been anyone."

"No, I know what you're thinking," she says, "but it couldn't have been anyone. They need a special pass to get past the gate; it's all secure around here, OK? They've all been checked. He came in the wrong way, that's all." She straightens her mouth and looks down at me. "Come on now, let's get you back on the straight and narrow. You know how important that is."

I close my eyes, take a few breaths.

"I can't do it. There's too much. I need more help."

An amplified crackle shocks my mind and flings my attention to the two speakers bracketed by the ceiling of the Baurice Hartson Rest & Recuperation Room. They fire out a burst of vaguely Eastern soothe music, and Karen is quick to drop the volume to an appropriately ethereal level.

"A bit of something to evoke a more pleasing atmosphere." She smiles.

She has a nice smile. And a clipped little accent. Not completely English, although almost completely. She says *esses* instead of *zeds*. Odd shape to her *ohs*. It sounds sweet. Swedish, I presume, if this is a Swedish massage?

"So if you could remove your pajama jacket for me, what I'm

going to do is massage your chest with this oil, which should help clear your airways and assist your breathing. Sheila tells me your breathing has been difficult?"

"Yes," I say, beginning to unbutton my pajama jacket.

"Well, this ought to help to clear those lungs."

Nod.

"I'll just close this…" She kicks twice, thrice, at the rubber doorstop, lets the door drop shut.

"Here we go," she says, helping me off with my jacket. "I hope you're not shy like all the English, are you?"

"Um, no, I don't think so."

"I'm glad to hear it. English people always seem to be so shy."

"Really?"

"Yes, it's very rude. Women come into our saunas in their swimming costumes. It's very unhygienic." She sounds like she's telling me off, but she's still smiling sweetly. They are difficult signals to interpret. "A body's a body. Why should you be ashamed of it?"

I get settled on the table and try to give off an air of nonshyness.

"Now, I'm warming the oil up in my hands here, so it's not too much of a shock to the system. Are you OK for me to start massaging you now?"

"Sure."

She lays her hands on assertively, smearing my chest with oil. She must be used to it, of course, but I'm not. I'm not quite prepared for the feeling. The contact. I close my eyes. Just her hand shapes impressed on my chest, this way and that, this and that, working up and around my chest. I can feel a surge of electrical tingles, my nerve-endings recalling when I was last touched like this. Ten full years since. Sensations so long locked I've forgotten they ever occurred. Far down in the sightless, silent deep, my muscles have retained lost knowledge. Physical, unthought, unforgettable memories.

"And if that's the way you think about your body," Karen is saying, "then it says to me there is something wrong in the mind. My mother, when she was very frail, we used to take showers together, and I would help her wash, in the same way she helped me wash when I was a baby. What could be more natural than that?"

I start coughing, and she leans away but leaves her oily hands in place on my chest.

"Sorry," I rattle.

"No, no, not at all. That's why we're here."

She starts up again when I have settled down, goes more gently, working her fingertips firmly into the top and middle of my chest.

"Is that pressure OK?"

"Yeh—" I gurgle and have to clear my throat. "Yes, that's fine, thanks." Superconscious now of my wheezing. Not coughing, at least.

Back to relaxing. Exhale, carefully. Forget the improvised audio, the magnolia walls, the failed double glazing, its condensation skulking around the lower left corner. Concentrate on her touch. Think of the feel of her hands. Steady rhythms swash, swash, on my chest. Yes, yes.

"So, how long have you been a resident here?"

"I don't know—I forget. My third week, I think?"

"It's hard to keep track, isn't it? Have you been happy with your care?"

"They've been brilliant."

"Yes, everybody says that. They're very good here."

"I love Sheila."

"Very smart woman," she says, almost confidentially. "Really knows her stuff."

There they are, the tips of your hair brushing my neck and cheek, your flat palms pressed to my chest, fingers clutching searchingly around my jawbone and earlobe, cupping my cranium, fingertips drawing up tight and scratching into my hair. Tracing your fingertips around my back until you find the place just below my ribs—the unbearable place…just…

No.

The table creaks rhythmically beneath me.

I open my eyes, see Karen's face working intently, concentrating on the job. She catches me looking, briefly smiles.

"OK?"

I do a smile, though I doubt it reaches my eyes. Close them again.

Positive thinking. Think something else. Anything, anywhere else.

But you're everywhere. The memories of you, the shape of you.

All the parts of my body seem to come together and remember you. I've got your textures at my fingertips, your scent in my airways, the balance of your weight in my arms and my back. In every part of my body, there's a space for you, and all I need is for you to come back again and fill it.

The electronic beep of the alarmed door strikes suddenly out in the corridor—my muscles suddenly tense, and my heart instantly starts thudding twice as fast. Karen's hands pause briefly before working on through the noise.

"Oh, it's only the door alarm," she calls through the noise. "They must be testing it."

The alarm stops abruptly after a few seconds, leaving a door slam to slowly subside and allow the music back through.

I have to relax.

"Can you think of any body parts that begin with *O*?" I say.

"Oh," she says, stopping her work for a brief moment with a knowing smile. "I see. Are you playing Sheila's little game?"

"Yeah."

"Yes, she likes to get people to play that one. Gets people to open up a bit."

"Yeah," I say, although it doesn't sound quite as nice to have it put like that.

"Let me have a think. *O*… I know what I'd do for *O*. Because I'm a qualified aromatherapist, I'd have lots to say about the olfactory nerve. Yes, that's definitely what I'd do."

I break out once again into gurgly coughing and hold my hand up in apology. "What's the olfactory nerve?"

"It's what enables you to process scent. It's an amazing thing, very mysterious. I've got reams and reams of research showing how your olfactory senses are some of the most effective in tapping into the brain. They're starting to utilize it with coma patients to lift them out through these associations."

O

Olfactory Nerve

I don't know what the olfactory memory of my life would be.
Vetiver: that's the scent of you.

I've caught it a very few times in the last ten years of working
on the checkouts, the scent of vetiver. It's an immediate hyper-
link back to you, to you and me.

No.

Something else.

Mr. Miller, holding out the polyethylene bag before him.

"In this polyethylene bag is one of those most incredible,

unforgettable smells known to man. It's astonishing, really, that it's possible to store it inside something so simple. Astonishing."

The whole class in the palm of his hand.

"Who wants to sample the delights?"

Twenty-four right hands shoot up. Four left hands. He comes to me.

"One scientific sniff, if you please."

He's acting weird. Why is he acting all weird and sort of... respectful?

I sniff tentatively.

"Fuck! Aww, fucking hell!"

Acid explosion in my brain and eyeballs.

I'm back. I'm backward, up off my stool, and I've just said fuck in front of everyone, twice.

Everyone is laughing. Kelvin, close by me, is laughing hysterically.

I snort out my sinuses, get rid, get rid. Eject the stench. Is my nose bleeding? I'm bleeding, surely?

Miller has the bag closed. He observes the spectacle before him.

"Ammonia. Now, if everyone will stop being so childish, please, what we have learned here is that we need to be far more cautious when sampling odors in the laboratory."

He holds the bag at a distance, wafts the odor toward his nose with a queenlike hand wave.

☙

Vetiver: it's the scent you've brought with you now, into my childhood bedroom at my mum's house—at my house.

We've talked those few times on the phone, but the fact that we haven't been in each other's presence since we split up—what, seven weeks ago?—is made absolute and physical by the fact that I can smell your scent.

So there you definitely are, a full-grown woman in a heavy, woolen outdoor coat, stylishly tailored for grown-ups who mean business, sitting on a young teenager's desk chair. You look awkward.

I'm sitting on my squashy single bed with its double duvet. There's nowhere else.

Rolling up the walls around us, the old wallpaper, James Bond–style rockets, carefully rendered. It had never occurred to me how carefully rendered they were. Like someone cared about the engineering. Just for a child's wallpaper. You wouldn't get that now. Mum has had no reason to redecorate, so the incongruous matchup remains.

This could be my past looking into my future.

"So you've finished your exams?" I say.

"Finally. Don't ask me how I did, because I don't want to think about it. I'm heading off back to the Lakes for a month to stay with my mum before I start work."

"Oh right. Well, give her my best."

"I brought this..." you say meekly, holding up the crochet blanket. "I don't really know why. You probably don't want it."

"No, I do. I do."

I take it from you and hold it, folded in my lap. It too smells of vetiver, and I remember you spritzing it before you went on your last work placement, months ago. You did it so I wouldn't forget you. Now it means I won't be able to.

"Thank you," I say.

"And I dug out some of my notes," you say, "and there's a few leaflets and things that explain the basics. Stage 2 kidney disease: look at these sections here—they're going to want to keep regular tabs on you, make sure there's no more loss of kidney function. But the main thing is to keep your heart in good health. Cut out the smoking, get some exercise."

And I can hear myself, my own voice, blundering and naive. "Yeah? Oh, that's a load off, I tell you—"

"It's *serious*. Please, please don't go getting complacent."

You shift a little in your seat. Maybe I was a shade snappy.

"Anyway," you say, "it's nothing that you can't fold into your life—and hopefully there won't be any more deterioration."

I flip through a couple of the leaflets and try to absorb some of it, but I'll have to leave it till I'm on my own.

"I brought you this too. A bit of light reading." You hand over a hardback coffee-table book: Piet Oudolf, *Planting Design*.

It's so easy for you even now to surprise me with kindness.

You smile happily, pleased I'm pleased. "It's only a library book, but I thought it would give you some good ideas, a few things to mull over while you start getting used to where you're at these days."

I set the book down on the blanket on my lap and pat it to show gratitude. I allow myself to look at you, and you smile.

"Thank you so much for making the effort, is all. I really appreciate it." I thumb the edge of the blanket.

"Happy to help," you say. "Just because we've had our problems doesn't mean I don't care."

"I'm sorry I leaned on you so much," I say.

You look down in your lap. "It's my baggage too. It's…it's not something I think I can cope with. That whole…*trust* area."

"I wasn't straight with you, and I'm so sorry."

"Maybe it needed to happen. It was just too much, hearing you say that, and seeing you not looking after yourself."

"That's not me. That's not what I want to be."

I look at you and try to sustain your gaze, but you look away.

"I can change, Mia," I say.

You look back at me, and some self-centered part of me had been imagining tears in your eyes. But they're dry.

"There are times when I want to let it all drop, Ivo. I do miss you, you know. But everything's so up in the air at the moment. I'm going away, and when I come back, there's the new job; you're coping with all this change with your health; and…it's not the right time. It'd be better, don't you think, if we just stayed friends?"

I look up into your eyes, and I see the kindness. And I realize I'd forgotten to tell myself what I should have been telling myself all along: remember never, ever to hope.

Crushed again.

"Better to be friends—better than to have nothing at all," you say.

No.

Not better.

"Maybe I'll give you a call from my mum's? In a week or two?"

Oh God, is it a good idea to string this out if it's not going to come to a happy ending? Shouldn't I just sever all ties now?

All I can think of is the photo Mal texted me shortly before you arrived. He's found an apartment.

But I can't bring myself to tell you.

"Yeah, yeah," I say. "That'd be nice."

p

Palm

Slip and slap of footsteps on the stairs. Bedroom door cracks open as my mum comes in.

I was awake anyway. I'm here where she left me, in bed, in my best church clothes.

It's dark now.

She reaches down by my bedside table and squeezes the switch to turn the lamp on. She twists it quickly to the wall. Keeps it low.

The house has been silent since the last of the mourners left, and since Laura slammed her bedroom door in tears.

Mum sits on the side of the mattress, and I slide involuntarily into the dip.

She quietly raises her hand and strokes my hair.

"How you doing, kiddo?"

I don't say anything. I tighten the curl of my body around

where she's sitting, the warmth sealed between us. I know I don't need to say anything. I know she understands.

"Brave little soldier, aren't you?"

I look up at her from where I'm lying. She's still got her posh earrings in.

"Are you OK, Mum?"

She looks down at me but doesn't answer straightaway. She's exhausted. It's the first time I've ever noticed tiredness in her face, though it can't be the first time, of course.

"I'll be fine, sweetheart. We'll get through, you and me."

"Yeah."

"Listen, you don't have to go back to school until you feel ready. Everyone understands you'll want to take your time."

I frown into the low light. "I want to go tomorrow."

"We'll take a few days to…to think about your dad."

"They'll think I'm silly."

"No one will think that, kiddo."

"I want to go and have it be like every day."

Mum falls quiet for a moment and sighs heavily. "OK. We'll see how you feel in the morning."

"OK."

She smiles down at me. "You're the man of the house now, eh?"

"Yeah."

"Your dad was so proud of you, you know."

"He'd want me to go to school," I say, and return to looking across the low-lit room. She carries on lightly stroking my hair, before her hand slows, and finally ceases, resting on the back of my head.

"Palm of calm," she says. "Can you feel my fingertips taking out all the worry and sadness? And can you feel the palm is pushing in warmth and love and happiness and peace? Can you feel it happening?"

I can feel it. I'm sure I can.

"Palm of calm," she says to me.

༜

I could do with a palm of calm now. The world is beginning to swirl around me. I can't remember the last time I felt normal. What is normal anymore? I imagine my mum's palm on the back of my head. If I close my eyes, I can almost feel it.

Or your hand.

Your hand in mine.

My hand in yours.

Palms pulsing together.

An anchor—you and me drifting hand in hand through the world.

It's the toxins. Karen said the massage could release toxins into my blood. The last thing I need is more toxins.

And the face: the face at the window has got me unsettled.

I'm vulnerable. I see that now. It's like my body just needs to be started off, and it stays pumped full of adrenaline. Anxiety. Panic.

Sheila's right. I have a panic-shaped hole in the middle. Fill it full of anything.

Q

Quim

There's nowhere else to go. What's *Q*?

I wish there was something else to say. What is there?

There's only one thing.

Becca, on her big birthday weekend up in Mal's northern stamping ground, her arms flung out, ten to two, standing in her bra and nothing else. No pants. Specifically, particularly, explicitly no pants.

"I'm Queen Quim!"

I look at her, and I look away. I look again, and I can't even quite get what it is I'm looking at. It doesn't register.

There it is, all things considered. The most mind-blowing thing I've ever seen.

I look at Mal, who's looking at us with this expression of fixed amusement. Laura's screaming and laughing, standing there in her black catsuit and cat's ears.

Sometimes, you know, when you see the worst of everything lined up before you, you've just got to go for it. See how badly you can crash it.

Push your body to the limit. Sometimes, sometimes.

So I stand here shivering in the stairwell of a nightclub some-where—I've no fucking idea where, or how to get back to the hotel—in some strange northern town. And I'm tripping. Tripping it out. Tripping you, tripping my health, tripping my future out of my system. Give up, give up. And it's been nice and easy to sur-render responsibility to Mal and Laura and Becca. If I shouldn't be doing this, it's up to them to tell me.

And anyway, one trip's not going to kill me. It's the general pat-tern that has to improve. And that can start tomorrow. If I want it to.

Becca strikes the pose just long enough to register for an eter-nity, her beaming white teeth in a Hollywood smile.

"My knickers didn't match my bra," she proclaims, "and it's my best bra."

I can't look at it. It's like the sun. A dark sun. Much hair, note. I don't want to have seen it. I want to be a gentleman. And now she's away, her buttocks revolving through the curtain and into the club beyond, followed by Laura.

What the fuck? I say to Mal.

"It's a fetish night," he says to me, and I'm focusing on his mouth by my eye. "They didn't want to let us in, because it's fetish gear only. So I struck a deal with them. We can go in if we wear one item of clothing only."

Tonight's been weird, I say.

"You heard Becca," he says. "We've come here to find action, so let's dive in."

Ah, yes, *that's* why I'm here. Becca. *You wouldn't want to disappoint a girl on her birthday, would you? I haven't seen any action for months, so let's have some fun!*

Becca the persuader.

Persuasive enough that me and Mal are now in a small side room with a wall of coat hooks, and he's throwing triangles as he wrenches his legs out of his trousers. He's hopping, and talking.

"Come on, man, it's down to one item of clothing or less." He looks closely at me. "Are you with me, fella?"

Mmm? Myeah.

"We're the lucky ones," he's saying, pointing at my over-skinny legs. "One item of clothing, so we can go in there in our pants. Not like Becca, eh? Hats off to Becca, man."

Pants off to Queen Quim.

"Ha! Yeah. Pants off."

The cool air shifts around me and tingles, my skin unused to expanse and exposure. I mean, it feels kind of…*good*. Feels a little bit *magical*. We descend the short flight of stairs into the color-washed club. A comfortable enshrouding darkness is flushed with primary-color lights in sequence, slow and simple. Sub-bass hip-hop throbs through, mellow, just nice. But, Jesus, what is this place? My eyes skip from one zone to the next, not wanting to rest, wanting to take in the general effect, follow the light pulse, illuminating now this group of people, now that group, now this. There are clusters upon clusters of squashy bodies, one or two completely nude, great folds of flesh, ruched up on the vertical from bum crack to cranium, pleats of flab hanging down and out.

"Make yourself at home, fella," says Mal, disappearing off. "I'm going to see a few people."

He has that look. He's on dealer duty tonight. That must be why they let us in. Got to keep the clients happy.

I wander around, my brain sloshing in my head. I take in the scene of merry carnage in front of me, pasty arses juddering as they rearrange themselves. The baldness, the red pates, now green pates, and the veins in their temples wriggling and throbbing, unembarrassed. I've got to steer myself away from this grimness, Britishness. Ugh. I don't want to be here.

Eyes on alert to seek a familiar face, a family face, Laura: Laura's there. There in her catsuit and cat ears. Almost familiar, switching deep red now green, her shiny stretched skin.

How did you know to wear a catsuit? I say.

She tips a wink at me. "I may have had a tip-off," she says. "Isn't it brilliant? Look at everyone! It's amazing."

And I'm looking around, and when I look back at her, she's still talking and—how long have we been talking? And her lipstick lips are all in my face, and she's talking and talking hard, her voice riding in and out of the bass beat.

And now I'm talking too, and all the words I'm saying are about you. I can feel myself talking fast, pouring out my problems, but the weight of them isn't getting any less. Laura now, and Mal now, they're hearing the sounds that I'm making, but my words aren't conjuring the shapes on their faces. Maybe they're not coming out right. Maybe I'm here just speaking in tongues.

"She's led you on," says Laura. "I know women like that; they try to control you. Make you into something you're not. They're all over you; they want to take over your life."

No, no, it's not like that at all.

Laura's head nods rhythmically before me, butting in her version of the truth, like I don't know what I'm talking about. But it's not true; it's not true.

"You want to watch women like that," says Mal. "They shit you up, and then they nail you down."

And here's Becca, chilled Becca, swimming up in the dark.

An arm slips easily around my waist. It's her arm.

"Are you good?"

Yeah, yeah.

She looks deeply into me, and her smile grows calmer, her eyes kinder. I can feel the dizziness rising.

"Come here," she says. "Come and give the birthday girl a dance." And she backs away and takes up my hands again, and we slowly dance, there, at arm's length in the middle of the room, as the bass pulses around us, through the air, through the floor, through everyone in this place.

"You miss her," she says.

Yeah.

And my throat is closed. And the tears—there are tears.

Becca places her forearm casually high up on my shoulder and rests her fingertips against my neck and ear, and we dance, close.

That was the thing, the Becca thing: *I'm Queen Quim!*

I'm aware. I'm so aware of what's going on down below in the blue light. I have it about me now to stand discreetly clear. Wish not to scrunch up against the Queen's quim. But the Queen's not ashamed. She holds me close, gently close, unabashed.

"Close your eyes," she says. I obey, and I feel her fingertips work lazily around my neck and earlobe and hair. "No need to see. Just feel. You need to feel better."

I feel her hand work down from my neck, slowly, and take my right wrist, and move it slowly in space. She lands it delicately on her shoulder, my fingertips touching her neck.

"It is so lovely to be held," she murmurs, turning, still constant in her movement, her naked bottom pressing into me. "The contact is everything; the contact is good. It's good to feel good, and that's just how it is."

Switch off, switch off. I don't want to think—I don't want to think about you. You must never know this. Nothing of this would make sense. All of this time, I'm thinking of you. If I want you to know anything, I want you to know that. I'm thinking of you.

We move, we move, and I feel Becca's fluid motion as my own, follow the shift and shimmy away across the room, my sealed eyes pulsing in the gloom.

"Hey," she whispers playfully in my ear. "Let me take you away from all the people. Come through here."

I open my eyes just as she disappears behind a heavy curtain hung from a scaffolding bar bolted to the black brickwork. I remain, swamped in deep green, switched now to harsh white. I lift back the curtain and step through into deep gloom and through a velvet drape into absolute black.

Rich black. Black like oily black. My eyes try to acclimatize by sending out blobs of color and swirls of disturbance and imperfection. I'm seeing the imperfection in my eyes.

Floating, I'm standing still, and I can feel the liquids, the movement in my brain, slowly, slowly clockwise, resolving slowly, slowly counterclockwise.

And with the all-encompassing black, the acoustics are dead. My attention is thrown on the small foreground sounds. People. More than Becca. There is breathing down to my left. Slight shuffle far right. Slurping. The ticks and sibilants of licks or sucks. Simple innocent kisses, maybe.

Maybe.

Where is—?

I hear Becca giggle, for maybe a quarter of a second, but I can tell it's her—her timbre. Her teeth. She's standing, over the other side of the room, straight ahead.

She takes my wrists, draws me forward, and down, and we sit, and she lets go of my wrists, shifts her hand down across my body, and she strokes me tenderly, her fingernails giving precision to every flex of her fingers.

This feels like the wrong thing to be doing. My thoughts flit to you, to my commitments to you—but they are redundant thoughts, leaking out into the dark, no home to go to. Any loyalty to you is only a habit now. You don't need it anymore.

"Poor boy," says Becca, plosives on my earlobe, "no need to think, just feel."

And from out there, from the pitch black, the rich black, unfamiliar lips press themselves passionately to mine. They open, and my lips open, open together, drive deeper, a tongue pushes between my lips.

This is supposed to be all right.

When I picked up the phone, it was still light outside. And still deep in the comedown from last night at the fetish club, I was so pleased to hear your voice. Like coming home. I can shut this down; I can shut it all down and bask in the comfort of your voice.

I've since slithered down to sitting on the stone kitchen floor with the big old phone cradle on my outstretched legs, and I'm clutching the receiver firmly by the mouthpiece like a cricket ball. My ear's getting hot, but I won't swap. Not yet. I press the earpiece against my ear until the plastic creaks in protest.

This silence has been going on surreally long. More silent than silence, because you can hear the electrostatic crackle poised and ready to catch any sound. I draw in a great breath, exhale through my nose, and the digital noise fills my head. And yours too, no doubt.

"This is nice," I murmur. "Spending time with you. Even when you're two hundred miles away."

"Yeah," you say. "It is."

I run my finger in between the numbers on the keypad of the phone cradle.

"I really miss spending time with you," you say. "Even more than I thought I would."

Silence. I can feel my brow furrowing. Are you trying to say something?

"So…I'm wondering if…"

You sigh, the bits and bytes flowing into my head, into my brain, making me close my eyes to tolerate it.

"Oh… What are you *saying*?" I groan.

"I don't know what I'm saying. What am I saying? I'm saying I look at us, and I ask, why can't they sort it out? And the only person I want to ask is you. I want to step back from it and talk with you about how you think it's going to turn out for them."

Short crackle. I risk a switch of ears with the receiver.

"You're not like the rest of them," you say. "But I have to be careful, Ivo. With a background like mine, you've got to understand, I have to be careful."

"I want you to be careful," I say. "I really, really want you to be careful. I mean, to the point that, if I'm going to bring you trouble, then…then I don't want it to be me."

Doot!

"What was that?"

"Oh, sorry," I say. "I had my finger on the five, and I accidentally pressed it."

There's an added crackle on the line, and I know exactly the breathy chuckle you've just made.

The heat rises from my relieved lobe. Imagine it now, glowing in the gloom.

Doot!

"What was that?" I say.

"That was a one out of ten for not saying anything positive. Say something positive."

"It feels lovely to laugh with you again."

"Yeah."

"I don't laugh anywhere near as much with anyone else."

"No, nor me."

Pause there.

That feels right.

That feels like what I mean.

You sigh, and another flood of static washes through my brain.

"What are we going to do?" you say.

"I'm not sure."

"Nor me."

Long, long pause.

"I can't be rushed," you say, finally. "I can only take it one day at a time. One *hour* at a time."

"Yeah. Yeah."

"And I suppose we have to trust that it's going to take us somewhere—somewhere better than this."

"Yeah."

"Let's work toward what makes sense."

There's another great long pause, and I have an ocean of relief dammed up and waiting to cascade all over me, but I don't want to let it. No, no. Let it drip.

"How do you think it turns out for them?" you say.

"I don't know. I really, really want it to turn out well."

"Me too."

"I love a happy ending."

"Me too."

"I'd better go," I say. "My mum's car just pulled into the driveway."

I start to climb to my feet to sound busy. No car. I just want to stop this now. Quit while we're ahead.

"I'll call again tomorrow. Is that OK?"

"OK. Yeah."

"I'd better go."

"Yeah."

You pause once more, and we both must realize this at the same time.

"I want to say I love you," you say. "That's what I used to say at this point."

"Mmm."

"Bluh blah bloo."

"Yeah. Bluh blah bloo too."

Shocked awake now, think—I'm fucking drowning.

Push the button, push, push… I—

Sheila in, with urgency. "Are you all right?"

"Drowning… I'm—"

"OK, OK, now…"

Mask pressed to my nose and mouth. Pressed firmly.

I don't know where.

Ask questions, ask—

What's the day—? It's—?

I have no idea. I don't even know where to start to find something like that out.

What was the day yesterday?

I—?

Sheila spiders out her hands and threads the elastic of the mask back over my head. It snaps tight above my ears.

"OK, lovey. Now breathing, yes? You know the drill."

"Breathing, breathing."

"And it looks like it's time for a little more of the morphine solution, OK?"

"OK, yeah."

Yeah, yeah.

She starts to move around in the now familiar morphine routine. Methodically get the bottle. Strange, formal little movements. She doesn't want to get anything wrong. Top responsibility, the drugs.

"Down the hatch."

༄

"Here we are, at last," I say, arriving finally on the crest of the hill.

You follow on behind, pushing down with your hands on your knee to lever yourself up the final incline. You fall in breathlessly beside me and slip your hands around my middle as I drop my arm across your shoulders and squeeze you tight: the anxious clinch of a couple once lost to one another, now reunited. It feels so good to be holding each other after everything we've come through.

A day at a time, then a week, and all's well.

All's well.

"My favorite place in the world," I say.

Up here we're more in touch with this deep, deep sky than the valley down below. Huge gray-white clouds bloom epically in the blue.

Beneath us, the land drops away and sweeps off down the valley. A tiny cyclist lends perspective, cranking herself east along the dirt track toward town. She's farther away than seems possible.

"This is where my dad's ashes are scattered," I say. "I remember me and Mum and Laura coming out here and doing that."

"It's a beautiful spot. Perfect."

"I think my mum left it a couple of years before we scattered him. She wanted us to be old enough to remember."

We carefully lay out the blanket on a clean patch of ground—the blanket now happily being used for what you intended—and you sit. I sit down behind you and thread my arms around your middle, rest my chin on your shoulder.

"Whoever first used the word *rolling* about hills knew exactly what they were talking about," you say. "These hills really roll."

"They're exactly the right size and roundness."

"And millions of colors. Really like a picture-book green, and then if you look at it long enough you start to see all the yellows and browns coming through. Purple skirting the bottoms."

"Could you make a blanket out of those colors?"

"Nature's got that one covered," you say.

You pull out an apple and bite into it. I lift my head from your shoulder, and you let me take a bite too.

"So," I say, "I've been invited to join the garden design course."

"Ah, really? Well done! I think you'll be great at it," you say. Then: "You're going to be sick through nerves again, aren't you?"

"Can't wait."

"No, I think you're going to get in there, and you're totally going to blossom."

You back into me for a tight cuddle and draw my arms tighter around you.

"This feels so good," you say.

"Yeah."

"It doesn't feel like living day by day anymore. Not to me. Does it to you?"

No… No, it feels…just right.

You draw in a deep breath and exhale languorously.

"Do you think, when you die—"

"OK… Nice—"

"—that the ash when you get cremated is the same ash people use on their gardens?"

"I don't know."

"Aren't you supposed to know things like that if you're going to do a garden design course?"

"I don't know. Probably."

I laugh.

"What?"

"Why do you always take us to the darkest places?"

"Do I? I think nursing might have broken my darkness filter."

"So, when you're a nurse, do you get immune to people dying?"

You chew thoughtfully for a moment.

"No," you say, "not immune. If you know you've done the best in your power to help this person, then…well, the alternative is that you weren't there and you didn't help."

"I suppose."

"You have a job to do, to help them, and you just have to do your best. Sometimes I almost think it's quite a selfish thing to do—the better job you do, the more self-respect you can have. I tried explaining that to one of the women on my course, and she looked at me like I was gone out."

You examine the apple to select the next best bite.

"I get that."

"I always think it's worse when you see the family. You can't do a lot for them. There's no time. And you can't really prescribe to take away people's grief."

"Not properly, no."

"And you see little kids, like the doctors and nurses might have looked at you when your dad died, and you think—there's a lot of loving that person needs, right there."

You fling the apple core down the valley, watch it catch now and nestle in the bracken.

Crickle crackle.

"Well, that's one way of deciding where you want to place your apple tree," I say.

You grin at me and give me an appley kiss, smack on the lips, and we lie down on the blanket, huddle in close.

"If I were ash," you say, your voice washed out as you talk into the air, "I'd like to be sprinkled under a fruit tree. Or if it's the wrong kind of ash, I'd like to be buried under a fruit tree. Worm food."

"Yeah?" My voice bassy and loud in my ears.

"Because then the nutrients from me would go to swelling the fruit. And then maybe the birds would peck at the fruit and get the energy to fly—so the same energy that is making me say these words now would be used to help the bird fly. I'd literally be flying."

"Yeah...yeah."

"And that to me is truly comforting. Seeing myself, launching off from this hill and diving down there into the sky, down there in the valley. Deep down, and up around. Everywhere."

You hold your hands up to the sky, cross them, palms

downward, pressing your thumbs together to make a bird. A fluttering bird.

I take my right hand, press it to your left, thumb to thumb.

A bird. A fluttering bird.

Hold our hands against the sky.

Fluttering, fluttering in the blue.

At that moment, I hear the signature squiggles of birdsong in the distance and a brief flutter of wings, and a look of childlike delight crosses your face.

Rib

Mal holds up a sticky sparerib and turns it about, before greedily stripping off the meat with his teeth.

"Mal," says Laura in a warning tone.

"What?"

"That's probably not very nice for a vegetarian to have to put up with."

Mal looks up at you and grins, dropping the bone on his plate and licking his fingers noisily. "You don't mind, do you?"

You shrug and continue with your risotto.

I knew this was a bad idea. All I've done is sit here and hope that Mal behaves himself. But he's in one of his petulant, contrary moods. Careful piloting required.

The look you gave me when he blatantly whipped the reserved

sign off the table pretty much set the tone for the evening. You're only here reluctantly anyway, and so now I have half an eye on you and whether you're having an OK time. Now we're all just tense that we're about to be found out. All of us except Mal.

"Have you taken your shot?" you ask me suddenly.

"Mmm? Yeah," I say and show you my insulin pouch as proof.

"That's probably enough potassium for a while, though, isn't it?" you say, pointing at the amount of tomato in my bouillabaisse.

Mal can't help but give me a look. An under-the-thumb kind of look.

"Are you sure you don't want a sparerib, fella?"

"Probably not a good idea. Not too good for me."

"Ah, whoever ate anything because it was good for them, eh?"

I hear you sigh beside me, and I pray that you keep it all in. Your head's down now, and I can tell you're concentrating on getting through this.

"Do ribs freak you out then?" asks Mal.

You pause and contemplate awhile, and I try to catch your eye to remind you of why we're here. *Building bridges, remember? For a sustainable and friendly future?* But you won't look at me.

"Not particularly."

"How's the chicken?" I ask Laura.

"Bit dry," she says graphically.

Makes me feel faintly queasy, so I get on with what I'm eating. We can make it through to coffee if no one says anything too—

"Did Ivo tell you our news?" you say.

"No…" says Laura, looking up all interested.

"It's not *that*," I say.

"No, we're looking at getting a place together," you say. "My contract's up in three months, and you're technically at your mum's still, aren't you?"

Mal drops a rib to his plate and looks at me, frowning deeply.

"Well… What about *our* apartment, man?"

"What apartment?"

"I've got a place lined up for us. We said we'd… Ah, Jesus."

"Sorry, I didn't…I didn't know you were going to go ahead and do anything."

"I've put two hundred down on that, man. Two hundred you've lost me."

"Anyway," I say. "I didn't think…that was going anywhere."

"Yeah, well."

We fall into an awkward silence, save the percussion of cutlery on crockery. Even the people at other tables don't seem to have much noise to make.

"So…where are you thinking of staying?" asks Laura.

"Somewhere up close by the hospital," you say. "At first, anyway. We can always try a few short contracts, see what's best."

We eat on, subdued, with Mal sitting back on his chair legs, pointedly chewing.

"So, how does it feel, as a woman then?" says Mal. "Being made out of the rib of a man?"

Laura frowns. "What are you talking about?"

"Adam and Eve," I say, a little warily. "Eve's made out of Adam's rib."

"Oh," she says, squinting to somehow summon up the memory. "I'd forgotten about that. Old Cecil Alexander taught us that at Sunday School." She turns to you. "He was the vicar at Mum's church before Mal's dad took over."

"Oh," you say.

"Is it true, then, that men have one less rib?"

"Yep," says Mal.

"No," you say. "Men and women both have twelve pairs."

Mal draws in a breath and raises amused eyebrows at me.

"So how does that make you feel," he says, "being a tasty offcut?"

I think you're not going to answer. I'm hoping you're not going to answer. "Well, it's not the best story, is it?" you say.

"No? You don't like this bloke being ripped open, and one of his ribs being snapped off, with all the jelly bits hanging off and dripping on the ground?" He takes another rib and starts stripping the tacky marinated meat down with his fingertips. "And that's what a woman is."

"Well, not only that," you say, "but then she goes on to ruin the whole of human existence. Let's hear it for the girls!"

"We do get it a bit hard in that myth, don't we?" says Laura.

"But it's not a myth, though, is it?" says Mal. "It did really happen."

"No, it didn't," Laura says girlishly.

He tears a strip off another rib and forces us all to await his explanation.

"The story had to come from somewhere, didn't it?" he says, pointing at you with his stripped rib. "So it came from women's bodies and all their weaknesses. And if it didn't have any truth to it, it would have died out centuries ago. Here's a man, and here's a woman, and the other is the servant of the one. That's what people feel. That's biologically true."

"It *must* be," you say.

Oh, this is all going horribly.

"It's nature," he says, drawing a circle in the air, using the rib bone as a pointer.

"Tell that to all the women who come into the hospital after a botched late-term abortion because they're expecting a girl."

I flash you a look. *Do we really need to go there?*

Sustainable and friendly future?

Yeah?

Again Mal raises his eyebrows at me, but I won't look at him.

Silence settles once more between us all, filled only by the gingerest of clinks of forks reluctantly hovering over flesh.

Maybe we should skip dessert.

"What are you *doing*?"

I look up to see that Mal has jabbed his rib bone into your risotto.

"What? I wanted to try a bit."

"Mal, she's vegetarian," says Laura.

"Oh, so what? It's not got any meat on it, has it?"

"Look," you say, standing, "I'm going to go, all right? I'm not feeling too good. There's twenty for my share." You turn to me. "Are you coming?"

"Here we...here we go," says Sheila, catching the telephone cart on the door frame and stopping up short. She unhooks it with a wiggle and wheels it into the room. "It's old-school telephony for us, I'm afraid. I'll pop that there. Now, I've given him the number, and he said he was going to leave it about ten minutes and then ring."

I look up at her and nod in reluctant acknowledgment. All of this, reluctant.

"Then it's up to you, lovey. Pick it up, or don't."

"Yeah."

"Listen," she says. "It's none of my business, but I think it's really good you've agreed to this. I know it might seem a bit silly, accepting a phone call from someone sitting fifty yards away in the parking lot, but...well, if you're willing to even think about being a bit flexible, well, that's real character in my book. That's real strength."

I smile an administrative smile. I can't do any more.

"I'll leave you be," she says.

She tidies herself out of the room, pulling the door softly shut behind her, and as soon as the light of her departure has shifted and settled in the frosted glass, the phone begins to ring. Cheap electronic chirrup. Annoying. I look at it for a moment, but the instinct is too strong. I can't let that noise carry on, troubling the other patients.

I let it go on.

Chirrup-chirrup.

I pick up the receiver.

"Hello."

"Hello, mate."

"Hello, Kelvin."

"How you doing?"

The habitual first question, not worth answering.

"You wanted to speak."

"Sorry, mate, it feels a bit weird talking from a parking lot. A bit Cold War spy."

"They still want me to see Mal."

"Yeah."

"I'm not going to, Kelv."

"No."

An awkward pause.

"I wanted to tell you the stuff that no one else is saying," he says.

He pauses again. I know he wants me to say something, help lubricate his way. But he can work for this. I don't need to lift a finger.

"I know this is the last thing you need, people coming up to you with demands when you're feeling so shitty, but I know you'd want to know. Even if you don't change your mind. I know you'd want all the facts."

More unnatural silence.

"No one wants to upset you, least of all me, but things are pretty bad. For his mum and dad, for Laura. They worry themselves sick about him all day every day. And the times when he does come back, he's usually in a real state. The last time he was shivering and crying because…well, you know, he'd run out of money and he hadn't had his fix."

My mind darts over this scenario, searches for an emotional response. Comes back blank.

"That's a lot for them to take. He's not the swaggering lad you used to know. He's changed. He's changed a lot. And he's paid heavily for everything that happened."

"So have I, Kelvin."

"I know you have, mate, I know. And I'm sorry to come to you like this when you're…you know."

"Dying?"

He can't bring himself to say it.

"Look, mate, you can't carry on going through life thinking no one's going to notice or care whether you're here or not. When you're gone, you're gone forever. There's a lot of people going to be very upset by that. Damaged by it."

"Why are you trying to do this, anyway? Why are you trying to make me feel guilty for this?"

"I'm not trying to make you feel guilty."

"He *killed* her, Kelvin."

There.

That's stopped him.

That's fucking shut him up.

"I don't see why you're so interested in all this anyway. Is it because you want to get in Laura's knickers? I reckon you want to see him gone."

Thick silence. Nailed him. I've nailed him there.

"You can take the piss out of me all you like, mate," he says quietly.

"I'm just saying it as I see it."

"Is that right?"

"That's right. And I've seen you do this over and over again to these people's lives, and if I can stop you from doing it again, I will."

"I'm not doing anything."

"Yeah, that's you all over, isn't it?"

The phone goes dead.

I place the receiver gently back in the cradle and press my buzzer.

Skin

"The skin," Kelvin reads from the textbook, "is the largest organ on the human body." He looks at me. "Well," he says, with his big stupid face, "it's not the largest organ on *my* body."

"Gah!" I throw my pen down, and it bounces off the kitchen table and rolls across the floor. "I knew you were going to say that!"

"What? It's true!"

Watching Kelvin's mind at work is like watching an oil tanker trying to do a three-point turn. I reach down and retrieve my pen and try to get back into my notes. I've got to stop this jitteriness. I'm starting to get really panicky about this exam.

"It's such a stupid joke," I say.

"So? All good jokes are stupid."

"No, but it's *bad* stupid. It's the first thing anyone ever says— and it's just impossible. It doesn't work. Even if you had a cock the size of Ecuador, the skin would still be the size of Ecuador plus one human, wouldn't it?"

Kelvin ignores me and flips the page.

"Skin renews itself every twenty-eight days," he reads.

"I know."

"My cock renews itself every twenty-eight minutes."

Laura is slumped, still in her dressing gown, in the middle of the sofa in the front room of her apartment, crying. The utter pitifulness of the expression on her face is almost funny. I feel bad for thinking it, because the state of her actual face isn't funny at all.

The skin looks badly scalded, angry red cheeks sweeping down to an almost bony yellowish color under her nose and around her mouth.

"I've got to go to a spa in three days," she says, dabbing at her nose with a sopping tissue, "and I look like Freddy Krueger."

"Well, why did you give yourself a chemical peel if you're going to a spa in three days, you dumb shit?" Mal says overloudly. I reckon he's showing off to hide the embarrassment that they've had to drag us round to Laura's for your medical opinion.

You tentatively settle beside her on the sofa.

"What exactly was it that you put on your face?"

Laura pushes a box at you.

"Glycolic acid," you read. "Did you follow the instructions?"

"Yeah." She nods sadly. "I just pushed up the percentage a little bit. Just a *little* bit."

You take up the minutely typed instruction leaflet and scan it. "Are you in any pain?"

"Not so much now." She sniffs. "At first it felt like my whole face was on fire. Now it's really tight. But it's how it *looks*. I don't know how long it's going to *look* like this."

Her tears well up again, and you tut sympathetically, flip the instruction leaflet over in your hand.

"It's stupid, I know," says Laura, "but I'm going with Becca for a bring-a-friend-free weekend getaway and I didn't want to look like some sort of dried-up old hag next to her."

"Oh, Laura, you've got lovely skin," you say.

"Yeah, except it's not on her face anymore," says Mal.

You glare at him.

"What?" he says. "I could have boiled the kettle and poured it over her head and had the same effect. Cheaper too."

Laura picks up her compact mirror and lifts and dips her head to assess the damage once again. "Becca looks amazing without even trying," she says, "and I spend ages—like when we went to that fetish club on her birthday?" She looks up at me, as if asking me to remember. "She didn't need to make any effort, and she was instant eye candy, and I stood there in a stupid catsuit and no one gave me a second look. And I thought, it'll be exactly like that at the spa."

There's a momentary process in your eyes as you meet my gaze. Something begins to unsettle in my middle. *Fetish club? Some explanation required?*

"It was her birthday, wasn't it? Ah, that was a top night," says Mal, with forced wistfulness. "She did look good, though, didn't she?"

"Thanks a lot, Mal," spits Laura. "That's exactly what I wanted to hear."

"Well, come on. That body in just a bra? Nothing else? Hats off to her."

"Were you there?" you say, looking across at me. "Where was I? I don't remember even hearing about this."

I squint at Mal, pretending only to dimly remember, broadcasting all the negatives I can at him.

"She said her knickers and bra didn't match, and it was her best bra," Laura explains dolefully.

"Oh no, I remember. That was when you were on your little break from each other," says Mal.

"I can't remember," I say.

"I'm not surprised, the state you were in," Mal says, laughing.

"When was this?" you ask, almost as if you hadn't heard him.

"My lips are sealed," says Mal. "I've said too much already."

"You were in an *S&M* club?"

We're marching along at a furious rate now. I'm starting to get a bit out of breath.

"I was down," I say. "We'd all trekked up north to a place Mal knew for a night out. I didn't want to go, but it was Becca's birthday, and… they all thought I should be having a good time. I didn't know that was their plan when we went out, but—when you're there, you're there."

"And had you taken anything?"

I look across at you, and your eyes are blazing. My first instinct is to look away. I try to suppress that instinct, but by the time I do, it's already too late.

"I was really low," I say.

The clock of our footsteps on the pavement echoes off the walls and parked cars as we square the slabs away behind us, off down the street. "I don't understand it," you say. "I do not understand first why you can't just *stop* it. You're not addicted, you're not dependent; it's just a bad habit you will not kick. And I don't get how these people, these friends and family, can stand by and let you do this to yourself. And to us."

"There was no us at the time. There was no us."

I can see your eyes are stressed and weary. It's happening again. The whole thing is going to shit *again*.

"Just…tell me what happened," you say.

"OK, look, you've got to try to remember how it was—it was a hard time. For us both. It was, wasn't it?"

You don't reply.

I sigh unsteadily.

Honesty. Full honesty.

Finally.

"We were in the club, and a woman was dancing with me, and I was feeling… I was upset over you."

You frown deeply, processing.

"And we went into a back room, and…I don't know what happened. We kissed. I remember we kissed."

"Do you know who it was?"

You're looking up at me with hard eyes, scanning, scanning, your irises moving minimally from left to right to left as you look in each of my eyes.

☙

"Time for more bedsore meds, I'm afraid," calls Sheila as she breezes through the door with a smile. She stops in her tracks. "Oh, lovey, what's the matter?"

I'm crying. What is it I'm doing, the grotesque dry twitch, voice, rasping awfulness. I cannot get it out. I want to shed tears, but I cannot drink enough water to make tears.

Sheila fixes the door shut and hurries around beside me, but she doesn't know what to say. She simply stands there and holds my cold hand, strokes the back of it.

"I should never have started this," I say.

"Started what, my darling?"

"It's too painful to remember these things."

"Oh, lovey, I'm so sorry. It was only supposed to be a silly game to keep you occupied."

"No, no," I say, steadily regaining some kind of equilibrium. "It's not you, it's not you. It's me."

Am I imagining it? I'm shocked to see she seems a little choked. Double shine in her eyes.

"Sheila, could I...? Morphine?"

"Oh yes, yes, of course. Give me a sec."

T

Tear Ducts

This is it: I cannot make the tears come. And anyway, boys don't cry, do they?

But if you don't cry, does it mean you don't care?

If I could just cry it out.

Maybe it's better I don't.

Maybe I haven't earned that.

Crying isn't about sadness. Crying is to sadness what cold is to a cold. Unrelated.

The stupid reasons I've cried.

I cried at my dad's funeral, but I remember absolutely that it wasn't for the reason everyone said it was. It was because everyone called me *poor little love*, and said *aw, bless*. And if enough different people say *aw, bless* to you in one day, it's going to make you freak out. A congregation of over one hundred fifty. Each and every one of them must have said *aw, bless* to me.

I finally broke down when my grandma offered me a cookie. I said I didn't want it. She said, "Come on, you can have it; it's yours." But I said no, because I was feeling like I wanted to honor my dad by not having the cookie.

"Go on! You know you want it!"

Everyone looking at me.

Me, flushing hot and unable to stop the tears from coming.

"Aw, bless…"

Fuckers.

Where are they now, eh?

So here I am, once again. I thought I'd escaped. I was stupid enough to allow myself to think that maybe you and I had finally got it together. But I find myself back in my boyhood bedroom, in my boyhood bed with its collapsed mattress, dressed up in my dad's old pajamas. I'm pressing your blanket to my face. Its scent fills my nostrils, and I am awash with a renewed wave of sorrow. Deserved sorrow.

There's no coming back from this.

There's no coming back.

I hear my mum on the stairs. The slip-slap of her slippers. In a moment she'll appear at the door, break the spell of solitude. I look up. There she is. Never changing, always the same.

"Can I come in?"

I say nothing. She comes in. She's carrying a bowl of chicken soup and sets it down next to my alarm clock. She sits beside me on the bed, and we creak in closer to each other.

I take the crochet blanket up, pull it safely toward me. I look up at my mum. "The blanket smells of her."

"Oh, kiddo."

We are crying.

She cradles my head, places her palm on my hair, and gently, gently presses all over.

She wants to talk about it, but I can feel my anxiety burning within. I don't have anything to tell her. All there is to tell would break her heart. She doesn't even know I smoke. How would I tell her about...everything else?

I can't tell her anything, so we sit there in silence as the soup cools before me. I don't have any appetite. I only wanted her to make it so she would have something to do. Something away from me.

I'm sorry, Mum.

I don't mean to be mean.

I'm just sitting here, pushing the crochet to my nose and mouth and tightening for crying.

Mum kisses the top of my head, my hair.

"It was cruel," she says now. "She was too cruel."

"No," I say. "No, she's not been cruel."

"Do you want me to wash it for you? I'm sure I could put it on a delicates wash or something, if you want to keep it." She starts examining a corner of the blanket to work out how best to wash it.

"No," I say. "No, thanks."

Mum leaves me.

I want this blanket to keep your scent. It will remind me. I can change. I can do this, and then you'll come back. And we will wrap ourselves in it.

Mum reappears at the door, holding a neatly folded blanket she's drawn from the airing cupboard.

"Here we are, kiddo. Why don't you take this one, eh? Have this blanket."

Laura's all in my face, and the people at the other tables in the café are starting to get a whiff of scandal. I wish I wasn't still in my work shirt.

"Why aren't you talking to my boyfriend?"

"Laura, I'm just trying to eat my lunch, all right?"

"Why aren't you talking to Mal?"

Mal stands sheepishly behind her, trying not to catch my eye.

"I'm not." I mean I'm not not talking to him.

"Yeah," she says, "you aren't. And I want to know why."

I consider my Cheeto-powdered fingers, at a loss as to what I'm supposed to say. She's giving me a soap opera, like this is how people are supposed to talk to each other.

"I think it's totally shitty, what you're doing," she says.

I'm not engaging with this. I start to methodically depowder each finger with a deliberate lip smack.

Mal benignly pulls out a chair adjacent to mine and sits.

"How is it Mal's fault?" demands Laura.

"No. Laura…" says Mal. "He's all right, yeah? I never should have said anything. It was a mistake, OK? I thought she knew. You told me she knew."

"No, I fucking didn't!"

"Laura! Keep your voice down," I say, casting a glance across the café to see if any management is in the area.

"You said they were being open and honest with each other about everything," says Mal. He looks awkward. Genuinely upset. Laura glares at me again.

"She and you weren't even together at the time anyway. I don't know why she thinks she can get all upset about it if she'd dumped you—"

I shake my head. No, no. I don't want her turning her fire on you.

Laura turns to Mal. "He's spent his whole life blaming other people for choices he's made. It's time he started taking a bit of responsibility."

"Fuck *off*!" I surprise myself, feeling the shout coming out of me. I catch a tut from a customer at a nearby table. "Will you leave me alone? Do you think I want to sit here and listen to all your bullshit? Look at you! Look at your own life for a change and sort that out before you start doling out sage advice to me about mine."

I think for a moment Laura's going to laugh as the words ring in the air around us. This is a game, right? Neither of us is really taking this seriously.

She fixes me a stare with her wonky face, and with typical extrovert silence, she suddenly gets up and sweeps off, leaving a big, stupid, empty space behind.

Making it all about her. Now she's the one who's been wronged. So typical.

So here's me and Mal.

Two bodies adjacent in the same space.

Not looking at each other.

I'm looking at the cart lined up waiting for customers' empty trays. I should maybe help the kitchen staff with that, perhaps wheel it through to them.

Mal's voice comes to me first.

"She's about to become more powerful than you could possibly imagine."

He's absolutely deadpan.

I snort, lightly.

"Don't I know it."

We sit and just… I don't know. Here we are. Again.

"Listen, man," he says. "She's only trying to defend me. You know what she's like."

"Yeah."

"I'm no good at all this, and I say the fucking—the wrong thing. But, I mean, it's coming from a good place, man. I'm just on the lookout for my mate. I just want to look after him when I see he's doing a lot of changing."

I look at him now, and he flicks a nervous glance at me. I've never seen him quite like this before.

"We've been through a lot," he says. "And I mean, it's true—I should have been a lot better of a mate about your health. You know what it's like; I like to look after my mates. But I didn't step up to the mark there. I didn't know you were having blackouts and all that. I didn't look after you. Diabetes and everything—it's serious news. You need to take care of that. Be a little bit strategic, like. But you're not an easy fucker to tell, you know what I mean?"

"No, I know. It's not that bad. I don't want to be treated any differently than anyone else. I'm not some like major special case."

Mal nods reflectively.

"Just so you know, if I'd thought you'd even wanted telling, I would have told you and made sure you looked after yourself."

"I'm fine, I'm fine. I can look after myself. I just need to…not do quite so much shit to my body, you know?"

"Yeah, of course, man."

He stirs his feet and contemplates. Maybe he's waiting for something from me, but I've got nothing. I don't want a scene.

"There was a moment back there where I thought…you know. We could get a place, move in together. Be a laugh."

I stare fixedly at my empty cup of Fanta. It sounds kind of pathetic, what's coming from him now.

"But you never got back to me when I said it. So I'm thinking, maybe he doesn't want to be friends anymore?"

It's true. I never did get back to him. But that's because—

"It gets pretty lonely when your best mate's vanished without a trace. That's no good, man, is it? Disappearing like that overnight."

As I lie here now, going over that scene after all these years, the danger I think of is his clear eyes and honest intonation, and I think, maybe I had more of an effect than I thought by simply not being around. Maybe you can't just switch yourself off from people's lives. Maybe I could be persuaded that he was being reasonable.

But no. No way.

It makes all the difference to be sitting here by the window, looking out at the magnolia tree and the lawn beyond. The robin's back, flittering around. There's something deeply comforting about seeing her little eccentric moves.

"So," I say, taking a small sip of water and swallowing it down with some effort, "how did it go? Your mum?"

Amber cannot keep the warm smile from spreading across her pale face.

"There was standing room only," she says, with glittering eyes. "It was really, really moving. Mum would have been totally amazed at how it went."

"Ah, Amber, I'm so pleased."

"A whole load of people she used to work with came along,

and all the people she went to church with, and all her drama friends. And there was this group of men from a place she used to work at like ten years ago, and they were saying to me, *Your mum was so proud of you, and she always used to talk about you when she was working with us.* People really loved her, you know?"

"How about your dad? How did he do?"

"Oh, he did brilliantly. He couldn't think of a reading, but he stood up there and he spoke in front of all of those people, and he was as brave as anything. He was telling them all about how he and Mum met, and how people didn't take to him because he was Japanese and she was English, but how she stood by him with all their friends and won them over, and how he was proud to call them all friends now, and it was just the warmest possible send-off."

"Brilliant," I say. More water. "I'm so chuffed. You made all that happen."

"No, it was you. You got me to think about it differently. Thank you."

"People can go through their whole lives without rethinking something."

She goes a bit shy, and…well, so do I. It feels strange to tell someone you're proud of them. But I am proud. And I'm pleased she thinks I've helped.

She smiles coyly and begins to gather her things together.

"I think I'd better get going. We're planting a tree for Mum this afternoon. I think she would have liked that."

"Well, that's lovely," I say.

"Would you like me to do anything for you—for Mia?"

I look down at my blanket, turn a corner, and inspect the neat edging. Take a sip of water.

"If you want, you could get your crochet going. Do a yarn bomb."

"Yeah?"

"Do it properly. That would make me really happy."

Teeth, tongue, tonsils, taste buds, throat

Teeth.

Tongue.

It's all mouth. Teeth, tongue. It's taste. Taste and texture. Taste and touch. Taste buds. Teeth and tongue, taste buds, throat, tonsils. All in there together. All *T*.

So dry. My teeth and tongue now thirsty. They're tacky and clicking dry. I need a drink. I want to flood my mouth with an ocean of relief.

Grandma: old as her tongue, not as old as her teeth.

Your taste buds change, don't they? As you get older. They change. When I was a little boy, Granddad gave me a sip of his whiskey. Awful, awful. Couldn't conceive of why anyone would want to drink that. Stomach bile. Awful. I knew that when I grew up I would only eat sweets. When I was old enough to eat what I bloody well wanted. Sweets and cake mix. Couldn't stomach it now.

"Morning, lovey. How are you doing today?"

Sheila. Quiet voice. Gentle voice. She works the room, looks at me. Tries to judge how I'm feeling.

"Can I get you anything? A drink, or…?"

No food. Food no longer on the menu. I have had my last meal.

"Tea?" I say. "Please."

"A cup of tea? All right, lovey, sit tight and I'll go get you some tea."

Cup of tea. Floods the mouth. Floods the buds. That's something to say. Cup of tea. Forever the first thing to get me moving in the morning. It's my—what do they say?—my control. My control state.

Cup of tea floods the tongue, teeth, throat, tonsils.

All the *T*s.

Six sugars in my cup of tea, I used to have when I was little. Couldn't do that now. Spooning out the sludge in the bottom of the mug. Happy days.

Wh—?

Sheila plants a teacup and saucer on the cabinet beside my bed.

"Here we go, lovey. I've brought a fresh glass of water for you too in case you'd rather have that, all right?"

I smile up at her. Hope the smile reaches my face.

She sits awhile as the tea cools beside us.

"Jackie tells me you had a bit of trouble in the night."

"Mmm, yeah."

"Breathing bad again, was it?"

"Yeah. Yeah, awful."

She tuts sympathetically and takes up my hand.

"What's, uh…what's the day?"

"It's a lovely bright Tuesday."

"Tuesday? I can't keep track."

"Still, at least you've got an excuse, eh? You're allowed to lose track when you're feeling a bit peculiar. I don't know what my excuse is."

"Heh, no."

"You feeling a bit better now, though?"

I nod. "A bit strange. Really, really weird dreams."

"Yeah, that's normal. That's quite normal for morphine."

"But…better than awful."

"That's good. We aim to please, eh?"

"Yeah."

"Well now, I can't hang around here gassing all day. I should get on."

"Right."

"Have you got your buzzer? It's there by your hand, look."

Look. My hand is next to the buzzer.

"I'm just outside, OK?"

"OK."

She leaves, leaves the tea steaming behind her.

I know I'm not going to drink it.

I can't taste anything anymore.

Tongue, teeth, and taste buds, all dead.

All dead already.

U

Urethra

Urethra? Ha? Urethra Flankrin.

What are you talking about?

Uvula

"Sash! Sasha, come here!" Mal calls through the booming music of our housewarming party. Very much his housewarming party. I don't want to meet anyone new.

The kid in the bowler hat meets up with Mal, and Mal throws his arm around his shoulder and draws him to me.

"Ivo, this is Sasha. Good mate of mine from up north."

I shake his hand, which is cold. He's got three spikes coming out from beneath his bottom lip and gouged earlobes. "How you doing?"

"Sash's the piercing king," says Mal.

"Oh yeah?" I say with effort. I don't want to start getting to know this stuff. I couldn't give a toss. "What you got?"

"Well, the ones you can see." Sasha smiles with a faintly nerdish choke to his voice. "I've got two twenty-six-mil ear gauges, the three in the bottom lip, two nostrils, and an eyebrow—"

"What about inside?" Mal says with anticipation.

"Tongue, gum, and uvula," he says.

"What's that?" I ask.

Sasha opens his mouth and flashes his tongue at me, before lifting his top lip and displaying a silver bolt that I think pierces his top gum.

"Ah, Jesus," I say. I've always been a bit squeamish for stuff like this.

"Show him," urges Mal.

Sasha opens his mouth wide and sticks out his tongue.

"Uvula piercing," says Mal, bright-eyed.

I frown and look in there, not knowing what to look at, and then I see it: the punch bag at the back of his throat has a bolt through the front.

"Ah, Jesus," I say. "I don't want to see that."

Mal grins, but Sasha looks offended. He death-stares me before pulling down his lower lip and showing me the inside. There, between the three bolts for the three spikes, is tattooed the word PAIN.

He disappears off into the darkness, an air of nerdish revenge having been exacted.

I don't need this. I never wanted a housewarming in the first place. But Mal insisted, of course. A prime chance to get all his mates and acquaintances around. Get his customers comfortable with his new setup.

This is my new stage in life. This is what I'm committing to. I've never felt so low.

I sit on the floor, lean against the wall. *My* wall. Half mine. All our chairs have been taken up by faceless freeloaders invited by Mal, and the buzz throbs through me, through the floor. This is not what I want.

Come on, come on now, positive thinking.

I pick myself up off the apartment floor and say to myself, *Bring it on.* Use the words: C'mon, c'mon, bring it on. Let's feel it. Gaze up at the lights through the smoke. Even though I helped Mal rig the old bicycle wheel to the light fitting, it still works. It looked rubbish, dangling down like a slipped halo. But hats off, man, the Christmas tree lights hanging off it, they're magical.

You can be the magician and still enjoy the trick.

Mal's dropped Coldcut, and the twentysomethings are up and bouncing around and shouting "Chooon!" and pointing at the ceiling. They're jumping up and down, and I can feel them through the floor.

Fucking Coldcut, though, man, genius, I'm on it now, the bass, as I pulse against the wall, I can feel it through the floor,

I can feel it through the wall, it's the bass drum, the belly that's speaking to me. It's living me.

I wish you could be here to feel this… I wish—

Sasha's grotesque dancing face looms up at me now. Aggressive. He's being aggressive. The only thing I can think is I want to turn him into a punch bag. Sucking, scummy leech.

I push at him with my fists, and I get him off balance. Puff of stink off him like damp-clothes smell.

I'm away now, shoved away by Mal, and he's shouting at me. He's trying to calm me down.

"Fucking prick," I say, looking over at the punch bag punk. He's regathered himself over the opposite side by Becca, playing freaky with her. She's paying as much attention to him as she has to me.

"Come on, man." Mal's still at me, I see, his face in my face. "You're in a bad space, yeah? We're going to take you out of this. Here, here, wait…" He turns around to the drinks table. "Here—get a load of this, yeah?"

I take the drink and down it.

"Little housewarming present from me, OK? Time to cheer up and chill out, yeah?"

"Yeah, right."

I look up, and his face is still staring, right at mine.

Thuds and colors and wailing faces slide past me, and I've burst out of the front door now. I'm on the street, and Mal's with me. He's talking to me.

I'm going to make everything all right, he's saying.

We're leaving the housewarming behind—no one's going to care, are they? Not this far gone.

We can sort you out, he's saying.

He's going to make it all right.

We can explain it to her. I'm going to take you there.

He's going to bring me to you. He says you'll be thrilled. And we'll be together again.

Listen, let's take my car. It's pissing it down.

Yeah, yeah, a car. We don't have to walk even.

And we're driving. I love driving. I love being driven. Since I was a kid, with my dad. The streetlights flung past, caught up in the animated rain on the windshield. How much time must it take your brain to render all that movement? It's amazing, amazing. Every corner is drawn in real time as we drive around it. All the angles perfect.

Where are we going? We're not going; we're coming. I'm coming to you.

Parked up, chunk-chunk car doors shut, and out on my feet now, yep, yep, I'm coming to you. I'm inhaling the pavement—long, straight terrace street, and I'm surfing it, every slab of it. Tiny ups, tiny downs.

We can straighten it out!

I'm thumping on your door, because I've got to tell you now, this is it. I should say, right, this is it forever, yeah? I'm done! I see you! I feel you! You and me forever.

Your door opens, and it's you! It's exciting!

What? Go home. Go home, it's four o'clock.

"We can work it out!" I say. "We can do it, Mia!"

Jesus, Mal, what state's he in?

He wanted to come see you. I've brought him to see you.

"This is it forever," I say. "I'm excited! It's beautiful!"

Go home, go on. We can talk about it when you're more together.

"I'm—"

Are you looking out for him? You're not stoned as well, are you?

Nah, nah. I'm fine.

Are you all right?

Are—

"I'm not—"

What is it?

Have you taken your insulin?

"I don't know—"

All right, stay there. I'm going to…I'd better call an ambulance.

Nah, nah. I'll take him in the car. You don't call an ambulance out for something like that.

Yes, you do.

Fine, well, you call an ambulance, and in an hour and a half when they get here, tell them I've taken him to the hospital.

Oh bloody hell, all right, let's get him in your car.

I'm in the back of Mal's car, and you're in the passenger seat, and Mal's driving. I'm trying to speak, but the first words won't come.

Your voice. *Come on, think of something. Keep thinking, now. You and me up in the valley. You remember? Up on the top, with the grass washing all around us, the sky above, and the sky below. Are you with me?*

I can't think. I don't want to think. Leave me alone.

I don't know what sounds are coming out of my mouth.

I can hear you. I can still hear you. You're not talking to me. You're talking to Mal. Your voice in the whirl.

There, there: there's the hospital sign. Do you know where the emergency room is?

Mumbles from Mal.

Your voice changes.

Are you all right? Mal?

I hear no response.

There's a big sustained heave, and my head and shoulders feel funny. Funny heavy.

I'm awake, I'm aware. I'm aware of the orange lights sweeping past. I'm lying on the backseat, and I can see Mal's towering silhouette, lurching and twitching around in his seat, and you're on at him to stop.

Stop!

And then there's a thump, and your voice and Mal's are silent suddenly, like a sudden sweeping intake of oxygen, and the weight on my head and shoulders is immediately immense, and then gone, and in one snap, I'm dumped down into the footwell and shoved, forced, hammered into the metal and the carpet and the cogs of the seat mechanism. I'm being crushed, and an immense and horrendous sound smashes all around us, of everything smashed and shattered.

☙

Your hand. I'm holding your hand with my hand.

The ventilator breathes out, you breathe in; clicks; in, you breathe out.

I'm here for you. Can you feel me holding your hand?

I want you to feel me holding it. My palm to your palm. Fingertips on the back, by your wrist, our thumbs turned around each other. Can you feel the life coming into you through my palm? Good energy, good energy coming into your palm from my palm.

I want you to know what's happening to you. You were in a car crash. You were hurt. You're at the hospital. They're keeping you asleep on purpose, because they want to see if your body can heal itself. Do you understand?

In; clicks; out.

But listen, it's really important you listen to me.

They're talking about turning off the machine. You need to get strong enough do this on your own.

So if you can just get a little bit better, just try to get on top of this—now's the time. Now's a really good time.

Your mum's here, and your…your dad's here too.

We all just want—

Baby, you can't go, you can't go.

Who's going to buy me silly stocking stuffers at Christmas?

I need you to look at my garden designs. For the course. I need you to approve them.

How could you leave me to do that?

Are you receiving me?

Can you feel my thumb stroking your knuckles? Can you feel my hand?

⤳∾⤳

"There we go," Sheila says as the burly young student nurse fastens the final buttons on my pajama jacket. "A bit of cleanliness makes the world go round."

"Yeah," I say. "Thanks."

"No worries," says the nurse. "Thank you." He turns to Sheila. "What should I...?"

"Take the water through to the washroom down the corridor on the right, and you can pour it away there."

The nurse flicks me a look and a shy smile before leaving.

"There we go," says Sheila. "Thanks for that."

"It's fine. Hard work being a student."

"Lovely. Now I'd better go check on the lunch orders and make sure—"

"Sheila..."

"Yes, lovey?"

"Do you have the number for Kelv? The man I spoke to on the phone."

"Phone number? Yes, of course."

"Will you call him? Tell him I want to speak to him."

Her face lets slip no glimmer of opinion.

I'm grateful.

I—What's that?

For a moment I could honestly feel the shape of your hand in mine. The softness of your skin. Are you back now, for me? Now that I am the one in the hospital bed? Are you holding my hand, like I once held yours?

I'm here.

I'm going to imagine you here.

I'm here.

My hand cradled in yours.

Your hand.

Your hand.

Your thumb tenderly strokes my knuckles.

I need you to tell me this is the right thing to do.

You know it's the right thing.

The quietest of knocks, just enough to make the wood of my door resonate.

My dull brain sharpens once more to see what's what.

"Hello, mate. How are you doing?"

"Hi, Kelvin."

"How are you doing today?"

"Not great."

"No, no."

There seems to be no hint of the bad feeling of our last phone call. Good. I'm glad of that. Life's too short.

"Sheila told me you wanted to see me."

I beckon him in, gesture him over to the chair.

The door, which he left open, is now fixed shut from outside, and I see the stipple of Sheila's tunic as she drifts away beyond the slot window.

"Well," says Kelvin, "it's a nice old day out there. Nice and sunny. Not too windy. Perfect, really. I'd take you out again today if I could, but I think you wouldn't thank me for that, would you?"

"No."

"Maybe next time then, eh? If you concentrate on getting a little bit stronger, you and I can go out there and have a bit of an old roll around the gardens."

His nervous jabbering slows to a halt. Of course, he wants to see why I've summoned him here.

And I'm not sure. I'm going to have to…

"I wanted to make sure we're OK."

"Of course we're OK, mate. Don't be daft."

"You're a good friend."

"Don't be daft," he says again and looks away.

"I want a favor."

"Oh, typical," he says. Forced amusement.

"I can trust you."

"You can."

"I want you to make sure they're all right. Laura. Mal's mum and dad."

"Of course."

"When I'm gone. I want them to be OK."

"Yeah. Of course."

This isn't going in the direction I want it to. Be more direct.

"My funeral."

Kelvin sighs and sets himself to say something.

"Listen," I say. "I didn't want one. I hate fuss. But it's…it's for others. Other people."

"People will want to pay their respects."

"Yeah, well, I want it to be me. I want them to…to know me."

"Ah, mate," he says. "I'm really pleased to hear you say it. It's definitely the right thing."

"So, music." I let go a wobbly sigh, look up at the ceiling. "'Introduction' by Nick Drake."

Kelvin scrabbles around for his phone and makes a note of what I'm saying.

"And I like Gillian Welch singing 'I'll Fly Away.'"

"Right."

"They're me. That last one's a bit happy, anyway."

"Anything else?"

"'Monkey Gone to Heaven'?"

He looks up at me a moment before smiling and shaking his head.

"I've always thought the cancan is unfairly overlooked."

I tense. Laughing, after a fashion.

OK, now we're getting somewhere.

"Something to make them feel better," I say. "I can trust you."

"Of course you can, mate."

"And...could you write some words? Something that means something?"

He looks genuinely taken aback. "Well...yeah. I'd be honored. Are you sure you trust me to do it?"

"I want you to do it. If you could just...just say—" Sudden unexpected choke in my throat. This is *hard*. "Could you just say that I knew...a bit late in the day maybe, but I realized that... you know, I shut myself away. And that...that wasn't maybe the right thing to do. I could maybe have...been around, you know? And helped people through. Does...does that make sense?"

Kelvin nods wordlessly.

"And that this funeral is my gesture—"

"Too much."

"Too much?"

"Yeah."

"OK, well, the rest of it, not too sad, not too hilarious. You know me."

"Thanks, mate. Thank you. I'll do that."

"Oh, and ashes."

"Ashes."

"Scattered up on the top of the valley."

"Up at the top, right."

"Somewhere that feels right."

"OK."

"There aren't many trees out there, but…if you happen to see an apple tree—"

"Apple tree, right…"

"Just there. At the root."

"Got it."

My mind drifts out the window again, and I push my fingers through my blanket, gather you up around me.

V

Voice

"Hello."

Wh—?

"Hello."

It's…it's *you*.

Clear as day. It's *you*.

Your voice. Your friendly voice. Where was that from?

Am I hearing that? Are you really there?

So completely familiar. Familiar voice. Familiar tailoring to the sounds. The tilt and tone, the lift and fall, the pitch and percussion of it. So clear, so clear.

I have a blueprint. Right here, a blueprint of you. No one can take that away from me. I love it, I love it.

"Hello."

I can hear you saying it now.

Illuminates my gray brain.

Makes my heart accelerate now. I can feel it pulse now. Through the sheets. Through the mattress. It slows.

"Hello, baby."

Pulse up quick again now, pound through the mattress. It's the tailoring to the sounds, my blueprint of you. I want to be close to you. I want to merge with you.

Hello, hello.

It slows.

Where are you?

Have you come to see me?

I say, "Mia?"

"Morning, lovey."

Oh.

Sheila.

Gentle Sheila.

That's a proper sound. Physical sound.

I can hear it with my ears. Oh, that feels different, hearing with my ears. Bass vibrations.

"I've got some fresh water for you here."

Cruel confusing morphine. It's confusing. Strange.

Sound. Gentle sound. Low sound. Stirring my gray brain. Strange brain.

"Let's wet those lips, OK?"

Cool mess on my lips, my chin. Low relief. It's dripping; it's dribbling.

Sheila still speaks to me. Lovely singsongy voice. Nice voice. But slow, gentle.

"I've been thinking about your A to Z," she says. "Where have you got up to now? *V*, is it? Or *W*?"

Voice, voice. Sheila's voice.

When did I last use my voice?

I want to say thank you. I'll try to say—

"Don't try to talk, lovey."

Too dry now. Too parched.

What were my last words? I can't remember.

I hope I've said enough.

Enough for them to be going on with.

Light flick.

Switch on.

All I can feel about me now is a heartbeat in a bed. I can hear it through the mattress. Faster, now faster.

It's sensed what I've seen through the window.

My heart beats out what I have seen.

Should I push the button?

Sheila? Is Sheila there?

No, no.

Faster now, my heart beats in the sheets.

My heart beats, and I breathe.

I breathe and I see.

That's all I am now.

I'm seeing now through the window and beyond. Beyond to the magnolia tree.

In the breeze between the hard-bitten branches of the little tree outside, there flutters and bobs a heart.

A love heart.

A crochet love heart.

It's there. Look, it's really there, in the tree.

I can see it.

W

Wings

I'm up above the valley.

I'm here. I can sense it here all around me.

I can feel the sun's warmth, my blood basking beneath the surface.

And it's you.

You, look, you're holding up your palms and crossing your hands now, pressing your thumbs together to make a bird. A fluttering bird.

I take my right hand, press it to your left, thumb to thumb.

A bird. A fluttering bird.

Hold our hands against the sky.

Fluttering, fluttering in the blue.

Two songbirds, fluttering on the eddies, energized by the fruit from the tree, out in the gasping yawn of valley air. That's when we'll be together, mingling in the wind.

You're smiling and widening your eyes.

Your eyes.

"Oh, it's so good to see you," I'm saying. "I thought I'd never see you again."

Let me look at you; let me drink you in.

"You look so well and so happy. Are you happy?"

"Really happy."

"Oh, I'm so pleased. This is amazing. You look amazing. I've missed you so much."

"Miss you too."

"I'm so sorry. I'm so, so sorry."

"I know."

"You were so straight and clear and good and honest with me. I'm so sorry."

"I know."

"I can't even ask for your forgiveness. You must never give me it."

"No matter."

I can't tell you what a relief it is. After all these years. You're exactly, exactly as I remember you, only clearer. Crystal clear. Your eyes glisten brightly for me.

"Will you give me your hand?"

"Here."

I can feel it! I can feel the soft skin. I can feel you stroking my knuckles with your thumb.

"Hereing me."

"Oh yes, yes. I am hereing you."

"Knowing my words."

"They sound just the same, exactly the same as they used to."

"Same sound, no sound."

"Can you hear me now? Do you know my words at the same time as I think them?"

"I know."

"Forgive me."

"Come."

"Where are you going? You're not going, are you? Please don't go."

"I won't leave you. Here for you. Don't worry."

Washed-out quality of your voice.

Signature squiggles of birdsong.

The flutter of wings.

Ohhh.

Still here.

Awake forever.

This breathing, this breathing.

Like through a drinking straw.

Sleep won't come.

Lying across the pain.

Pain like a branch through my back.

Sharp twisted tree branch.

Tinkle cart.

"Hallo, lovey. It's only me. It's only Sheila."

Tinkle tinkle.

There it goes. Hmm.

Tinkle tinkle.

The people don't speak to me now. Not Jef, not Jackie. Only Sheila.

Good good.

Speak stirs the chemicals, busy head.

Keeps me awake.

No more.

Good.

They're good people.

Good people.

Angels.

Night now.

Shhh.

Shhh shhh shhhut up.

"Morning, lovey."

Tinkle, tinkle.

Here comes the cart.

Drink, I can't drink.

Good, go.

I like it when nothing happens.

What was I…? What was I suppose to be…?

I?

❦

"Hallo, lovey. It's only me. It's Sheila."

Sheila.

"I'm just going to take your blanket, OK? Let me unhook it from your fingers here, so we can sort your bedding out, OK?"

Mmm?

"I'm just going to put it by your bedside, all right? It won't be far away."

No. I—

No…no, that's not right.

I don't feel right.

Cold.

Cold now.

X

<u>X</u>

Wh—?

Familiar sound of the double doors slipping shut off down the corridor.

Doesn't feel quite—

Who'd be walking down there now?

It just feels…wrong. Seems…against the routine. What's…?

Ridiculous. Stop, stop.

Stop thinking.

I have it in my mind that Mal is approaching, wafting through the double doors, unchecked, unbalanced.

Ease off now.

That's mad thinking.

Mini squeak of shoe rubber on glossy floor. Trapped and amplified by the shiny walls.

He is out there. That's enough for me: these two things. Door slip, wrong time of day; squeaky shoe.

Who else could it be?

No.

Fix eyes shut.

Think of other things.

X. X-ray.

Xylophone. Ribs as a cartoon xylophone.

Xs for eyes.

X chromosome.

"All right, fella."

Wh—?

Brain on.

Flicks on like a security light. There's… Was there movement over by the doorway?

Anything?

Is anybody over there?

My ears listen out, but I'm too asleep to open my eyes. I'm realizing I'm more asleep than I thought. Can't…move.

There's nothing there.

Same old night terrors.

Brain off.

"Y'all right, are you?"

On.

Over by the doorway, at the foot of my bed, definitely.

The room remembers the sound.

Paintwork resonates.

"Nice place you've got here. All the gear."

Gray matter now fully lit up and active.

Mal's voice. Definitely Mal. Gravellier, but same tones. Same tune.

He's there. He's there in the doorway.

Alert now. Alive to the room.

I can't… There's nothing I can do.

Sickening twitch accelerating in my chest.

Push the button. I want to push the button. Find my hand. Find the button to push.

My hand reaches, grasps…nothing. Blanket wasteland.

"I wanted to come and see you."

Low voice. Anxious. Slight edge to it.

Silence. Shit, shit.

Air conditioning ceaseless, ceaseless breath.

Unseal my eyes. Painful light. There he sits. Simply sits. He's just there.

Can't see if it's him, but it's him, isn't it? Everything tells me it's him.

Shit. Shit, Sheila. You said he'd never get in.

Maroon jacket. Yellow lettering top pocket. NRG. Wh—?

Has he wh—? Is it Mal? I'm confused.

"It's Mal," he says. "It's Malachy."

"M—?" I mean Mal. I mean Mal, but my lips stick together.

"That's right. Don't talk if you can't talk."

"N—no."

"What?"

"Don't—"

"Don't what, fella? What…what are you saying? I can't under-stand you."

He leans over. Looms over.

"S—s—"

He's frowning down.

There's a smell off him. Outside smell. Football pitches. No, like…football terraces. Makes no sense. Cold smell.

He leans in, dangerously in.

"You what, fella?"

I push, push out at him, push him away.

He steps back, sizes me up.

He thinks I'm delirious.

I'm not delirious.

"Stop," I say. I think I say it.

He's stepped back.

"All right… I'm not going to hurt you. Easy, man. Easy."

He's still frowning. Trying to work me out.

"I've just come here to see you. I've just come to say hi."

He lifts his hand and scratches through his hair—a familiar motion. A Mal move. Shows me he's stressed. Anxious face.

He looks hesitant. Nervy.

He looks genuine.

Benign.

"I just wanted to say hi," he says again.

The longer I look at him, the more I resurface. Relax. Relax a little. Reality.

He looks scared. Seems almost timid.

"Do you mind if I sit?" he asks. "Stay awhile?"

I close my eyes. It's not my decision whether he stays or goes. In time I hear him choose. Tiny knock-scrape. Plastic exhalation. He's sat himself in the visitors' chair.

"Fuck me, man. I'm not going to do you any harm. You didn't think that, did you?"

I shake my head. Yes.

I open my eyes again, rest them on him.

He looks quickly away, out of the window.

Perhaps he can't take the vision of me, lying here, this mask strapped to my face.

That's fine. I'll look at him looking away.

"I don't know what to say in places like this," he says, still gazing out at the magnolia tree. The heart, the fluttering heart. Can he see it too? "I hate hospitals. I could talk about the weather."

Pause a moment.

"Inclement."

He snorts to himself.

I'm going to say something. I need to try to say something.

But it won't come.

"Here," he says, standing and coming forward.

I can't stop him—

He carefully pours a little water into the teacup on my table and places it to my lips.

"C'mon."

He places his hand behind my head to lift it, but I can't…

And he has tears in his eyes. I can see, closeup, he has tears.

"Wait a minute," he says, setting my head gently back down. "I'll just… Here." He unwraps a clean sponge from my bedside table and dips it into the teacup.

"Here we go. That's better, isn't it?"

Lips moistened. Better, yeah, better.

Try again now. Say, "Where you been?"

Clear my throat. Clear a little with the water.

"I've been staying with Becca for a bit. Giving myself a bit of head space, bit of brain space. She wanted to come and see you, Becca, but, y'know. Bit scared, I think. She hates hospitals. You know what it's like. People hear the name St. Leonard's, and they think…they think a certain thing."

I close my eyes. Yeah. Come out feet-first in a box.

The silence swells in between us on the air conditioning.

He wants me to say something. Give him a sign.

In all the world of words, I can't think of a single thing.

"Do you know why I'm here? I hoped you'd know."

Here we go. Here we go now.

"I want to make everything better, but I can't make anything better. Can't say anything. Some stuff is too big, you know? Too complicated for words. But I didn't just want to leave it, man. You need better than that. I wanted to be here. I haven't got all the fancy words, you know, but I thought, if I bring myself and something good might come out of it. Do the right thing, yeah?"

He snorts quietly, nibbles anxiously at a cuticle.

"But fucking hell, you know, even saying this, man, feels fake. *Oh*, you know, *I don't know what to say*. It feels like I'm just saying it to make you feel sorry for me, but I'm not, I don't want you to feel sorry for me. I'm sorry for you. I'm sorry *to* you."

He chokes suddenly, unable to continue.

I look at him. Sympathy.

"I promise I was trying to do the right thing, but…well, it's just words, isn't it?"

"No."

"I wanted to say, there's a lot of things I should have said and done, you know? And a lot of things I shouldn't have said and done. I've had a lot of time to think about it. Too much time. You know that. I bet you've been through that, haven't you? I know you have."

I have.

"You find suddenly you've done all these terrible things for…for no reason, almost. Things that didn't seem terrible at the time, you know? And not for a long time. But you find that, you know, your whole world's changed because of them. Lots of people's worlds. You've made your mark, whether you like it or not."

I look up at him now, and he seems small. It's like I'm looking at him from a long way away. The little man. A little man in a chair, next to me, here, a little man in a bed.

"So here I am, you know? Here we are."

"Mmm." I frown and attempt to swallow. Get halfway and unswallow.

I can't—

"I don't know why I'm here, man, if I'm honest," he says, looking over at me almost shyly. "All those years, you know, of imagining what it would be like to meet up again, say what I've got to say. I knew it'd never be the same as I'd thought. I had loads of things to say. Sitting there. Thinking it all up. It's gone, you know? It's not important, is it? Words don't change anything. Don't change what's happened."

"No."

"You know, man, if I could I would—in an instant I'd go back and change everything. I wouldn't have let you stay at that party. I wouldn't have let you leave that party. I wouldn't have fucking got in that car. I wouldn't have done any of it, man. It was all my fault, man."

No, no. Too raw. I don't want to talk about this. I don't want to have this out now. Have it out later if we've got to have it out at all. Have it out later. But he's focused on me, intent on going through this. He's going to sit there and make me go through this moment by moment.

"No," I say.

"It was. I was right there; I should have stopped it. I know I should."

"I don't—"

"You're a dying man, yeah? Let's not fuck about with this.

You're dying. And that's my fault too, isn't it? I never told you, did I? When you were fucking yourself up in the clubs every night, I never said anything. But that's because I didn't know, man. I didn't know how bad things were with you. But I should have known. I should never have stood by and watched, and I'm so, so sorry."

He's fixing me with a desperate stare.

"And if there was anything, *anything*, I could do to make it all better, I would do it, straightaway, you know what I mean?"

The piercing glare in his eyes flickers and is finally diluted, and a tear swells in his right eye, breaks over the lid and flees down the side of his nose. He drops back now, back into the seat. Exhausted with the effort of it all.

I close my eyes again.

It's me. The outline of me, could have been a chalk mark, scrawled on the floor of our apartment. Our shared apartment. I'm looking up, amazed at the bicycle wheel hanging crappily from the light fitting. Amazed at seeing a vision. A vision of glow sticks and smoke.

Amazed enough to propel me to your front door, declare myself amazed.

Your face, not amazed. Not amused.

Your voice, alarmed. Trip to the ER for me.

Backseat of the car for me, looking up at you.

You and Mal, uneasy alliance.

All for me.

All because of me.

I am a passenger.

You, there in the hospital bed, me cradling your hand.

Me, here in the hospital bed. Because of me.

It's because of me. All of it.

I look over at Mal. He's not looking.

I need to get him to look at me.

"Mal." He looks up.

His face is gray and drawn. The trace remains of the fallen tear.

I hold out my hand. He edges toward. Takes it. Takes my hand by the outside. His palm to my knuckles. Wraps it gently into a fist.

"You're all right," I say.

He exhales and sniffs graphically. He doesn't try to snatch back the blame. In truth, I think it lies between us. But...no use for truth.

A large stream of snot begins to dangle from his nose.

"Ah, shit, man. Sorry," he says, clapping his hand to his face and wiping with his cuff.

I smile. It actually makes me smile. I can feel it spread across my face.

"Sorry." He laughs.

I breathe.

It is good. This feels...it feels good.

It was the right thing to do. All things fall into place.

A broad, happy smile fills his face, right to the eyes.

And the relief, the *relief* in him. I didn't expect that.

And they were right; of course they were right. Sheila. Kelvin. Laura, even. About...about what?

To see him so broken… He looks—*forgiven*. And that's not right.

"Sorry, man," I say.

He looks back up at me. "Don't be soft."

And oh, the relief of it: in him and now in me… I can physically feel it here in my body. I'm lifted with it, the weight of it gone. That's what they told me would happen. A weightlessness, it's true. This is definitely a thing. Definitely a real feeling.

It's you I want now. It's you I want to forgive me.

I cough. My body coughs without me. I have to wait to let it pass.

I look beyond him, gaze over at the window. Painful light.

One fluttering relief: the heart, there. Your heart in the tree.

Close my eyes.

So, so glad this is all over.

Seems so easy, it's embarrassing. I can feel from my heart up through my back, through the pain, through my limbs to the fingertips an overwhelming surge of love and goodwill.

Drifting, I can feel the time slide around me.

The coffee machine works up again and ceases, and Mal, close by, remains. The sense of a hand in my hand remains.

And I don't know if it's there, and I don't know if it's you, crossing our hands to make a bird. A fluttering bird. Up against the sky, fluttering in the blue. Mingling in the wind. No more blur.

The relaxation, I can feel it, creeping up my spine and into the base of my cranium, up through and around the thick bone of my skull, around to the deepest recesses of my brow. But in the depths of my deep frown, I can feel the resistance. I'm trapped in the room. We're still in the beige, dry, air-conditioned room.

Overwhelmed by the surge. I can feel my face crumpling, but no tears come. Tight throat.

"Oh, man, are you all right?" says Mal's voice, close.

I open my eyes, and he's there. Still there.

And I'm still here. I look at him, and…are there tears?

No, still.

"I know, man," he says. "I know."

"Just—"

"I know."

"River Severn."

Silence—save the endlessly exhaling air conditioning.

"You what, fella?" His voice, dry in the silence.

I open my eyes wide. Look at him. Look at him hard. Does he remember? Does he remember everything I remember?

His gray face holds still, rough and unshaven, shapeless hair encroaching on every side.

"Hephzibah?" I say.

His addled eyes grow clear, sharp. I'm reading him, reading. Willing him to remember what he said to me.

"Hep-hep-hooray?" I say, urging, urging him to recall.

The clearness freezes in his eyes. A memory registers. He *must* remember. Wheelbarrow me up to Hephzibah's Rock…a couple of spins around, hammer-style…fling me down into the Severn…

"You got me?" I say.

"Ah, no, man." He's looking at me. Scanning.

"You said."

Still scanning. He's afraid.

"Don't ask me, man."

"Please. Mal."

"It's not fair to ask anyone that."

It isn't. It isn't fair.

I sigh deeply—deeper than I can—and cough. Crumble into what coughing I can manage.

My clamoring thoughts sink, defeated, to the back of my head. All I want now, all I need, is to be with you. I close my eyes and dump my head back into my pillow.

Listen to the silence.

"Come on, fella," says Mal's voice, renewed with brightness. "I can make you comfortable anyway. Is…is this the same blanket? Is this Mia's blanket?" Slight waver in his voice. "It's no good folded up by your feet, is it?"

I sense him lean across me to gather it up.

"Here you go, man. Let's get you settled, yeah?"

Subtle shift of cool air.

"Shall we take this off?" I open my eyes and lift my head and allow him to prise the oxygen mask from my face. He hangs it carefully on the top of the canister beside me. Cool, dry air on my nose and mouth, the clammy shape of the mask subsiding.

"Close your eyes, man, yeah?" he whispers. "Close your eyes."

I look at him: fix my gaze onto his eyes. Another tear drops from his eye as he leans over me. I feel it land on my cheek.

He looks at me, and I look at him. I can see it in his eyes. I can see what he's asking me.

"Close your eyes."

I close my eyes now; close them.

The sight of his face, the twisting branches of the tree in the daylight, cropped by the window beyond, all remain, fading on my vision.

Luminous eyelids darken now.

His hand now cupped on the back of my cranium, holding my head in his palm.

Palm of calm.

Faint familiar scent—vetiver. Still detectable, after all these years.

You.

Soft wool on my face. Alpaca and merino. So thick and heavy, pushed, pushed by Mal, tight, tight. Tight enough. Just right.

Consistent stitches.

Strong sense of you.

Dry that tear.

My hand now reanimated. He's holding it. Gently, gently. Warm hand cradling mine, mine I'd forgotten. Mine so cool.

"That's better, yeah?"

Stronger now, the scent.

Pushed, tighter.

Strong sense of you.

That's it, that's what I can do: deep inhalation.

Draw deep.

Sleep down deep with you.

Reading Group Guide

1. Why do you think Ivo chose to address his stories directly to Mia, referring to her as "You"?

2. How did your perception of Ivo change throughout the book? As the picture of his lifestyle, choices, and friendships came into focus, did you grow to like or dislike him more?

3. What do you think appeals to Mia about Ivo?

4. What could Ivo have done to salvage his relationship with Mia? Would it have changed anything, or would the outcome of the book still have been the same?

5. Mia and Mal are arguably the two most important people

in Ivo's life, but between them, they have a complicated relationship. Why do you believe their interactions are so difficult?

6. Who is to blame for Mia's death?

7. What do you think happens to Mal after we leave him?

8. *The A to Z of You and Me* jumps back and forth in time through Ivo's life. In your opinion, did that help to paint a fuller picture of him, or did you wish the book had followed a more linear structure?

9. How does Ivo's humor and attitude change as the book progresses? Does the seriousness of his situation reflect back in the body parts and stories he chooses?

10. To what extent do you blame Ivo for the situation he is in?

11. Was there a story in the A to Z game that resonated more strongly with you than others? If so, why was it particularly affecting?

12. Ivo's death doesn't come as a surprise, as the novel revolves around his stay in hospice. How did your general expectation of the ending affect your experience of the book?

13. If you had to pick a letter of the alphabet and tell a story of your life, what would it be?

14. In your last days on earth, what would you choose to remember?

15. "Love ends at death. Does it?" Discuss what you think and how Ivo, Mia, or other characters throughout the book support your opinion.

A Conversation with the Author

What was your inspiration for writing *The A to Z of You and Me*?

Its structure is really a series of answers to a series of questions. I began with the tiniest thought, that it was interesting that a great deal of mathematics is contained simply within one's fingers. Ten fingers point the way to a decimal system and a whole way of thinking. You have digits and points. Beyond that, drinks can be measured in fingers, horses can be measured in hands, and so on.

It was a natural development to wonder how interesting it might be to have a whole anatomical dictionary made up of such anecdotes, which might then combine into a coherent story of someone's life. The shape of the life would necessarily be dictated by the stories.

Questions arose that I needed to answer:

- Why would my character be dividing himself up like this? It's a game. He's creating little biographies for each part.
- Why would he be playing this game? He's trying to calm his fretful mind.
- Why would he be trying to calm his fretful mind? He's dying.
- Why is he dying?

"Why," I asked a doctor friend of mine, "is he dying?"

"Well, if he's lucid enough to tell tales right up to the end, and is not too sedated or confused, it sounds like he might have a kidney problem. Often, you get quite young people with kidney failure because they haven't managed their diabetes well."

So, I had my character. He has Type 1 diabetes, which is not his fault, at an age when all he wants to do is go out with his friends and have a good time. He finds managing his condition almost impossible, as his friends are not capable of providing the support he needs.

This basic structure of the story emerged from an entirely mechanical process. I like that any other author would answer these basic questions differently and end up with another book altogether.

There comes a time, however, when one needs to release the original concept to allow the idea to support itself. When I began to improvise around the body part ideas, I found that other, freer, more spontaneous ideas began to flood the book, gave it heart and warmth, and indeed began to force the main plot to account for itself. That's where Sheila, Amber, and Old Faithful come in.

Although Ivo's situation isn't ordinary, his emotions and yearnings are universal. How do you hope your readers relate, and what questions should they ask themselves?

Certainly, Ivo isn't blameless in his choices, but who among us has not acted in a self-destructive way and simply gotten away with it? *Tonight, I'm going to eat that whole tub of ice cream, drink that whole bottle of whiskey, blow all my savings in a casino, buy that expensive gadget I can't afford.* The most excessive of us might be branded as lovable rogues. If you've ever tried to maintain a diet through January, you'll have some idea of how hard Ivo's diet "for life" might be, especially without the support of the people around him.

Personally, I think Ivo is a good guy. He's kind and thoughtful, but unfortunate and misguided. His aspirations are certainly to better himself.

So I guess I'm hoping readers will look at Ivo's situation and question precisely how much he is in control of it, and how likely it was he would have been able to meet his aspirations with the resources at his disposal.

What research did you do to add depth to Ivo's sickness and his experience in hospice?

Given that Ivo's "narrative condition," if you will, had been diagnosed by a doctor from the very beginning, I needed to shore that up with research about how he would be feeling. I kept checking with a renal consultant about what would be happening to Ivo physically—the assault on his dignity, his state of mind, what the doctors around him would be thinking, and so on.

I have a couple of friends who are managing diabetes, and they were good enough to show me their everyday routine, what was involved in injecting insulin and whatnot. I cannot convince them that the book is not some incredibly unsubtle and doomy hint to them to stay on a healthy track.

Much of the stuff that happens with Sheila and Amber and Old Faithful came from my observations of life and death in St. Catherine's Hospice in Preston, UK—a place of many heightened emotions, including love and laughter.

If you had to pick a letter in the A to Z game and tell a story about that body part, what tale would you tell?

I already did. It's in the book.

As a debut author, what was the most surprising discovery you found on your journey to becoming published?

The most surprising thing was that I was able to interest previously uninterested friends simply by telling them the concept of the book ("a character reveals the story of his misspent youth by recounting little tales about each part of his body") before I'd even written a word of it. I was accustomed to friends switching off if I started talking about writing, so it was surprising that they were still engaged when I'd finished talking. All I had to do was preserve and nurture that little spark of interest while I wrote it.

What does your writing space look like?

The A to Z of You and Me had a real hodgepodge of writing spaces, though almost all of them were beds. My bed in Shropshire. A friend's futon in Walthamstow, London. A cheap hotel room in Stevenage. I would stay over with my brother in Northampton each week and would write in a child-size bed with a Power Rangers cover and Bratz curtains while my nephew and niece camped out in the garden.

Which authors inspire you? Why?

I'm not a flag-bearer for any particular author (although I do have a master's in Samuel Beckett studies, which is more of a certificate than a flag). So much of it has depended on where I was as a reader and what I'd already encountered. I think it was pure luck whether I encountered the writer I needed at a given time.

Roddy Doyle's *Paddy Clarke Ha Ha Ha* achieved the sleight of hand of appearing to get inside my head and talk in my voice (a common response to this book, I've subsequently heard), and Doyle is altogether humane, which appeals. Kurt Vonnegut's humaneness too. Beckett's appalled amusement hit me at exactly the right time and absolutely feeds my need for core rhythms in expression.

I'm drawn to warmth, and when I really needed some warmth and brightness and positivity, I happened to read Maya Angelou; she's really stayed with me. For some reason, I always feel a great urge to write when I watch anything by TV writer Dennis Potter;

his 1980s Singing Detective series is unsurpassed in the size of splash it made in my writing development.

I'm always drawn to complex ideas approached with a youthful enthusiasm: Douglas Adams, certainly. And Caitlin Moran feels very good at this on a social/cultural level.

If there's one thing you'd like readers to take away from *The A to Z of You and Me*, what would it be?

I don't know if I could say that. I think it's much more about readers bringing a part of themselves to it. And it depends on where they are as readers and what they've already encountered. They might find something here; they might not. Maybe the thing that leaps most readily to mind that they could take away is that laughter and tears are incredibly closely linked. And it's possible—no, it can be extremely helpful—to laugh at how utterly hopeless a situation has become. If you don't already know that, it's very helpful to realize it.

❧ Acknowledgments

"Team…"

Thank you first of all to my two brothers, who have put me up and put up with me; to my mum and my dad, who afforded me time and space; to my bandmates, inspirations all; and to the Jolly family of Preston, who had me over for Christmas once.

Thank you too, Catherine O'Flynn, for support, positive discouragement, and inadvertently giving me the title.

I am grateful for the advice given to me by Dr. Alice Myers, David Abdy, Sally Quigg, Ian Abdy, Shonagh Musgrave, Carolyn Willitts, Simon Wheatley, Sara Grainger, Su Portwood, Frith Tiplady, Anna Davis, Chris Wakling, and the autumn 2011 cohort of the Curtis Brown creative writing school.

I am indebted to many people for taking and making this

book: Susan Armstrong, Jane Lawson, Alison Barrow, and the talented teams at Conville & Walsh and Transworld; Shana Drehs, Heather Hall, Jillian Rahn, Adrienne Krogh, Brittany Vibbert, Nicole Komasinski, and all at Sourcebooks.

I have never met John Murray, author and benevolent editor of Panurge New Writing. But I am grateful for a few typewritten notes from him back in '94 and a phone conversation in '03. It takes only a few words to change your world.

This novel has been tested on, discussed with, and occasionally bundled past the incomparably marvelous Christine Jolly. Jols, I cannot thank you enough for everything you've brought to this book. But I can try: thank you times, like, fifty.

About the Author

James Hannah has an MA in Samuel Beckett studies. *The A to Z of You and Me* is his debut novel. He also sings and plays guitar and drums in various bands with friends. He lives in Shropshire with his family. www.jameshannah.com